Dominic

Cerberus MC Book 4

Copyright

Extras:

Cover design by: Essen~tial Designs

Synopsis:

Dominic Anderson knows exactly what he wants in life: simplicity, safety, and solidarity with his brothers. He's vowed to spend each day living his life exactly how he chooses since the day his wife betrayed him and his four year military career turned into twenty.

Returning home after retirement from the Marines, he's traded the sand in the Middle East for that of the New Mexico desert, Humvees for a motorcycle, and the comradery of men in uniform for the occasional woman at his feet.

Life was perfect until Makayla "Poison" Evans, Renegade MC Princess, knocked on his door, bruises on her face, neck, and arms, and no money to pay the cab driver. Pink hair, perfect body, and a mouth that Dom yearned to teach a million lessons, Mak asks more from him than he's conceded to a woman in decades.

She needs his help, his protection, and against his better judgment, she expects him to keep her secrets. Only her secrets are deadly, dangerous, and have the potential to start a war between two MCs.

At what point does safeguarding a woman become a betrayal to the men Dominic calls his family? More importantly, can he get back the sanctity of his home once Makayla is no longer in the picture, or will he be forever tainted by her poison?

Acknowledgements

Man, book #14…

So many people make my dreams possible… I hope I don't leave anyone out!!

Mr. Marie James… what can I say that hasn't already been said. You're my perfect book boyfriend. The power and consistency of your love is what makes me able to write these books. The knowledge of love and experiencing it daily allows me to write loving characters with little research on that part!! Thank you for your dedication to my art and continued support!

My wonderful PA's, Laura and Brittney… without you I'd spend all my time pulling my hair out than spending it writing… your friendships and help are priceless!!

Wyoming… Has recently become one of my favorite states. MaRanda, Steph, and Renee… if it weren't for the daily chats, ears to vent to, and allowing me to be the person my PR company says I can't be on social media I'd literally go insane. Daily, you keep me from giving up and throwing in the towel. You can't even begin to imagine how dependent I am on you ladies!!

My BETA team, Renee, Laura, Brittney, Brenda, Sadie, MaRanda, Steph, Michelle, Rachel, Sally, Miranda, and Sara…. You helped make this possible. Thank you from the bottom of my black heart for supporting me and making Dominic the best it can be!!

Linda, at Sassy Savvy Fabulous, thank you for not only talking me down when I'm in the mood to speak my mind even if it means upsetting some people that support me, but for also becoming someone I would consider a friend. I take your guidance, albeit sometimes with a scowl on my face, very seriously and I'm eternally grateful to have you on my team!!

TE Black, I love the teasers!! Thank you for being a part of my journey!

Give Me Books, you ladies are amazing! Thank you so much for being there each and every time to support my releases, even when I flake and don't get you what you need in a timely manner!!

BLOGGERS!!! What can I say? Without you I'd just be a women sitting on manuscripts that no one would ever hear about!! You gals/guys get the littlest amount of praise when you honestly deserve the most!! Thank you so much for doing what you do!!

ARC team reviewers!! I cannot thank you enough for your excitement and speed at which you read and share your experiences!! You help me become more visible in the hectic Indie world and there are not enough thanks in the universe for you gals!!

READERS!!!! Thank you for once again taking a chance on one of my stories!! Reading this book, whether you purchased or read on KindleUnlimted, helps make the next one possible!! On that note if you bought this book loan it to a friend. It's totally a thing and everyone is doing it...

Word of mouth is the best way to spread author love. If you enjoyed this book (hell, even if you didn't) tell a friend, write a review of share a post! I hope to bring many more books to you, and this helps a TON in making sure that's possible!!

Prologue
Dominic

There's nothing in the world that can knock the grin from my cheeks. I only have thirty-six hours to spend with my wife before heading back to the sand pits, but it's better than nothing. This surprise, albeit short, leave couldn't have come at a better time. When I got off the phone last night with Karen, I could hear the agitation in her voice. She didn't even try to hide her feelings about me heading out again.

Joining the Marines right out of high school was always our plan. I wasn't the only one involved in that decision, she was right there beside me. She wanted to be married and have children. Those were her life plans, ones I was happy to give her.

What we hadn't anticipated was how easy being a Marine was for me. Leaving civilian life and becoming a soldier was the easiest transition of my life. Combine that with Operation Desert Strike, and I found myself in the Middle East not long after finishing The Crucible. Deploying wasn't the issue. The Corps had trained me to fight, to save, to die if necessary. Leaving Karen behind two weeks after our simple courthouse wedding, which was only days after our high school graduation, was the hardest part. We'd seen each other nearly every day since we became an official couple in the cafeteria in seventh grade.

Three years of quick visits, leave that's never long enough, and short phone calls have put a strain on our marriage. I'm hoping this impromptu leave will have the ability to bandage up the cracks that have been created from time and distance before my final year in the Corps. Four years is what I promised to give them. I'd wanted to make a career of the military, especially since I was so good at it, but the months away from Karen weren't something either one of us was handling very well.

I breathe in the fragrant air surrounding our modest home. Early spring has always been my favorite time of year. Karen has expressed her distaste of living on base, complaining that everyone was too close, neighbors were nosy and intrusive. I reminded her that she's safer on base than anywhere else. Frowning when I open the front door, I find myself making a mental note to speak with her again about keeping it locked. Crime still happens on base more than it should, and her safety is my number one concern.

The sound of the shower perks my ears, my body already humming at the mental image of my wife naked and soapy under a warm cascade of water. My cock thickens in my utility pants as I make my way across the open floor plan.

No sooner do I get fully erect before I begin to deflate. The playful baritone of a man's voice assaults me right outside of the bathroom door. People say there are moments in their lives that they know a second before something happens that everything they once knew would be destroyed. They know their path in life will change in an instant, in the next breath. Sometimes that second is right before the deer jumps into their path on the highway, or the fire detector going off in the middle of the night, only to wake up already engulfed in a thick blanket of smoke.

For a soldier, it's the clank of the pin being pulled from a grenade or the reflection of the sun as it hits the scope of a sniper rifle, the bullet already traveling into your gut before the sound registers in your ears.

Today that second is the soft whoosh of air as I push open my bathroom door, the humid air and steam from the shower making a hasty escape from the enclosed room. More times than not, when your world turns upside down, you're in a state of shock. Your eyes seeing, your ears hearing the evidence right before you, but your brain hasn't caught up yet. The complex mass of gray matter in your skull refusing to accept the sight as it fights to understand and explain away what every other sense in your body has already accepted. That's not my wife bent over in the shower getting fucked by the next door neighbor, a man I'd consider a friend, a man who I asked to keep an eye on Karen while I was away. For the briefest of seconds I realize how disappointed in her I am, not only for cheating and ripping my heart out, but also because she didn't choose another Marine to do it with. No, the man pounding into my wife as she moans like a whore is the *husband* of Second Lieutenant Sara Estes. He's not a soldier, and for some reason that makes this feel like an even bigger betrayal.

My knuckles crack as I fist my hands at my sides. I don't try to hide the loud pounding of my boots as I cross the tiled floor to the civilians who can't even be bothered to pay attention to their surroundings. I nearly rip the glass door off of its hinges, as it pulls open and moans against the action.

Mid-pump, Samuel Estes raises his head and looks me right in the eye. I've never seen a human lose color so fast as the blood drains away from his face, not even soldiers on the battlefield when their bodies are nearly ripped in two by a spray of bullets.

Seconds is all it takes after I reach out and grab him by his unruly hair and pull him off of and out of my wife. She yelps in surprise at his loss, and I have to remind myself that hitting a woman is something I'd never do as my brain tries to reason that sometimes a bitch just needs to be smacked.

I close my eyes briefly, assaulted by the memories of my father beating my poor mother for crimes as simple as dirty shelves in the fridge, and the images are enough to calm my aggression toward the woman I thought I'd spend the rest of my life with. Instead, I focus my rage on the naked man at my feet.

Two punches are all I manage before Karen is out of the shower and attempting to pull me off of her consort.

"Please," she begs with a trembling voice. "Don't hurt him!"

I kick at the quaking pussy near my boots, feeling pride as he moans in pain.

I can't even look at her as bile rises in my throat. Three years of marriage, going on ten years of being together, and this is how she repays me. I've been in the sand, trying not to die while fighting for my country, and she's been here fucking a man while his wife does the same.

"Pack your shit and get the fuck out of my house," I hiss as I walk past her and across the same path I just traveled minutes ago.

"Stop, Dominic. I can explain!"

Ignoring her pleas, I walk out of that house and away from her. At the threshold, I leave any and all emotion that could hurt me this bad again. One year left in the Marines turns into seventeen as I keep my vow never to trust a woman again.

Chapter 1
Makayla

"I can see it in your eyes, Makayla. You want to tell me everything."

I glare across the small metal table at DEA agent Dean Ryland, unable to hide the sneer my mouth has been set in since he scooped me up off the street when I left the clubhouse to grab a cup of coffee that wasn't made by one of the club whores.

"You clearly need to be trained better, Detective. My eyes aren't saying any more than you should expect my mouth to say."

I smile inwardly as his dark green eyes flit to my lips. If he even has an ounce of ability to read the minds of criminals, my ability to detect arousal and interest in a man is a hundred times greater. The barely noticeable hitch in his breathing and the way he shifts on his feet every time I lick my dry lips betrays his inability to hide the fact that he'd trade my silence and any knowledge I may have of the Renegade MC for a quick fuck.

Men are so easy. Thinking with their dicks instead of the organ between their ears. I shift my weight in the hard metal chair, spreading my legs just a few inches wider. The action doesn't go unnoticed as Ryland attempts to clear his head with a quick shake. Heated eyes run the length of my body, and my confidence with the situation multiplies.

"It's Agent," he corrects with a hoarse voice.

"Well, *Agent*, you don't know shit about me. Am I under arrest?" My mind races to try to imagine what he could have on me. There are a million things I can think of that would put me in this small room and probably double that I can't recall.

He frowns. The simple action of his lips turning down informs me that he doesn't have shit, other than an egotistical attitude and the misconception that a woman from the club would relinquish information quicker than one of the men.

The swift laugh that escapes his mouth is unexpected and causes an unwanted shiver to run along my arms.

"I know more about you than you think, Poison." I recoil at the use of my club name. It doesn't go unnoticed, but I don't give him the satisfaction of insisting he call me Mak.

I cross my arms over my chest and lean further back in my chair as silence fills the room.

He takes a seat on the other side of the table which feels more dangerous than when he was standing, leaning over into my personal space. From that position, he could easily look down my low-cut shirt. My tits have gotten me out of more than one delicate situation, and I was banking on them helping me again this time. No such luck.

Ryland's position across from me now seems more official, more ominous. My pulse raises as his fingers splay out on the nicked metal of the table top. Somehow, even without a folder or a file box of documentation in front of him, his relaxed posture causes more alarm than I thought possible.

Without the aid of even a notepad, my blood runs cold as he begins to list off things from my life.

"Your mom overdosed on heroin when you were sixteen. As the bastard child of Adam "Breaker" Hanigan, your on-again off-again childhood trips to the Renegade MC clubhouse became a permanent thing. After your father died for betraying the Dirty Slayers MC by fucking the president's wife, your brother, Brooks "Scorpion" Hanigan, took over the Renegades at the ripe young age of twenty, a year after you moved in." He raises a perfectly manicured eyebrow at me, checking to see if he's made a mistake. He hasn't, but I wouldn't correct him if he did.

I school a passive look on my face, so he continues.

"From the look on your face, you don't seem to be getting along with many of the people there." I barely resist the urge to bring my fingers to my split lip. Large sunglasses remain in place, hiding the fresh black eye behind the tint. He cocks an eye when I tug the long sleeves of my leather jacket past my knuckles.

"Your injuries make it clear that you don't have your brother's protection. As the sister of the President, one would think any man or woman in the club wouldn't lay a finger on MC royalty."

His words give a voice to the girl inside me that has wondered the same things since the second I packed my beat up suitcase eight years ago and headed to the Renegade clubhouse. The girl inside me who left a rundown house just as the coroners were pulling my mother's decaying body off her sheet-less bed.

Hatred and disgust due to our father's betrayal for cheating on his mother are the only two emotions my brother has shown me. Even tolerance at my presence in his clubhouse is something he doesn't always have.

"Okay? You know some shit about my family. Big fucking deal, *Detective*. That still doesn't explain why I'm here, why you've unlawfully detained me to give me an afternoon rendition of my fucked up life." Thankfully, my voice is stronger than the internal battle I'm fighting within.

I part my lips slightly, exhaling through my mouth after sucking in deep breaths through my nose, an attempt to calm my pounding heart rate. I hesitate lying to him, if only for the briefest second. I allow the fantasy of getting out of the MC alive fill my racing thoughts. That's all it is, a fantasy. Scorpion would be more than happy to see the back of me, but Grinder will hunt me down and torture me just like the many men and women he's forced me to watch over the years.

Leaving alive isn't a possibility. Staying is another brand of misery. Better the devil you know.

"I know your brother's club is running guns, dope, and possibly trafficking women. I know you're not as in the dark about that shit as you want to pretend. The question is, do you want to get away from it all or are you just as involved?" His relaxed posture begins to strain a little, his shoulders hitching just an inch, the rhythm of his breath changing slightly as he waits for my response.

"I don't know a damn thing about anything, other than my brother and his crew run a respectable business in town." The lie falls easily from my lips as it has for years.

"Right," he says without an ounce of belief. "The gym. The *legit business* where only members of the MC come and go, yet the tax roster shows revenue from hundreds of members."

I quirk an eyebrow at him, my answer to his question as to whether or not I'd snitch on the MC.

"Are we finished?" I push my chair back and stand on wobbly legs.

Cops make my skin crawl, they always have. I can thank my mother, father, and every man I've been around my entire life for that. They're pigs, rats, and the scum of the earth hiding behind badges and civil duty, only out to destroy families and keep people oppressed as they pick and choose who goes down for a crime and who doesn't. It's taking everything in me right now not to spit in his face before walking out.

With my back to him and my hand on the door knob, I speak. "Unless I'm under arrest, don't ever speak to me again."

Trembling legs carry me out of the small police department the Drug Enforcement Agency has been working out of since they arrived in Durango. For months they've been lurking around, attempting to hide their investigation of my brother's MC. Scorpion knew they were in town the second they rolled out of their dark-tinted SUVs. Having several police officers on the MC payroll helps in situations just as this.

I keep my head high, refusing to meet the eyes of every uniformed officer who glares my way as I walk through. They haven't been able to get anything on me since that time I fucked up as a juvenile, but knowing if they dig too deep they'll find a slew of shit to charge me with makes my chest burn, terrified one of them will stop me and slap those steel cuffs on my wrists.

On the sidewalk, finally free of the hostile looks from the boys in blue, I take in my surroundings, trying to decide which way to go. Ryland brought me to the police department from the local coffee shop a few miles away, where my car still sits.

I turn right, heading toward the school administration building, knowing cabs tend to hang around the intersection of Twelfth and East Second.

A sense of unease travels over my skin, and I pull my leather jacket tighter around my chest. Doing my best not to jerk my head around looking for the cause of the edginess, I dart my eyes repeatedly left, right, and in front. The familiar sight of a ragged leather cut catches my eye on the opposite side of East Second. My blood runs cold, my pulse pounds louder in my ears than the DEA agent had caused it to only moments ago.

Grinder, my brother's Sergeant at Arms, sneers at me, keeping pace on the sidewalk across the street. The menacing smirk on his scarred lips means I'm completely fucked. He's watching me walk out of the police station, and the threats I made yesterday that earned me the black eye and busted lip that I'm sporting today seal my fate.

I walk slower, huddling amongst a group of tourists as they walk down the crowded street gazing at things they consider historical. To the locals, these old buildings are just a reminder that Durango, Colorado hasn't moved into modern times as fast as other tourist locations in the state.

Grinder slows when I do. The only safety I have in this ridiculous group is knowing he won't try to grab me in a crowd of people that he can't control. Letting him get his hands on me isn't an option. I'm dead if he catches me. I know it, and he knows it. I won't be given a chance to explain. He'll gag me, and my body will be in the desert, food for the buzzards within the hour.

On a stroke of luck, the small group enters one of the small shops, and I trail in along with them. Keeping myself hidden behind a tall rack of t-shirts touting Durango as the best town in the state, I watch as he crosses the street, paying no mind to the vehicles slowly meandering down the road. Horns honk, and one man yells out his window, only to stop mid-rant when Grinder's dark eyes turn to face him.

I ignore the yells of the shop owner as they insist I need to go back to the front when I cross through the door leading to the "Employee Only" area of the shop.

"Fuck off," I mutter.

The front door bell chimes just as I'm opening the back door. I don't have to look back to know he's entered the shop because the sinister aura that constantly surrounds him reaches me even through the wall.

I contemplate running back to Agent Ryland, begging for him to rescue me, but I know that favor would come only in exchange for testimony against the Renegades, something I'd never be willing to give.

My feet move unsteadily along the broken pavement behind the row of shops.

"No sense in running, Poison." The sureness in Grinder's voice nearly causes me to stumble forward, but my fight or flight instinct is in full effect, even if my efforts are useless.

My small purse falls from my arm as I turn around the end of a building. I leave it lying there, knowing I can't waste a second trying to grab it. Relief washes over me as a flash of white catches my eye. The distinct logo of the local cab company gives me false hope of survival as Grinder's pounding boots close the distance between us.

The driver isn't even at a complete stop when I tug open the door and jump inside.

"Go!" I yell as he turns around to ask me where I'm heading. Slowly joining the leisurely pace of the other cars, his eyes catch mine briefly in the rearview mirror.

I crouch lower in the seat, turning my eyes back to the man who's haunted my nightmares for the last six years. Anyone looking at him right now would think that the smile on his face is misplaced. I know better. I know that I've just given him exactly what he wants, a chance to hunt me like prey, a sport he not only loves but also excels at.

I'm as good as dead.

Chapter 2
Dominic

Trying my best to ignore the relentless pounding on my front door, I squat deeper, letting the nearly three hundred pounds on my shoulders drag me closer to the floor. Anyone in my life of importance has a key to the door, so the idiot that is relentlessly knocking away serves no purpose other than to annoy the fuck out of me.

I swing the bar back on the rack and head to the door, prepared to release every frustration my two-hour workout hasn't been able to alleviate on whoever has enough balls to interrupt my life unprompted.

"What the fuck do you want?" I sneer as I swing the door open. Only it isn't a Jehovah's Witness wanting to spread the Good Word on my front porch.

Familiar pink hair catches my eyes. Poison Evans tilts her head in my direction. The woman standing in front of me is more dangerous than any messenger of God could ever hope to be, even when my soul is already damned to Hell for the things I've done in this life.

"No," I say immediately and close the door in her face. Whatever bullshit she's bringing to my home isn't worth the trouble, no matter how gorgeous she is.

Kincaid has had dealings with the Renegade MC for years, for some reason turning a blind eye to the criminal ways they're constantly involved in. Hell, I've even taken several of their club girls to bed in a pinch, but this woman, alone and more than an hour away from her own club reeks of a burden I'd be an idiot to get involved in.

No sooner does the door close and she's pounding away on it again. Rolling my head on my shoulders, a failed attempt to relieve the tension that built at the sight of her, I pull open the door again. I don't speak, but take a moment to inventory her. Slim fit jeans she's poured herself into, low cut top with tits for days, and her well-worn leather jacket fills my vision. Jesus, what is it with untouchable women that make my cock throb?

My thoughts change suddenly when my eyes land on her busted lip, and I know this woman is going to say something that's going to fuck with my calm world when I look over her shoulder and see a taxi idling in my driveway.

"I lost my purse. I don't have money to pay the cab," she whispers. Her cheeks pink with embarrassment as she asks without saying the exact words if I can take care of the fare.

"Get inside," I hiss as I walk back in to grab my wallet off the table near the door.

She scurries past me as I head in the direction of the cab. Flipping him off when he bitches about the income he'll lose having to travel all the way back to Durango to find his next customer. Fucker knew what he was getting into when he agreed to bring her this far in the first damn place. I smile inwardly knowing what the sweet tits on Poison could easily convince me to do. Poor bastard didn't stand a chance.

I lock the door behind me and find her pacing the length of my living room. The normal bounce of her long, wavy hair I remember from seeing her at various gatherings is nowhere to be found. In its place is a mess of tangles and unruly, unintentional curls.

"I don't have time for drama, Poison." I stand near the threshold where the foyer meets the living room, arms crossed over my chest

"It's Makayla or Mak. Never Poison," she corrects.

Even the dim light coming through the French doors facing the lake doesn't hide the bruise covering her eye when she pulls her sunglasses from her face. My weight shifts uncontrollably when she removes the leather from her body and bruises on her arms and neck are exposed.

There's no way this woman knows my history. She wouldn't have a clue that I left home at eighteen, leaving my mother and brother in the hands of my abusive father because I was too much of a pussy to stick around and stand up to him. No chance that she knows that only two years into my service that my mother was beaten to death by that same man, a fucking realization that haunts me every day of my life.

Even though our actions prove the men we are now, there's no possibility that she knows of the vow Diego and I both made to protect women and children from those who would want to hurt them. Yet, here she is, standing in my living room, pleading with her eyes for me to get involved.

This isn't a mission sanctioned by the government. This isn't a call to action against some asshole in the community who is taking marital liberties and beating his wife. Those situations I don't have an issue getting involved with. Those situations are easily handled, allowing me to return home without a doubt in my mind that I did the right thing.

Makayla in my house is the equivalent of shitting where I eat, getting involved in something that has the potential to not only blow up in my face but could manage to fuck the club my brother has spent years building. But I can't turn her away. Not even knowing what's going on, I don't have it in me to tell her to fuck off, even when every part of me is demanding I do just that.

I grab my cell phone from the table near the front door.

"Scorpion's going to fucking kill whoever hurt you, Makayla."

This is going to get bloody. I know there is no love lost between her and the president of the Renegade MC, but he'd never allow for his sister to get hurt like this and not demand the life of the person who inflicted the pain. An assault against her is almost as bad as an attack on him. He won't tolerate the disrespect. No matter the situation, no matter the explanation, someone will die, and that shit will be another thing on my conscious since she involved me by just showing up on my doorstep.

She whimpers and takes a few steps closer to me as I pull up my contact list.

"Please, don't," she begs covering my hands with hers, preventing me from seeing my phone screen.

"He'll handle this," I insist, even as the words taste like shit in my mouth.

Having her closer, I get a better look at the fresh bruises that seem to travel the entire circumference of her throat. The blood on her lip has dried, but I can see how the wound has been opened and closed more than once since it was inflicted. The sight of her injuries makes me want to step up and take the place as the avenger for the damage her body has suffered.

"Please," she begs again.

I pull my eyes from where her hand still covers mine and look up at her. Watching her busted lip tremble in fear guts me. I've seen that look more times than I'd like to admit over the years. Panic stricken eyes plead with me, terrified that I'll turn her away. How could I at this point? What man exists that could force a woman back out into the unknown with injuries like this? *The same man who inflicted them to begin with*, my conscience tells me.

"Who did this?" My attempt at calm and comforting isn't reflected in the gruff demand.

She takes a step away from me, releasing my hand. I notice the lack of warmth immediately as the cool air surrounding us hits the area our hands were connecting. She shakes her head in refusal, cowering slightly when I take a step toward her. I'm near insisting she tell me every sordid detail, if only so I can hunt down the motherfucker who thought it was okay to lay a single damn finger on her.

"Damn it," I mutter when her eyes widen in fear at my approach. I back off quickly, hating that she could even consider I'd hurt her. I clear my throat and attempt again to portray some level of control. "Who hurt you, Makayla?"

"I can't tell you," she insists backing up to the point her body is flush against the backside of the couch.

"You can," I cajole.

"They'll kill me," she whispers. "Promise me you won't call any of them."

"Who?" I ask, refusing to make a promise I'm not certain I can keep. I know she's talking about the Renegade MC, there's no one else she would be involved in. A sickness settles low in my stomach when the realization that her very own brother could be the piece of shit who hurt her. He's acted his part when around the Cerberus boys, but I can see the evil in his eyes. I know Diego can as well, certain he's maintaining the keep your enemies closer when he's invited them into his clubhouse on the occasions that he has.

"I just need a place to stay for a few days. Please, Dom? I won't be any trouble. I swear."

"Trouble started the second you stepped out of the cab and your boots hit my front lawn," I mutter as I motion for her to follow me down the hall to an empty guest bedroom.

Chapter 3
Makayla

Agitation is rolling off of Dominic by the time I step into the room he's gracious enough to let me use. He hasn't said much since I showed up, but the constant tick in his jaw and tension in his shoulder betrays just how annoyed he is with this situation. What I can't decipher is if he's annoyed I'm here or livid someone has hurt me.

I'd like to think it's the latter, but I'm well aware of his semi-reclusiveness and antisocial tendencies, so there's a greater chance he's pissed that I showed up at all. The idea to leave Durango and come to him hit me as the cab sped away from Grinder and my certain imminent death.

Shorty, one of the Renegade's club girls spent a couple of hours with him at a party a few weeks back, and she let everyone know. It seems bagging the loner brother of the Cerberus MC President is a feat needing to be bragged about. Scorpion didn't let me go to many functions they participated in with the Cerberus men. I knew from the few times I've been around those guys that Dominic didn't stay at the club often and had his own house on the lake, assisting in his demand for privacy and separation from the goings-on at the clubhouse.

The idea, while riding in the back of the cab, seemed genius, until he slammed the door in my face. He's my last chance of survival even though I have no right to ask him for help. When that door closed, dread, like I've never felt before, filled my body.

My eyes scan the room, realizing very quickly that it is better than the room Scorpion allowed me back home, and it also has a feminine touch to it. The throw pillows on the bed and sheer curtains a clear contrast to the gruff, manly biker who owns the home. It immediately makes me wonder if he's got an old lady here as well. The thought is unsettling since she may take issue with another woman staying in her house even for a few days.

A room to the right of the bed reveals a full bathroom, and I can't get my clothes off fast enough. Not only the time traveling and running through the back alleys of a less than stellar neighborhood in Durango, the sight of Grinder along with the memories of him from years past make me feel absolutely filthy. The insistence to get clean every time my eyes meet his hasn't been stunted even after the hour-long drive away from him.

Keeping my eyes open, even under the warm spray of the water, ensures that the flashes from the past aren't able to take hold. I've spent years avoiding Grinder and the attention he sometimes insists on showing me, but I know the next time I see the man will be the last, ending unfavorably for me.

All-in-one body wash and shampoo is the only thing available in the shower, and I use it twice to wash my hair and every inch of my skin until red splotches are visible. No amount of scrubbing will make the feel of his hands on me go away, but I don't have the luxury to dwell on the past when my future is so unsure.

I towel off quickly, only to realize I have no clean clothes. I'll stay in this bedroom naked before I put the filthy jeans and shirt back on. Wrapping the oversized towel around my body, I open the bedroom door, sticking my head out into the hall trying to figure out where in the house Dom may be. The unintelligible hum of the TV floats down the hall, so I quietly make my way in the direction of the den.

The top of his head is visible over the back of the couch, but rather than making myself known, I stand silent and watch him. No one knows much about the enigma that is Kincaid's older brother. He's military, that much is clear by the way he talks, stands, and commands the attention and obedience from everyone around him, even if his hair is slightly longer than I've ever seen it before.

I've only seen the man in passing at a few parties. He's always had an air of solitude to him, one that is so strong you walk out the front door and around to the back if you encounter him obstructing your path through a room. Only the bravest, or stupidest, girls from the Renegades even attempted to speak with him. I never found the courage, until today. The first words I'd ever spoken to Dominic were the ones on his front porch when I asked a man I don't even know the favor of paying for a very expensive cab ride, which he did without hesitation or explanation. There isn't a man in the Renegade MC that would ever do that, including my older brother.

I've heard the Cerberus members were good men. I'd even encountered their gentlemanly ways at a fundraiser Scorpion let me attend in the park last year, but it wasn't until he helped me earlier that I'd ever been on the receiving end of it. It was that rumor, the one the girls whisper about how those men treat women with respect. They stop when you say no; they listen when you have concerns. That's brought me here today. Seems it's paid off.

"Lurking around my house isn't the best way to instill the trust I'll need to let you stay here."

Even as quiet as I've tried to be, Dominic knew I was in the room the second my foot hit the threshold. I don't respond to him, because at this point what can I say? I don't have an excuse or a lie that comes fast enough to seem reasonable, and the truth that I was wondering what it would be like to have a gorgeous man like him in my corner isn't something my lips would ever confess.

He turns his head until he side eyes me. The lick of his lips as he takes in my towel laden body doesn't go unnoticed. I would use his attraction to my advantage. While watching the girls at the clubhouse, I know so many things can be solved with me on my back or on my knees. Realizations Grinder was certain to make sure I understood at a very early age.

Dominic's scrutiny, however lustful, doesn't seem to fit a situation where a blow job would get me what I want, a fact I'm grateful for due to lack of experience. At this point, I don't even know what I'd ask of him other than to keep me safe. Him showing me to a guest bedroom has already established his willingness to help, if only temporarily.

"I don't have any clothes," I whisper, suddenly embarrassed to be standing here in a towel even though it's covering more of my cleavage than my tank top was earlier. I hold the knot of the towel higher on my body, my strangling grip assuring it doesn't fall to the floor.

Steel gray eyes follow the line of my body from the black polish on my toes to the mess of pink hair piled high on my head. A shiver of arousal hits hard before I can shut it down.

He glides graceful and silent from his position on the couch and stalks toward me. Chills run up my arms leaving goose bumps in its wake. I hold my breath as his hand reaches out, unsure of what his expectation of me staying here would be. I learned long ago that nothing in this life is free, payment always has to be made, and if fucking Dominic to stay safe in his house even for the briefest of time is the requirement, it's one I'd not feel completely ashamed for doing.

Rather than reach for the towel as expected, his long calloused finger traces one of the numerous bruises on my upper arm. The tip of his finger travels along the easily recognizable outline of another man's handprint on my skin.

"Did Scorpion do this to you?" His voice is menacing as he waits for the confirmation I'm sure he wants to justify killing my brother.

I shake my head.

"He'd never lay a hand on me." I try to swallow the truth unsuccessfully. "Hating someone enough to hurt them is an emotion he couldn't even spare me."

"Who then?" he asks not responding to my admission. His lack of concern is what I'm used to, a familiar response when an unspoken cry for help is made, one I'm used to being met with.

When I refuse to answer, he continues, "one of his men?"

"I just need something to wear," I mutter.

His finger pulls away, and a confusing mixture of relief and regret hits me. His eyes search mine as if the answer to every one of his questions is hidden in their depths. Not finding what he's looking for he turns from me and heads down the hallway.

"I have some sweats and a t-shirt you can wear. They'll be baggy as fuck, but at least your ass won't be hanging out."

I follow him down the hall, passed by the open door to the guest room he deposited me in. The thumbprint security access required to get into his room isn't surprising. Most guys at the clubhouse have some sort of security in place to keep people out of their personal space. What's odd about the lock on that door is this is a home, not a clubhouse frequented by various people with low levels of trust.

Or maybe it is. Maybe Dom has parties at his house. I wouldn't have a clue, but the lock on his door speaks of his distrust in people.

I stand in the doorway, knowing I won't be welcome in his private sanctuary. He's walked out of view, but I can hear him in the closet wrestling around. I let my eyes wander over the dark linens on his massive bed, the softness of his duvet a contrast to the level of masculinity that seeps from his pores. If I had to guess just by the way the man carries himself, I'd thought he'd be on a twin sized bed with scratchy sheets, not the luxury I'm looking at right now.

"This is the best I can do," he says coming back into view with a small pile of clothes in his big hand.

I take the proffered clothing from his hand as he looks past me down the hallway.

"Thank you." I turn and walk back to the open door of the guest bedroom. I feel the air from his body moving past me. "When will your old lady be home?"

He stops in his tracks but doesn't turn to face me. "I don't have an old lady."

"Oh," I say with more surprise than I feel. "This room is just decorated with a light touch."

Why am I still talking? It's clear he doesn't want to interact. Hell, he could've had a woman before that's now gone. His personal life isn't my business, and if I'm honest, I don't need his shit in my head as well.

"Rose decorated the guest bedrooms. If it were up to me, they'd all be empty." He begins walking back toward the living room, but I hear him mumble, "If they were empty I wouldn't have people showing up expecting to stay."

I close the door quietly. If he thinks saying shitty things and letting his opinion about me being here known is going to run me off, he has another thing coming. Being unwanted isn't new to me, but an everyday way of life. Unless he just insists that I leave, I'm not going to let his discontent with me being here faze me. Not much at least.

Chapter 4
Dominic

"What the hell are you doing?" Most men would be ecstatic at finding a gorgeous woman wearing nothing but a long t-shirt cooking breakfast in their house. I'm not most men.

"Making you breakfast," she says over her shoulder as she pulls the skillet from the fire and plates a pair of amazing looking eggs beside a pile of hash browns and thick cut bacon.

"I don't expect to be catered to while you're here," I grunt but reach for the plate when she offers it, my mouth already watering. The only time I wake up to breakfast like this is when I get too drunk to drive home at the clubhouse. The girls there always make a huge spread, and even though I don't stay very often, the home cooked food always soothes the hangovers that seem to get worse the older I get.

"It's the least I can do," she offers as she turns back to the stove and breaks another egg into the frying pan.

She hums softly as if in a world of her own and not the kitchen of a man she doesn't even know. She may be more comfortable this morning, but I heard the lock click on her door after I gave her clothes yesterday evening, so she's not as relaxed around me as it appears on the outside.

My eyes glance from the food in front of me to the tan expanse of her toned legs. The borrowed t-shirt hits about mid-thigh and for the first time in my life I wish I were a foot shorter. Her hair, now clean, hangs in long waves down her back, the pink hues contrasting with the dark navy of my shirt. I turn my eyes from her as the thought of wrapping it around my hand and using it to guide her mouth down my cock hits me hard. I grumble to myself. She's come here for help and refuge, and all I can think about is getting her on her knees. The thought of my mother rolling over in her grave at my desire is a sobering thought.

The last thing I need is this woman in my home, stirring my cock, when I have no idea why she's here in the first place. Seductive without even trying, she slides the egg onto another plate and turns the stove off.

"Thank you," I mutter as she hands me a cup of steaming coffee and sets her plate, with only half the amount she's served me, down next to mine at the table.

Her proximity makes me realize just how small she is. I'm sitting now, but I know if I stand, the top of her head wouldn't even reach the bottom of my chin. Petite, sexy, and full of fire, a trifecta of appeal that I know is going to somehow turn my world upside down.

"Eat," she insists, sitting in the neighboring chair. I nearly groan when the fabric of the shirt raises a few desperate inches further up her legs. "It's going to get cold."

I begin to dig into my food if only to distract myself, once she's lifted the first bite of hash browns to her mouth. She quirks an eyebrow at my manners, and I give a shrug.

"You ready to tell me what the fuck is going on with your club?" The yellowing of her black eye lights my blood on fire even more than it did yesterday. I'd lain awake last night imagining what I wanted to do to the fucker who hurt her.

"It's Scorpion's club, not mine." She says with an exasperated huff. "Just because I live there doesn't give me ownership or any say. That dumb DEA agent couldn't seem to understand that shit yesterday either."

I stop mid-chew and tilt my head to her. "DEA agent?"

She frowns, fork paused halfway to her mouth. I can tell by the dart of her eyes she's said something she didn't want to disclose, and she's trying to think of a quick lie to cover her tracks.

I assess her injuries again. Federal agents usually have more restraint, especially when dealing with women, but it's not unheard of for an asshole agent to rough up someone in a bid to get information from them.

"Did the DEA hurt you?" I ground out letting my fork click on the plate as I release it from my hand a second too soon.

Her head shoots up, but the indisputable look on her face tells me I'm way off mark. "Ryland? I could snap his neck in a split second."

My eyes run over her tiny frame. Either Ryland is a minuscule little shit, or her overconfidence is in full force this morning. Her breath hitches when my eyes linger on the prominent tips of her breasts, hardening under my stare. I look up in time to see her licking her lips then dragging the lower one between her teeth. My cock, on full alert, begins to strain against my sweats.

I clear my throat, failing at an attempt to redirect the conversation. "If the DEA didn't hurt you, who did?"

She shakes her head and grins. "We don't have to talk about that."

Her fingers, the softest of touches, graze my thigh causing the muscles to jump and beg for more attention. Thankfully, I've never been a man who could be lead around by my dick.

I clutch her wrist hard enough to know I mean business but not too tight, cognizant of the injuries she has there.

"Answer the question, Mak." Her eyes search mine as if she's trying to figure out a way to avoid the questions once again. I let her yesterday because it was clear she'd had a fucked up day, but her staying here without knowing what I'm facing isn't going to happen.

"The DEA agent didn't hurt me," she confirms, a fact I've already worked out for myself.

"Who did?" I growl, growing increasingly frustrated at her continued avoidance.

She shifts in her seat, turning her body in my direction. My eyes land at the naked flesh revealed when the shirt shifts at her movement, glorious bare flesh. Catching the direction of my gaze her thighs part another inch.

"I'm very grateful you're letting me stay here Dom. I'd love to thank you properly." The fingers of her free hand trace up her leg, and my eyes follow as if it's the most enthralling thing I've ever seen. "But I'm not sure I should tell you what's going on. I don't want you to get involved."

Trance broken.

My eyes snap to hers, finding a seductive lilt of her head and a knowing smirk, as if she's pegged me for one of the idiots in her brother's club.

"You involved me the second you showed up on my damn doorstep." I release her hand and push myself up to standing, needing distance before I become the man who thinks with his dick.

"Come back here," she pants with a provocative hint in her voice.

"Close your fucking legs," I sneer. "And if you're going to be outside of your room, you need to wear more fucking clothes."

I grab my plate of half-eaten food off the table and damn near break it when I slam it into the sink. Frustrated, I grip the edge and hang my head. Deep, drawing breaths fill my lungs but do nothing to calm my annoyance or flag the stiffness in my cock which makes my normally easy temper flare.

"I'd appreciate it if you didn't flash your pussy around my house when you're here," I say driving the point home as I turn back to face her.

"I'm not a whore," she mutters, turning her face away from me and back down to her plate. Seconds tick by as she picks up her fork and pushes the cooling food around on her plate.

"Yet, you're the one offering it up in payment for room and board." I wince as the harsh words leave my lips, regretting them instantly at the jolt of her shoulders.

I'm an asshole, a fact concreted when she turns her head back to mine, and I find her eyes shining with tears.

"Fuck," I grumble. "Listen—"

She stops me with an upturned hand.

"I shouldn't have said—"

Her hand goes up again. "You're right. I shouldn't have propositioned you, but I do feel like I owe you something for letting me stay here."

"All I want is an explanation."

False, my dick says. *You want to fuck her too.*

I watch her, waiting for her to explain, but she doesn't.

"I'll get you some more clothes," I offer as I turn to walk out of the room.

"Thank you," she says.

"I'm heading to the clubhouse. If you're running from something, you'd probably do best staying inside." I meet her eyes once more. "Or don't. Your choice really."

"Dom?" I stop in my tracks but don't turn around to face her. "Please don't tell anyone I'm here."

I want to use her need to remain undisclosed as a means to pry information from her, but I'm not that big of a manipulative bastard. The thought of keeping her hidden even from my brother and his guys makes me uneasy, makes my mind imagine all sorts of scenarios that have no business in my head.

I nod in agreement and head into my room.

A change of clothes and a quick call to the department store we use when we have to get clothes for battered women later, and I'm on my bike and driving through my small community, grateful she wasn't still in the kitchen when I had to grab my cell phone off of the counter.

Chapter 5

Makayla

The second his bedroom door clicks closed, I'm out of the chair and down the hallway to mine. I don't even bother putting my plate in the sink. I'll worry about it after he's gone, hoping he takes the embarrassment I feel at how I acted with him.

He's being a dick, which I understand. Most bikers are assholes, especially when faced with women. We're almost like a sub-species, only around to serve and pick up after them. I didn't figure cooking breakfast this morning would put me more in his favor because I was expected to be in the kitchen with his hot meal on the table when he sat down.

The difference today, which would never be found at the Renegade Clubhouse, was the thank you and assurance that my kitchen skills weren't a requirement. I'll be there again tomorrow if he doesn't kick me out by this evening.

I listen, with my ear to the door, when he leaves his room and walks down the long hallway. He pauses just outside of my door. Taking a few quiet steps back, I wait for him to enter only to hear his boots begin to move further away. I can't determine if I'm relieved he didn't open the door or disappointed.

The roar of his motorcycle is muffled through the wall, and before long it fades to nothing as he heads away from the house. Although I was happy to get away from him, being alone in this house brings its own emotions of abandonment and fear.

I take a seat on the edge of the bed, pulling at the hem of my shirt as it rides up my thighs. The action felt so right in the moment as Dom's eyes hungered at the sight, but shame fills my blood after his reaction.

I never would've acted that way at my own club. My brother and Grinder would've lost their shit if I propositioned a man there. Why I did it today is beyond me. At the Renegade clubhouse, I do my best to stay away from all the men there, but something foreign is drawing me to Dom.

He's attracted to me, that much I know. I could feel his eyes burning into my back as I cooked. I'm not an overtly sexual person, but I know my tiny frame and disproportionate breasts turn the eyes of many men. The men at the clubhouse would watch me, leer in my direction, eating me up with their eyes. Dom is no exception.

I shudder, a literal chill running over my skin when I think about the men at the clubhouse and how their eyes follow me, the words they whisper when Scorpion isn't around, and the way Grinder rules over them. He's claimed me, happened years ago. So as much as the men talk and make disgusting innuendos, I know they won't touch me. Just like myself, they're terrified of him and his psychotic behavior. I'm not worth risking his wrath, so they stay clear.

Just the thought of Grinder and the last eight years of my life makes my skin crawl. After locking the bedroom door even though I'm alone in the house, I enter the bathroom, strip to my skin, and climb in the shower. No amount of scrubbing can clear my head of the things I've done, witnessed, and been forced to do, but the symbolism of coming clean eases my mind.

I take my time showering, toweling off, and getting dressed back in the t-shirt Dom provided yesterday. Not interested in TV, I clean the mess in the kitchen, opting to wash the dishes by hand rather than use the dishwasher simply because it will kill more time.

Footsteps and a thump on the front porch almost cause a heart attack as I'm wiping down the kitchen table. The echo of the doorbell off the walls makes my heart stutter, and I do the only thing I can think of in the moment. I hit my knees and crouch behind the kitchen island, praying whoever is on the porch doesn't come around the side of the house and look through the large picture window over the sink.

Frightened, I huddle, hunched over my knees, making myself as small as possible while waiting for the imminent attack. I knew better than to run to a person who knows Grinder. He'll leave no stone unturned looking for me. I'm a liability, knowing too much that will either get him killed or land him in prison.

My breathing rattles in my ears, seeming louder than it actually is, and I wonder if the person outside can hear the harsh inhales and exhales. I shriek like a frightened child at a horror flick when a phone on the kitchen wall begins to ring.

Eyes darting in the direction of the front door, I fully expect a combat boot to kick it in any second, especially after my reaction to the phone. It rings five times and silences, only to begin again ten seconds later.

"Mak?" Dom's familiar voice soothes me more than it should.

I stand from my kneeling position and look over the island, fully preparing to explain my reaction now that he's home.

"Mak!" His voice is louder but seems just as distant. "The box on the damn wall woman!"

Noticing a small silver box on the far wall of the living room, I slowly make my way over there. Trusting nothing, my eyes dart left and right as I take measured steps across the room. There's no looming shadow showing through the front door or boot steps on the porch, which aid in calming my raging heart.

Is it possible to have a stroke at twenty-four?

"The box, Makayla." I shuffle faster as the irritation grows heavier in his voice. "Push the button to talk."

"Fuck's sake," I mutter before obeying his order. "What?"

I shouldn't be disrespectful, not after he's let me stay here, but it's an automatic reaction after having the shit scared out of me.

"Don't test me, woman," he grumbles. "I just got a notification that the store delivered the clothes for you. They were told to put them on the porch and ring the bell once."

I'm an idiot.

"Y-yes," I stammer. "Someone just rang the doorbell. It scared the hell out of me."

His chuckle at my expense, although manly and admittedly sexy, rubs me the wrong way.

"You need to go out and get them. It's suspicious for bags from a women's clothing store to be sitting on my porch."

My head whips in the direction of the door and the thought of opening it and someone seeing me makes my blood run cold.

"No one's out there, Mak. They're leaning against the door. You don't even have to open it the whole way."

What is he a damn mind reader now?

"Now, Mak. I don't have all damn day."

"Fine," I say with a stab of the button on the wall.

I pretend to wring his damn neck with my hands as I walk to the door, but stop in my tracks when his laugh follows me. I side eye the silver box, but continue my trek across the room. Standing off to the side of the door, I unlock it and grab it, bending at the waist and dragging them inside. Leaving them by the front door, I go back to the box.

"There's underwear in there, Mak. So I don't have to see you bending over like that and flashing that pretty pink pussy at me." The words come across the intercom before I can assure him I have the clothes.

I peer around the room, wondering if he's hiding somewhere fucking with me. I would've never taken him for the type to play practical jokes, but people surprise me every day.

"Cameras, Mak. They're all over the house." My cheeks flush, and my hands instinctively pull my t-shirt down more. "None in the guest bedroom, but I did enjoy the little dance while you were washing the dishes."

I jab the button, but words fail me at first.

"Something you need to say?" The humor in his voice, such a change from his asshole attitude this morning, almost makes me laugh.

"What are you some kind of fucking creeper?" I face the box directly with the hope that it hides my smile.

"You think I'd leave a woman I don't know all alone in my house without the means to check and see if she's rifling through or stealing all of my shit?" Back to the same indignant jerk he was this morning.

My jaw hangs open. "I'm not a thief. I haven't stolen anything since that one time I got popped at Wal-Mart when I was fourteen."

I don't bother explaining I was a late bloomer and my mom refused to buy pads, even when I refused tampons the first time I started my period. The Asset Protection Officer at the store saw how embarrassed I was and even offered to buy them for me. Mortifying.

"You'll have to tell me the story when I get..." he pauses. "Shit. I gotta go."

Silence over the intercom, makes me realize just how much I was enjoying the interaction, even though he practically accused me of being an untrustworthy criminal.

Not feeling like providing him with any more entertainment, I grab a yogurt out of the fridge and close myself back in my borrowed room. Every connection I have in life is inside the Renegade Clubhouse and only one person in this entire situation that keeps me from running across the country and never looking back.

Chapter 6

Dominic

"Gotta go," I grumble into the phone before closing out of the security app on my phone, tucking it into my pocket just as Bri sashays up to me.

"Hey there, Dom." I give her a quick head nod, normally interpreted by everyone else around here to leave me the fuck alone, but Bri ignores it.

Brighton Griggs, the older sister of Shadow, the Cerberus VP, has been around for months, using the excuse of helping her brother and Misty with Griffin, their almost sixteen-month-old son. Problem is she doesn't know shit about children. She mistakes my grin about the story Kid told me about how she put Hershey's fucking syrup in Misty's breast milk as directed at her.

"We don't normally see you during the week," she coos, sitting down beside me without an inch to spare between our thighs. The Clinique Happy she's over-sprayed on herself assaults my nose. The same shit that Karen wore all through high school. I thought that shit went out of style in the nineties, but then again Bri is only two years younger than my thirty-eight, so I guess it shouldn't be surprising.

"You staying the night?" Bri asks when I ignore her by keeping my eyes down, feigning interest in the app screen on my phone.

"Nope," I answer, wishing I hadn't even come over. "Was just about to leave."

My eyes dart up, finding Kincaid, Emmalyn, and several Cerberus members walking through the front door. The pinks and purples of the late fall sunset serve as a backdrop to their forms before the door closes. I smirk as my love-struck brother guides his very pregnant wife through the room.

"Hey, Dom," she offers without pausing.

"Let me get her to bed, and I'll be out in just a few minutes," Kincaid says, his arms at the ready to fend off anything that could stand in her way.

I chuckle when Emmalyn rolls her eyes at his overprotectiveness. She's told him a million times to back off, but after about the sixth month she gave up when he wouldn't relent.

I thank the Lord above when Snake, Snatch, and Ace take seats in the living room. Bri huffs and excuses herself less than a minute later.

I look over at Snatch. "What were you guys doing?"

"Doctor's appointment," he answers.

"More like a security escort and convoy to the damn hospital," Snake complains with an exaggerated sigh as he plops back on the sofa. "Prez is getting worse the further she gets."

I cock an eyebrow at him. I can laugh at the way my brother is acting over the woman he married two months ago. Snide comments from someone other than a blood relative make me want to punch him in the face.

"They went through hell to get those babies," I say instead of getting violent. "Just because you knocked up a club whore and she chose to get an abortion six months ago, doesn't mean that there aren't people out there who want their children."

Snake grumbles something under his breath as he stands and leaves the room.

Snatch kicks my boot, forcing me to pull my eyes from his back. "Asshole thing to say, man."

"It's true," I begin.

Snatch shakes his head. "She didn't even tell him she was pregnant until after the procedure. He's pretty fucked up about it."

"Shit," I grunt. "I can't get shit right today."

Including keeping my attitude in check where a certain pink-haired girl is concerned.

"Five weeks," Kincaid says coming into the room rubbing his hands together. "I can't wait for my girls to get here."

A sharp knock on the door has Kincaid tilting his head at Ace as he sits down. It's only then that I realize Ace, one of the newer members of the club has a pistol at his back and another strapped to his leg, his hand on his side piece as he peeks through the peephole.

I go to grin at my brother for the show of force at the damn doctor's office, but Ace's announcement, "Renegades" before he pulls open the door snaps my neck in that direction.

I hate the ease Ace must feel as he pulls his hand from the gun on his thigh to swing the door open as if he's welcoming an old friend.

Kincaid shifts beside me, scooting to the edge of the couch. Nervous energy is rolling off of him, and I know then that he doesn't trust the Renegade MC as much as he makes the other Cerberus members believe. I see his eyes dart to Snatch who's on his feet in less than a second.

"Beer?" he asks me as he heads further into the room toward the kitchen and closer to the entry into the hallway where Kincaid's pregnant wife is resting.

"Sure, man," I respond not taking my eyes off of Grinder and two of his lackeys as they clear the threshold and walk toward us.

It doesn't go unnoticed that Snatch doesn't offer the interlopers a beer, a clear indication to everyone that they're not welcome to stay.

"Grinder," Kincaid says standing from the couch. His nonchalance betrayed by the way his hand rests on his belt, right above the glock he's got in an appendix carry against his stomach. "Unannounced is really unusual for Renegades, especially without your Prez."

The warning in his voice beyond apparent. The Renegade MC is invited to community functions, being the closest MC to Kincaid's. They come over by invite only, usually for barbecues or parties, the last one being when I retired from the Marines last year. Since finding out Emmalyn is pregnant, Kincaid hasn't invited them back. The pixie like woman alone in my house is the reason for this unannounced house call, and I hate that I promised Makayla I wouldn't speak to Kincaid or any of the Cerberus about her being there. Protecting her is one thing, but at the expense of this club when I have no fucking clue what's going on, isn't something I'm remotely comfortable with.

"Prez's sister is missing," Grinder says with an emotionless expression that makes my skin crawl.

Damn near graying hair and numerous scars on his face make his words more sinister than I'm sure he's intended. The Renegade's Sergeant at Arms has been around longer than almost all of the other biker's in the group. He was Breaker Hanigan's SAA before Scorpion took over years ago.

"How long?" Kincaid asks with concern etched in his uninformed voice.

"Nobody's seen her since yesterday, about mid-morning," Grinder replies.

"Less than thirty-six hours," Kincaid says after a quick glance at his watch. "Can't be the first time she's taken a break from the clubhouse."

An eerie sense of dread hits me when Grinder's scarred lip twitches as if he's barely holding back his rage.

"She tends to stick pretty close to home," one of the other guys says, but is halted from speaking when Grinder throws a death glare over his shoulder.

"We've had some trouble with a few assholes in town. She went to get coffee and never came back," Grinder shares.

Kincaid cocks his head to the side, confusion in his eyes. "If you got trouble in Durango, I guess I don't understand why you guys are looking for her in Farmington."

Grinder's eyes dart from Kincaid's to mine and back to Kincaid's. "We wanted to see if you've seen her. Ask if any of your girls have had contact with her. Scorpion's getting nervous. She's never been gone overnight before. He's afraid she's in a bad way."

She's safe motherfucker.

"Most of the girls here are gone for the week. Some lipstick convention in Tulsa. Been gone since Monday. Won't be back until next week."

"Fuck," Ace groans from across the room and I look over in time to see him grabbing his dick through his jeans as if he's pained by not having pussy at the ready for a week. Lazy fucker may have to go out and actually convince a woman to fuck him.

"I can put in a call," Kincaid adds. "But I can guarantee they haven't heard from her. Poison doesn't come around here. Never has."

The mention of her name makes the hairs on my arms stand up.

"So you're not going to look for her?" Agitation is evident in Grinder's voice as he darts his eyes between my brother and me.

"Let me do some checking," Kincaid placates. "I'll call you if I find anything."

Grinder nods and turns to leave, his gaze staying on me a couple seconds too long. I know he can't read me. I've perfected my ability to keep my emotions locked down, playing someone I'm not from years in the Corps, but the way he's looking at me makes me question if I've kept my face calm when ideas that he's somehow responsible for Mak showing up on my doorstep. The fact that she can compromise years of training concerns me.

We stand, silent, and watch the three Renegade members exit the clubhouse, not speaking until the sound of their motorcycles are no longer heard.

"Hmm," Kincaid hums as he takes his seat once again.

"They usually come to you with shit like that?" I ask as Snatch comes back from his post near the kitchen and sits across from us.

"Never," Snatch answers for Kincaid.

"They usually keep their club business to themselves," my brother adds.

"It seems more like they're hunting her, not looking for her," I reply.

"You caught that too, huh?" I nod even though the question is rhetorical.

"Let me know what you find out," I say standing from the couch. "I'm going to head home."

"Got big plans or something?" My brother, always attentive knows I'd normally stay later than now.

I shrug. "I feel like I need a shower after being around Grinder. That guy gives me the creeps." Which is saying a lot considering the people we interact with on recovery missions and encounters I've had in my twenty years of military service.

"See you later," he says also standing from the couch.

Snatch laughs as he heads back to his room to check on Emmalyn.

"Later," I tell Snatch as I head for the door.

The slow fifteen minute ride back to my house does nothing to abate the feeling in my gut that Mak's being in my house and the injuries on her body have everything to do with Grinder.

Once home, I don't even bother knocking on her bedroom door, but I'm surprised it's unlocked. She bolts up to sitting in bed the second the door opens.

"Cover yourself," I hiss when she just sits blinking up at me with her glorious tits on full display.

"Don't like my tits?" she teases but pulls the sheet up to her chin

"You have amazing tits, Mak. We both know that, but they happen to be attached to a woman who's in my house hiding out from a deadly guy, and I'm left in the dark."

She startles at the nugget of information I'm just making a stab in the dark at.

"If I'm going to have to look at your tits, you need to talk." She clutches the sheet tighter against her body as her head shakes left and right. "Eventually you're going to have to tell me what you got me mixed up in."

"You're not mixed up in anything," she whispers.

"Bullshit," I say rubbing my hand across my forehead. "Tomorrow you talk. Tomorrow you tell me why Grinder and two of his lynch men showed up at the clubhouse tonight hunting for you."

I back out of the room when she whimpers at the information. The urge to hold her, beg her to tell me what the fuck is going on, and promise her I'll protect her is too strong to stay in the room with her.

Chapter 7

Makayla

"Take it," the hot rancid smell of Grinder's breath rushes over my shoulder as he kicks my legs further apart. I know how this ends, but I can't keep myself from fighting him. Refusing to give in and just let it happen isn't in me.

One arm pinning my shoulder over the table, his other comes up and connects with my face. Searing pain blasts behind my eyelid, the warm trickle of blood already flowing down my cheek.

My lip is bleeding from biting back the screams in my nightmare when I finally break free of the entanglements of sleep. The nightmares are always the same; violent, horrific, and linger long after my eyes open. I rub the side of my face, phantom pain from his last strike against it as real as if he were in the room with me.

Even away from the clubhouse, the torture follows me, as does the morning routine. I barely make it to the toilet, completing the first step of almost every morning since I was sixteen. Next comes the scalding hot shower, which even if it were hot enough to peel my skin away, I'd still feel dirty.

The third is only accomplished after drying off and dressing, from head to toe this time. I grab the throw from the end of the bed and as quiet as possible make my way to the kitchen to caffeinate against the night of restless sleep. The sun hasn't even peaked over the horizon, but the peaceful calm of the dock and lake out back have been calling to me since yesterday. With coffee in hand, I check out front ensuring that Dominic is still home and sneak out back. My socks and the bottoms of my thick pajamas dampen as I walk to the dock, the morning dew clinging to them. I smiled when I pulled out the clothes he had delivered to the house. You'd think he was dressing a Mormon convert with how much skin each piece of clothing covers. I'd never complain though because the flannel I'm wearing right now is perfect for the chilly breeze of the early morning.

Sitting Indian style at the very end of the dock, I drink my coffee and look out over the water. The ducks, having noticed my presence, begin to wag feathered little tails as they swim in my direction, only to seem insulted and swim away once they realize I don't have a crumb of bread to share.

My mind wanders back to the clubhouse, and I smile but also want to cry when I think about Jasmine. The innocent little girl born into a life no one in their right mind would choose, the life her coked up mother chose for her from birth. Although she doesn't have the life experiences to know any different, she has spoken to me more than once about the things she's seen, the things she knows aren't right even though she knows no different. She's the reason I just can't disappear and never look back. Guilt fills my blood for being gone as long as I have, even though I know I had to leave when I did because I can't help either one of us if I'm dead.

"What the fuck are you doing?" the grumble of Dom's voice behind me nearly jolts me to the point I end up drenched in the lake.

I whip my head around, spilling coffee in my lap in the process, fully prepared to yell at him for scaring the shit out of me. Only no words come out, my throat only allowing the tiniest of squeaks when I see him naked except for a thin layer of black boxer briefs covering him. I don't question the gun in his hand; it's a regular sight with all of the men I've grown up with.

"I asked you a question," he says on a yawn pulling the back of his armed hand to cover his mouth.

"Drinking coffee," I tell him holding up my now nearly empty cup. "Contemplating my next move."

"Yeah?" He sits down beside me even though he has to be freezing.

I do my best to pull my eyes from the bunching and rippling of his abdomen as he settles beside me but I fail. Jesus, he's kind of ripped for an old dude.

"How old are you," I blurt.

"Forty-five," he answers.

"Bullshit!"

Chuckling at my answer he gives me the 'what? Don't you believe me?' look. "Thirty-eight. Thirty-nine in a few months."

"Really?" I ask emphasizing my disbelief, thinking he was thirty-two, tops.

"Why do you ask it like that? You're cracking my self-esteem."

I huff. "I seriously doubt that," I mutter. "You're just..." I wave my arm up and down indicating his incredible physique.

"I'm what?" His mouth quirks right in the corner, but he stops himself before full out smiling. The playfulness is in full contrast to how he treated me yesterday, bi-polar almost, and it concerns me more than him acting like an asshole twenty-four seven. I can't help but wonder if he's manipulating me into talking which is worse than being a douchebag and demanding things from me. I know how to deal with men like that.

Ignoring his question I turn my eyes back out to the water. "You should wear more clothes."

He laughs, actually laughs at my words. "Too tempting for you?"

"Fuck you," I grumble. "You're the one who turned me down yesterday."

When I look back over at him, I notice his face is no longer playful, but his mask of seriousness is in place. "You set the alarm off when you came out here, Mak. Excuse me for not wasting time getting more clothes on when I was afraid something was wrong."

I look over my shoulder back to the house. "I didn't hear an alarm."

"It's silent. The app on my phone woke me up." I nod my head in understanding. What he says seems feasible, but the Renegades don't have that level of technology back in Durango.

"Sorry," I whisper. "Didn't mean to wake you up. I just needed some fresh air."

He doesn't respond just looks out over the lake like I was doing a few moments before. I watch him, noticing the dark stubble on his jaw, as if I need another reason to find him attractive.

"Here," I say opening the blanket around my shoulders and offering him half. His torso and arms are covered in chill bumps, and technically the blanket is his. "No sense in freezing."

Surprisingly, he takes the offering and wraps it around his back. "You smell like me." The gravel in his voice and the absence of the full wrap of the throw now covers me in gooseflesh, the tingle settling low in my belly.

"The soap in the bathroom is for men," I explain. Knowing it's the same thing he uses makes me want to go back to the house and live in the bathroom with it.

"I'll have some girly shit delivered," he offers.

"You don't have to do that." I resist the urge to lean against his big shoulder. The scent of his body wash has been wrapped around me for almost two days now, just the smell bringing a sense of safety and respite from the horrific things at the clubhouse.

"You said you were out here contemplating your next move," he begins, changing the subject to one I knew he wouldn't avoid for long. "Any clue what that's going to be?"

"No," I answer.

"I can help you if you tell me what's going on, Mak. I'm not one to get in anyone's privacy, but you leave me no choice."

"I can't," I whisper. Tears sting my eyes at the thought of the trouble that I've brought on Dom and the Cerberus MC. "He'll kill you."

A genuine laugh fills the air around us, and I'm close enough to him that I feel the blanket shaking.

"You mean Grinder?" I stiffen. "I spent twenty years in the sand as a Marine, sweetheart. If those fuckers over there couldn't stop me, some disgusting old biker won't be able to either."

I want to correct him, tell him the things I've seen that demented bastard do, but I bite my tongue to the point that I have to swallow the taste of blood when it wells against my teeth.

I shake my head again when he turns to look at me.

"Okay," he says as he stands, the blanket falling limply to the wooden dock.

He doesn't threaten me, insist I leave, or treat me badly to get the information he wants, but for some reason, the sight of his back as he walks away causes more fear than I'll ever admit to.

Chapter 8

Dominic

Frustrated beyond words, I walk away from Makayla. I've never met a woman more obstinate in my life.

"Please," she whispers. "H-he raped me."

Warm blood, giving me life, runs immediately cold at her words.

"I'll fucking kill him," I seethe without even turning around to face her.

I allow myself a few long breaths before turning around only to find her looking out over the water as if she wouldn't be able to speak the words if she were looking at me.

"The bruises," I begin, but her humorless laugh stops me.

She shakes her head then turns her beautiful face up to look at me. "This is what I look like when I fight back, and he doesn't have enough time or privacy to finish the job."

"The last time he—" Fuck, I can't even get the words out. I've dealt with hundreds of women who've suffered sexual assault, but can't manage to form a sentence with Makayla.

"A month or so ago," she answers filling in the blank.

"The first time?" I know I'm going to hate him even more if that's even possible when she answers, but I have an unexplainable need to know everything. I want to be able to look in his eyes, fully informed when I choke the life out of him.

"H-he," she begins but has to take a moment to clear her throat and force down the emotion before she can continue.

I pad back down the dock, veins filled with rage and no longer feeling the chill in the air. I sit down beside her and pull the blanket back around my shoulders, if only to be near her, the only form of comfort I can offer right now.

"He used to touch me before my mom died, but never got the chance to go very far. My dad's wife at the time was actually pretty decent. Calypso, did you know her?" she asks raising her eyes to me once again, close enough that I can feel her warm breath on my skin.

I look away, out across the water where it's safe. "I didn't. Cerberus didn't start up until after she was gone."

I remember the stories, though. "Breaker" Hanigan was always an asshole. As president of the Renegades, he believed any and all pussy belonged to him. Women were props, fronts for the police, and only good on their knees and backs. I know Calypso killed herself when now

President Scorpion was only fourteen, his dad following her to the grave six years later in some kind of drug deal gone wrong.

"Calypso treated me like I was human. More than I can say for my father. I was eleven when she died. My dad didn't want me around after that. I was sad that she was gone but grateful every day that I didn't have to go back over there." She turns her attention to the wringing hands in her lap. "I was sixteen when my mom died. With no other family, I had no choice but to go to the clubhouse. Two weeks after getting there, Grinder raped me the first time."

The warmth of her body near mine is the only thing keeping me from jumping on my bike, driving the hour to their club and blowing the whole damn thing up. "I can't fucking believe Scorpion allows that kind of shit in his clubhouse. I mean, I know everything they do isn't above board, but I never imagined it was anything like this."

"Scorpion doesn't have a clue," she explains. "Grinder would literally kill me if I spoke a word of it. Some of the other members have suspicions, but no concrete evidence that he's been hurting me."

A million questions run through my head. Why didn't she just leave? Why would she stay quiet? Would Scorpion protect her if he knew? I know from my experience with this sort of thing that many women in these situations don't always think straight. The pain and assault that they know may be better than what they will face if they leave.

"He saw me." I feel her eyes on the side of my face, but I don't have the strength to look at her. I'm already fighting every muscle in my body not to pull her to my chest. "DEA Agent Ryland pulled me off of the street and brought me in for questioning. Grinder saw me leaving the police station. I know he thinks I snitched him out."

"Why would he automatically think that?" It's been my experience in dealing with one percenters that they don't let the women in the clubhouse know too many details about their illegal dealings. I can't imagine Renegades are any different.

She huffs a laugh. "I told him I would. I told him the day before when he was hitting me that I'd had enough and I was going to the police. I didn't mean it. I'd never jeopardize my life like that, but I couldn't have predicted that the fucking DEA was going to snatch me off the street."

"But you have shit on him? Things that would get him arrested?"

She nods. "He has shit on me, too." A tear streaks down her cheek. "He's forced me to help bury bodies. Held my finger on the trigger when he's shot people. I've cleaned up more blood and entrails than I could ever remember. He's threatened to go to the police. Says he has video evidence of the things I've been involved in."

I shake my head. "You were under duress. Grand jury would never indict you."

She gives me a knowing smile, one that says I'm a complete idiot. "You seriously think a biker princess has any pull or sympathy from civilians if it ever came to that? They'd lock me up and throw away the key."

"And I'm sure that's something that Grinder's ass has been telling you for years?" Her face falls, and I know the truth without her verifying.

"I'm as good as dead," she mutters like it's a fact rather than a possibility.

"I think if Scorpion knows, he'll be the first one to put a bullet in that motherfucker's head. He's a cocky asshole who doesn't treat women with the respect they deserve, but I've never seen him be abusive or condone that shit from his men."

She shakes her head again. "Scorpion isn't concerned with what happens to me, brother or not, he has his own set of sins to answer for."

"What aren't you telling me?" I try to keep it casual, my eyes staying on the water, so she doesn't feel interrogated.

"What do you mean?"

I finally turn my eyes to hers. "You came here. You didn't run to another state. You haven't asked for money. I can give you everything you need, you know that right? If you want another identity, it's done. We can relocate you, and you'll never have to think about the Renegades again."

"He'll never stop looking for me, and he'll find me. He always finds them, like a hound dog with a nose that sniffs out lies and the smell of fear." At her words I see her eyes dart over her shoulder toward the house as if talking about Grinder will conjure him from thin air.

"Does he need a body? Because we can do that, too. Fake your death that is, give them something to bury so he knows the trail has ended." She shakes her head again. "Give me something, Mak. I don't have a damn thing to work with here. I don't mind you staying here, but I also don't know how you see all of this ending. There has to be a resolution."

"This was the only place I could think to go, Dominic. I have no intention of bringing you in on anything. I don't expect you or Cerberus to do a damn thing to help end the bullshit I'm in the middle of."

"It's a little late for that, sweetheart. If you think I can just sit by while you're in danger and Grinder is still breathing, you don't know me at all."

She glares at me, and I love the fire in her eyes. It's so much better than the tears and self-recrimination. "That's just it, Dom. I *don't* know you. I have *no desire* to know you. If you want me out, just say it."

I remain silent as she flings the blanket off of her shoulders and storms off the dock back toward the house. Sassy isn't something I'm used to dealing with. If any other woman spoke to me that way, I'd tie her ass to my bed and spank the shit out of her until she relented. Control is usually something I always have, but knowing her story, I don't imagine that would work out in my favor. Hurting her is the last thing I want. She's been hurt too much, neglected for quite some time it seems. That shit stops now.

Her sulking off, saying that shit to me, however, will not go undealt with. I wad the blanket up and stand, following after her into the house. I may not be able to whip her ass like I want, but I'll put an end to this nondisclosure bullshit.

Chapter 9

Makayla

My hands are trembling to the point I can barely get them to work to open the back door to get into the house.

No desire to know him. I don't think a bigger lie has ever been told.

I place my empty coffee cup in the sink with more patience than I feel and head back to my room. I scurry faster when I see Dom heading back into the house. Refusing to meet his gaze through the glass of the back door, I enter the borrowed bedroom and lock the door. The urge to sleep for hours hits in a wave, so I shrug off the too hot pajamas and climb into the bed.

His footsteps bypass my door only to return thirty seconds later. The key in the lock has my eyes narrowing, glaring at him as he opens it and walks in like he owns the place. Well… damn it.

"Can I help you?" I mutter pulling the covers up to my chin.

"That little tantrum you pulled out there isn't going to stop me from getting the truth out of you." My eyes dart to his hands as he opens and closes his fists. It's not predatory or aggressive, but more like he wants to touch me but is keeping his distance. I'm sure my admission on the dock is governing his lack of action.

"You don't want a new identity," he begins taking a seat in the chair near the door. "But there's something that's keeping you close. You need to tell me what that is, Mak. Now."

I hate how the low grumble and commanding tone of his voice makes my insides melt. It makes me want to defy him more, just to see how far he'll take his insistence. Licking my lips, lost in the baritone, I hear him grumble something incoherent and turn his eyes from me. The quick glance at the door almost makes me chuckle. This huge biker, more than twice my size is planning his escape route when he initially came in here to give me the riot act and *force* me to tell him the information he wants.

My mind wars with itself. The fight between coming up with a resolution on my own, which I know I won't be able to just to keep them out of this, and telling him the truth and having no control of the outcome of the situation.

I opt for the latter because I'm out of options.

"There's a little girl there," I say.

"Your daughter?" His eyes dart to the blanket covering my stomach. "With Grinder?"

I recoil at the implications. "Hell no. She belongs to one of the club girls. Jasmine is eight, and her mother has been around the club for as long as I can remember."

"Does her mother want out also?" I shake my head. "You're sure about that?"

"She's picked up a pretty serious coke habit the last couple of years. She won't leave out of fear of losing that." I look down at my knotted hands. "I can't leave before getting Jasmine out of there."

He nods when I fully expected him to tell me some other woman's child isn't my responsibility. My heart, surrounded by walls built from years of abuse and neglect softens just a little.

"Jasmine is my sister," I disclose. No reaction from him. The determination in his eyes to help Jasmine is the same before he knew she was a blood relative. The walls crumble a little more. "Her mother denies it. Says the girl belongs to some guy she met at a bar."

He quirks an eye at me. "What reason do you have not to believe her?"

"Jasmine looks exactly like Scorpion and me. Just like us, there's no denying our paternity."

He leans closer, elbows on his knees. "She's not safe there? Renegades are hurting kids now?"

I swallow, trying to force down the lump forming in my throat, combating the sting of tears behind my eyes.

"Grinder mentioned in passing once that nine is the perfect age to start grooming girls to be *good little whores*." I avoid his eyes even though I can feel them burning a hole in the side of my head. "I was nine when he first touched me."

The sound of his knuckles cracking pulls my eyes from my own hands over to his.

"I didn't leave before," I continue, "because I knew I had to stay there. I may not be able to do much, but I could keep an eye on things. When Grinder saw me outside the police station, I had no choice but to run."

A renewed wave of guilt crushes me, but I speak through my sobs, wiping at the tears running down my face.

"I try not to think about the things I've gone through that he's planning to do to her next."

"I'll kill him before he lays a finger on her." His words are full of a promise so firm, I have no choice but to believe him.

"There's more," I admit. "He and two of the other guys are running an online porn site from the club."

He chuckles. "Mak, there's nothing I can do about illegal porn."

"Some of the girls are underage." The laughing stops immediately.

"Fuck," he grumbles. I watch his large hand rake over the top of his hair. "He's running child pornography?"

"The girls are fifteen and sixteen. Mostly hangarounds with daddy issues. As far as I know, he's not forcing any of them, but I know he plies them with drugs when they don't want to participate in certain activities. He's only a couple of bad ideas away from deciding to use girls Jasmine's age to feed the hungry fuckers who are into that disgusting deviant shit."

I jolt when he stands so fast the chair he was sitting in bangs against the wall. My eyes follow him as he paces like a caged animal around the room.

"I never trusted those motherfuckers. Pieces of shit, every last damned one of them." His eyes lock onto mine. "Has he forced you into porn? I'll fucking kill him twice if he has."

I shake my head. "He's threatened it, but he wouldn't want to share me like that." I clear my throat again. "He says I'm his. That he owns me."

He mumbles something that sounds a lot like. *If anyone is going to own you, it's going to be me*, but I can't be certain because his back is to me. I watch as his head tilts up and he focuses on an imaginary spot on the ceiling.

"Who's fucking the girls? Is he bringing in underage boys as well?"

I shake my head, but then realize he can't see me. "No. It's the oldest guys in the club. The members that have been around since my dad was president."

He growls his dissent, so I decide to lay it all out. Hopefully, we won't have to have this conversation again if he knows everything today.

"The website is Grinding Daddies." This information turns him around to face me, so I continue. "As far as Grinder's concerned the younger the girl, the older the guy, the better."

"Sick fucks," he spits. "And your brother is right in the middle of this shit?"

"I don't think so. All of the information I have was from listening in on a conversation last week. I confronted Grinder that same day."

He shakes his head. "Not very smart, Mak. He could've killed you."

My face softens. "I thought he was going to." I point to the healing black eye, busted lip, and marks around my neck. "My point is he was adamant that if I uttered a word to Scorpion, I wouldn't see the light of another day."

"What kind of president doesn't know this shit is going on right under his nose?" He searches my face as if trying to decide if I'm lying to protect my brother.

"You have to understand that the Renegades are like rabid hyenas. Each one is only out for themselves and what they can benefit from, even at the expense of the other members. The only time they stand united is when threatened by an outside force. Scorpion has no control over the men in his club. He's distracted at best most days. Disappears dealing with shit on his own agenda. The club is falling apart."

"Best fucking thing I've heard all day," he mutters.

"Those underage girls, Jasmine, some of the club girls don't deserve to just be left in the wind. Many don't see a way out. Some have been in it too long to know any different. There are club girls there my age that were born into all of that chaos and abuse by their mothers." I sigh, deciding to tell him what's on my mind even though it makes me just as evil as some of the men there. "My only concern is Jasmine. If worse comes to worst, she's the only person in that club I give a damn about. The whole thing could burn to the ground, and as long as my sister is safe, I'd call that a successful day."

"I can't let that happen, Mak. I would be no better than Grinder if I didn't take into consideration the other people there."

"I just want my sister to be safe," I say as guilt pushes more tears from my eyes.

He takes a long moment to look at me, and I've never felt more scrutinized than in this moment.

"This shit stops today," he seethes. "I'll get the guys together and put an end to this shit today."

"No!" I yell reaching out for him.

Chapter 10

Dominic

"Someone will get hurt," she cries as the blanket falls from under her chin.

Perfect, milky-white tits with the most suckable dusty-rose colored nipples are on full display. I push down the idea that I'm just like Grinder and his "daddies" since I'm close to fourteen years her senior. She's in her mid-twenties I bargain with myself as my throat clenches, mouthwatering excessively at the idea of my tongue on her.

"I can't have it on my conscience if you or one of the guys from your club got hurt because you don't have time to plan." I don't correct her about the *your club* part. It's Kincaid's club; I'm not even a patched member. I just like the excitement some of the missions they get involved in brings, a way for me to fulfill my need for the adrenaline rush that comes along with shooting and bringing pieces of shit to justice.

The way she's looking at me, I don't think she even realizes she's showcasing herself, but being the asshole that I am, I can't stop the words inching out of my mouth.

"You can't tempt me with those gorgeous tits of yours, Mak." I grin when she hisses and yanks the blanket back up to her throat. "I can fuck you all day and still save every one of those girls by nightfall."

"They're heavily armed," she whispers.

"You don't have to worry about us, sweetheart. It's what we do."

She shakes her head as if she's speaking a different language and I'm not translating it correctly.

"No," she urges again. "You don't get it. Renegades aren't like Cerberus."

"You got that shit right," I mutter.

"They're different," she continues, the narrowing of her eyes the only chastisement I'm provided at my remark. "Every single person in the club with the exception of Jasmine has something to hide. They've all committed a criminal act of some sort. There are some members who are on strike number two. It's every man and woman for themselves if you go in there half-cocked."

I grin at her tirade and just barely resist the urge to grab my dick to let her know that I'm, in fact, fully cocked and willing to prove it. However, the seriousness of the matter is no time for my dick even if I can't get the image of her tits out of my head.

"What's so damn funny? There's nothing about this that is funny. Grinning like that is exactly why I know someone will get hurt." I sober immediately.

"Sorry," I mutter even though I have no idea why I'm apologizing.

"But seriously, Dom. Everyone there has something to lose. Whether it's their freedom or their dope habit, no one is going to come willingly. It'll be an absolute blood bath. You say you don't want to just concern yourself with my sister, that all the women and girls there are important? Then you need to have a strategy." She blows out a long breath and leans against the headboard, unfortunately pulling the blanket with her.

"What do you suggest?" It's an olive branch. I have no need for her help in figuring out what to do in a situation like this. We spend our lives rescuing women and children from more insidious places than Durango, Colorado.

"If I knew, I'd have done it already," she mutters. "Even with Grinder in prison, I'm not safe. I've seen what some of the members are capable of from behind bars."

I hate the Renegades even more as the tears begin to flow down her cheeks once again.

"He's not going to prison," I promise. The words left unsaid aren't lost on her.

A softness fills her eyes, a small smile playing on her lips, and the whole look makes me uncomfortable. I can't negate the fact that she's a crime lord's daughter and she was raised in that environment. I'm trained to detect deception. I don't see any on her face, but that doesn't mean she's as innocent as she's portraying herself to be. The fact that I want to fuck her into next week doesn't help my ability to remain unbiased either.

"Some of the members," she begins after a long silence. "They may not be the most law-abiding, but they have honor. They're not one hundred percent bad."

I glare at her as she backpedals. "Really? The ones that put guns and drugs on the street? The ones who supply the dealers who then distribute dope to teenagers and kids? That's honor?"

I shake my head when she drops her eyes back down to her hands.

"Honor, sweetheart is protecting those under your care. Honor is never putting them in harm's way or supplying them with things that will eventually kill them. There is no *honor* in destroying lives to make a buck.

Your club wouldn't know honor if it showed up on the clubhouse steps waving a bright white flag."

Her eyes snap up to mine. "That is not my club," she seethes. "You think I asked for this life? That I wanted to be repeatedly raped by a man old enough to be my father? That I counted it a blessing that my father ignored me every day before he died? That I woke up at sixteen to find my strung-out mother dead in her bed and the piece of shit beside her leaving without so much as a call to the police to deal with the body?"

I take a step toward her, ready to take back what I'd just said but she holds me off with an upturned hand. "Don't even," she hisses. "You can't take it back. It is what it is. No one was there to get me out of that place, but I refuse to let my sister grow up any longer in that kind of environment. I won't turn a blind eye to the destruction of her soul from seeing the terrible things going on when people think no one is watching."

My jaw ticks at the picture she's painting. The guys at Cerberus are all for pussy, and sometimes things get heated before they move to one of the available rooms, but before Griffin showed up, there were no children. Things have calmed down a lot since his arrival, and I imagine after Kincaid's daughters are born, things will simmer even more.

"Mak, I'm sorry. I—"

"It's done," she whispers turning her eyes from me. I miss the blue stare immediately. "I appreciate the honesty. It's always good to know where I rank with people."

"Let me speak," I hiss, my feet moving me closer to the bed of their own volition. "Defending criminals and comparing them to honorable men went too far. Good men die every—"

"There's more you should know if you plan to get my sister out," she interrupts, and I can hardly fight the urge to yank her up and let me explain.

I decide, with both tempers ablaze, now is not the time to try to get her to see the light.

"They only film the first three days of the month," she continues.

"Today's the sixth."

She nods. "Exactly. I found out about all this shit on the first." She points to her face as if I need the reminder. "They don't keep the teenagers there the whole month. So if you go in now, there's no telling what will happen with those girls. I don't know where they're keeping them, and if you move on Grinder when they're not there, you may never find out."

Smart and beautiful, a deadly combination.

"So you have time to come up with a plan." She still denies me her eyes and every dominant bone in my body wants to grab her by the chin and insist she speaks to me eye to eye. I don't. For some unexplained reason, I want her to trust me, and I'm certain manhandling her is not a way to gain it.

"You know I can't do this alone." She finally raises her expectant eyes to mine, and I can't tell if she thinks I want her to help me or she knows which direction I'm going. "If they are as volatile as you say they are, the entire Cerberus team needs to be brought in on this. We'll need surveillance, floor plans, all sorts of shit to do our best to keep everyone safe."

"You're going to tell them where I am?" The fear in her eyes and tremble in her voice makes me cringe, but I know getting complacent is the last thing she needs. It's the fact that she's worried about Kincaid's men knowing she's here causing the fear that irks me. I have to remind myself that she's grown up around pieces of shit, and in that environment, she's smart to not trust anyone. It also forces me to realize the amount of faith she's put in me just showing up at my house.

"For now, I'll leave it be. We don't need a month to get ready for something like this. A couple of days is generous compared to the timeframe we're usually given, but yes, Mak. Eventually, they're going to have to know that I'm harboring the runaway Renegade Princess."

"I don't trust any of them," she whispers. "I know some of the Cerberus guys are friends with the Renegades, turning a blind eye to the criminal aspects of the club. Someone could tell Grinder where I am. Hell, some of them could be involved with the Grinding Daddies."

"Stop," I ground out. "Cerberus is keen on young pussy just as much as the next MC, but they draw the line at getting dirty with teenagers. If you doubt me, you need to talk to Kid and Khloe. I'm sure Kid still has an ache in his sac from the blue balls he had waiting for that girl to turn eighteen."

"How can you be sure everyone can be trusted? Your club girls could get wind I'm here, and they'll track me down. Please, Dom. You can't tell them."

I almost refute everything she's just said, with an extra reminder that the girls at our club don't get intel on things like this, but Snapper and Wrench come to mind. Wrench is long dead, teaming up with Emmalyn's abusive husband, but Snapper is a wild card, a snake who's not fooling anyone but tends to be super resourceful.

"I can easily convince them that I came across this info after looking into finding you since Grinder came by the club last night." She nods, wiping at another tear that's forced its way out. "But I won't compromise Cerberus to keep your secret."

"I understand. I wouldn't expect you to choose me over your men."

"Your secret," I correct. "This isn't about choosing, Mak."

"I just want my sister safe and away from that life."

My heart beats faster at her devotion. "I know you do, baby."

Baby? Why the fuck did I say that shit?

I clear my throat, hoping she didn't catch the slip. "I've got things to do today." I turn and walk out, needing distance and time alone to clear my head.

Chapter 11

Makayla

"Please, please," I beg, hoping that this one time he'll listen to my pleas and leave me alone. I don't know why I even entertain the thought, he never has before. "I don't want this. I'll tell my daddy."

He sneers, gripping my arms tighter, the evil in his eyes almost a tangible thing. "This was your daddy's idea."

I shake my head, rejecting the thought. He wouldn't, would he?

"Open up for me little girl," he gurgles, the smell of hot beer on his breath enough to make me sick, even if his fingers weren't trying to pry my thighs apart. "I'll be gentle if you cooperate."

I wail, unwilling to give into him, my body just won't allow it. I shriek, beg, plead with whoever may be around and can hear him hurting me. I know no one will rescue me. They didn't the first two times he came into my room and touched me. I shouldn't expect a miracle the third time.

"Mak. Makayla!"

Arms wrap around me, but the voice in my head turns from the taunting and torment of Grinder to the soothing and reassuring baritone of a familiar voice I can't quite identify.

"You're safe," he whispers. "He'll never hurt you again."

I calm as he consoles me in the safety of his arms.

"Dom," I whisper as my eyelids flutter and sleep threatens to take over again.

"I'm here, baby. Go back to sleep." The warmth in his tone comforts me more than I have the energy to analyze right now.

"Don't leave me," I whisper. "Don't let him hurt me."

"Never again," he vows.

"I never wanted it," I mumble as sleep clings to the edges of my mind.

"I know, I know," he chants softly until my mind eases completely and restful slumber pulls me under.

***

If someone would've asked me if I'd enjoy waking up in the arms of a half-naked man, I would've denied it. Never having experienced the act myself, I would've been sure that just their body heat alone would be too much to bare. I would've been lying. What seemed like a bad idea before the actual participation is complete heaven. I snuggle into Dom's side, trying to get a few seconds of pleasure before he wakes and shoves me away.

His scent, the soft sound of his breath, the long cock against my thigh, all overwhelm my senses.

I press myself harder against him, the tingling between my legs almost too much to ignore. With eyes closed and not allowing my brain to overanalyze the situation my hand travels over the bumps and ridges of his perfectly defined abdomen. Humming deep in my throat, the hair on his stomach tickles the tips of my fingers. I've never invited a man into my bed, and even though I didn't encourage Dom last night, my nightmare pulled him to me. I'm not mad that he stayed. In fact, I'm happy he's here.

Temptation prevails, and I reach lower tracing the outline of an undeniably thick cock. The tingles turn into a clenching need, but the fear of rejection, like the other day in his kitchen makes me unsure. My body demands attention, to the point my hips move against his leg, a desperate attempt at friction as my fingers grip him over the fabric of his boxers.

His husky groan and the tightening of his arm around my back are the only incentives I need to tug the band of his boxers away. Eyes finally open, they find my grip on his body.

"Jesus," I huff, the sight of wetness on his tip is my destruction.

Stroking from base to tip, I relish the small circle of his hips.

"You shouldn't be doing that." The warning is a contradiction to the gravel and urgency in his voice. "Scorpion wouldn't like me fucking his sister."

I smile against his chest, keeping my eyes low on his cock. Looking in his eyes right now seems too intimate, and intimacy is the last thing I'm looking for. Right now is about feeding the necessity my body feels when he's around.

His legs fall open a few inches when I cup his heavy sac, but my eyes are drawn to the bead of precome on the crown of his dick.

I begin to move down his body, pushing the limits until he tells me to stop. The words never come, and my mouth is around him seconds later. A full body tremble wracks his body when I pull him deep and swallow around him. I smile at his reaction and almost gag when his hips jolt up, forcing him deeper.

"Look at me," he pleads.

I ignore him, knowing the eye contact isn't something I can handle. Maintaining my attention down south is much easier than facing him, much easier than seeing what I do to him. I'll long for him when he's gone, and wanting something that's impossible to have is the greatest torture. It's how I feel about my freedom from the club. The desire is toxic, especially when you know you can never have it.

"Now, Mak." The command in his voice pulls my eyes open and up until the hazy gray of first-morning sight looks down at me. I exhibit no control over my choices when he uses that tone with me, a natural reaction to his demands. "Fuck, that's good."

A strong hand grips my messy hair and the other is gentle against my cheek. The sensations war against one another, rough with the bite of pain on my scalp, but beautiful and accepting against my face. My mouth waters as the need to please him sinks inside my blood. His lips part, and it's almost as if I can feel the warmth of his breath all over my body even though he's several feet away.

"Enough," he grunts, tugging my hair until he slips free of my mouth. I sweep my tongue out to get in one final lick, but he's out from under me and pushing me up on my hands and knees within the same breath.

I moan when he rips the panties he had delivered right down the middle, and nearly die the most blissful death when his hot mouth finds my center. He alternates between long leisure filled licks with soft sucking on my throbbing clit. My fingers ache from gripping the soft sheet in my hand, but he doesn't relent. I quake, tremble, and come violently as he mumbles praise against my flesh.

"Fuck, hold on," he grumbles, almost incoherent to my hazy mind.

The bed shifts. Certain he's thought better of what we've done and is leaving, I can't stop the sting of tears behind my eyes. It isn't until the bedside drawer opens and closes and then the sound of a box being opened and foil being torn hits my ears do I realize he's not leaving but preparing to take me all the way.

Warmth, once again, against my thighs sparks a lust in me I'd only thought had waned after my release. Uncontrollable need has my hips pushing back as his fingers graze my entrance.

"Ready?" He asks but slams into me before I can confirm my assent.

I whimper, my hips darting forward to ease the ache he's created with his intrusion.

"Don't," he says with a quick slap on my ass. Both of his hands grip my hips to prevent me from pulling off of him again.

My mind is arguing that being hit during sex isn't right, physical pain doesn't go hand in hand with sex which is supposed to be sweet and loving. My body, however, grows slicker, greedier for him to do it again.

The sting at the nape of my neck when he wraps my hair in his fist and pulls is another sensation I can't analyze right now because his hips are relentless.

"Fuck," he hisses. "I've wanted my hands tangled in your hair since the second you showed up on my porch."

My hips slam back, colliding with the front of his thighs. He grunts each time he shoves into me, and I weep each time he pulls away. A mist of sweat covers my body, muscles coiling, preparing until they grasp at him, pulsing with my release.

He withdraws and what I think is going to be repositioning turns into hot bursts of come on my ass and back as he groans and increases the pressure of his weight against the back of my thighs.

I crumple in the sheets, now cool from the circulating air. I can't imagine anything that could wipe the smile from my face.

It falters when I hear the bedroom door open and close, and falls away entirely when I hear his door open, and the lock clicks into place. I swallow back the tears, refusing to allow him to cause me pain, but when it dawns on me that not once did our lips meet, not once did he whisper sweetness, not once did we do anything short of fuck, I can no longer hold them back.

Silent tears leak from my eyes, mingling with the water from the shower when I finally get over the shock of being deserted. I wonder as I wash him from my body if he would've acted the same if he knew he was the first man I'd willingly given myself to, the first man I'd desired enough to wrap my mouth around. He may have been my first in those respects, but the outcome is the same. I'm always left crying and filled with a self-loathing no amount of hot water and time can wash away.

Chapter 12

Dominic

Regret is soul deep by the time I make it back to my bedroom. I can't regret the sex, and I won't even pretend I do. Something that amazing doesn't allow for it.

Smacking her ass, forcing her to look me in the eye while she sucked my cock like a common whore, and leaving before even offering her a washrag to clean herself up after I degraded her is causing the regret to swim in my gut.

She's no comparison to the countless women I've been with, each one before her nameless and forgettable. Kicking off the boxers I couldn't be bothered to strip off of my body when I fucked her as I walk across the room, I know I'm going to hate washing her scent off of me. It's why I walk faster and turn the shower scalding hot.

Only here a couple of days and she's in my head, somehow managing to climb into almost every thought that consumes me.

Dangerous.

Not in a physical sense, even taking the issues with her club into consideration.

Deadly.

For the way she makes me feel, compromising the life I've chosen to live since walking out on my wife and her fuck buddy.

Holding my breath, I let the water cascade over my face until my lungs are begging for air. The sensation of drowning is better than the desire I have to go to her and apologize for treating her the way I did. I don't make amends. Women know what they get when I give them even a fraction of my body. My head chooses this moment to remind me that conversations along those lines were never discussed with her.

I scrub myself clean, my cock inflating when I imagine her in the other room doing the same. The thought making me scour my body with harsh swipes of the wash rag. I will her from my mind, push her right out of conscious thought, a skill perfected after losing so many brothers in twenty years of constant war in the Marines.

It isn't until the water runs cold, sending chills over my body that I climb out. Even with the softness of the towels stocked in my bathroom, drying off brings a stinging sensation to my overheated flesh. I relish the feeling. Bad decisions or not, what's done is done, and there's no going back.

Pushing her from my mind, even after her scent is long gone from my body, is an impossible feat. I can still feel the tug of her gorgeous hair in my fist, see the satisfaction in her eyes when she sucked my cock.

"Damn it," I grumble as I get dressed, the echo of her orgasm still alive and well around my cock.

Sitting on the edge of my bed, I hang my head into my hands. I'm not a stranger to fucking things up, making the wrong call in the heat of a moment that results in tragedy. As many times as a decision has gone bad in my life, I can't help but feel like this one is going to have drastic consequences.

Staying in my room, hiding out like a chick with morning after regrets is an impossibility, and I refuse to even hint at the chance that she's gotten to me. I vow as I get dressed and leave my room that I'll apologize to her.

I need her to know my intention when I came into her room last night while she was in the throes of a violent nightmare was not to fuck her. I almost pulled away from her numerous times last night as I lie awake for hours plotting the death of several Renegades. Each time I attempted, she clung to me tighter, whispering, begging me not to leave her, not to let them hurt her anymore.

Getting up and walking out was the only thing on my mind when I woke with her hand on my stomach, those thoughts nothing but smoke in the air when her hand wandered down to my cock. I shut my brain off then, refusing to listen to the small voice in my head that knew nothing good would come from it.

I resist the urge to punch the wall as I leave my bedroom. I'm not one to have buyer's remorse, but fuck if this isn't a jacked up situation.

My steps falter as I make my way into the kitchen, not feeling human without coffee, no matter the eye-opening orgasm I'd had not thirty minutes earlier. Fully dressed and standing at the stove, Makayla doesn't look over at me when I pour coffee in the empty mug sitting on the counter.

"Thanks for making coffee," I say with genuine pleasure.

"No problem," she answers in a chirpy voice.

My eyes narrow as she smiles and turns her attention back to the eggs in the skillet.

"You're out of bacon, but I found some thick sliced ham in the fridge." She points her spatula at it on the counter. "I'll fry that up for you after the eggs are done."

"Mak," I shake my head. "I've told you, I don't expect you to cook for me."

I'm more worried now, afraid she's thinking in some kept housewife capacity, and that thought alone makes me want to throw her out on her ass regardless of the danger she's in.

Fuck, I'm an asshole.

She shrugs as she scoops the eggs out of the pan, placing them on a plate she has to the side. "I'm living here with no way to repay you. Cooking is the least I can do."

The least?

Oh, fuck no.

"Is that why I woke up with your hand on my cock this morning? Is that part of the least you think you have to do?"

My brain can't process how fast she turns from the stove to look at me. Her eyes narrow with indecision, but the smile she's had plastered across her gorgeous face since I walked in here never wanes. "That was... scratching an itch. Sex. Nothing more, nothing less."

Not what I expected from her, but I can't do anything but take her words at face value. Turning back to the stove she places two pieces of ham in the sizzling skillet.

In an attempt to keep my eyes off of her even though she's fully clothed in pajamas, I sit at the dining room table and look out over the lake.

"How often do you have those nightmares?" She's pretending that nothing happened last night and this morning, and it may just be another form of torture, akin to her staying here, but I need to know.

"They usually only last a week or so after... each assault." She shoots for indifference, but the pain around her is palpable.

The sound of my ceramic coffee cup cracking under the pressure of my hands is the only outward emotion I show. I don't mind her knowing how pissed off her abuse makes me, but after this morning I have to be more cognizant of my reactions to prevent her from thinking there's more going on between us than there is.

"You said he didn't rape you this time, but he hurt you pretty bad."

She keeps her back to me, and for a while I think she's ignoring me, refusing to talk more about it. I understand her hesitancy, but my need for information is too strong to let it go.

"It's not as bad as it has been before. No broken bones this time at least." She gives me a quick reassuring smile over her shoulder, but the hurt is there.

He's already broken you more than you realize.

"You confronted him about the underage porn." She nods. "How much does he know that you know? Scheduling? Will he change his filming schedule now that you're in the wind?"

She shakes her head as she pulls ham from the pan, places it on the plate, and walks over to set it in front of me.

"I'm not eating," she says when I don't make to pick up the fork to eat. "You should go ahead."

"You need to eat." I cringe at how fatherly that sounded, not wanting that picture in her head at all.

"I'll grab something later. I'm just not hungry right now."

I keep my eyes on her until she pours herself a cup of coffee and sits down across from me at the table.

"He only knows that I'm aware that he's filming," she begins when I pick up the fork. "I questioned the age of the girls, but he denied they were underage. I'm only twenty-four, and they're sure as hell much younger than me. He insisted they were seventeen and older."

"I'm no expert, but I'm pretty sure you have to be eighteen across the board to be in porn," I tell her around a bite of food.

"I thought the same thing, and it was confirmed after I looked it up online. He thinks I just walked in on filming and beat the shit out of me for questioning him." Her eyes glaze over, and I see she's looking past me rather than at me when she talks. I hate not having her eyes, but who am I to command her attention. "He's threatened to kill me before, but I never truly felt it was a possibility until this last time."

"What does he tell your brother when you show up with marks all over you? Unexplained broken bones?" I shake my head at the inattention her brother has.

"When he broke my arm, he staged a car accident. My brother called me an idiot for wrecking a car and said he hoped I'd learned my lesson. I was disgusted, but I don't see my brother much and when I do Grinder is around. I haven't bothered to tell him because I honestly don't think he'd care. I've never seen Scorpion outwardly abuse a girl before, but he's his father's son, and my dad was one of the vilest, most brutal men I've ever met."

She pauses, finding her steaming cup of coffee easier to look at while she speaks than chancing catching my eyes.

"The things Breaker used to do to my mother." She shakes her head. "My mom was his side piece for the longest time. He'd have a falling out with Calypso and take his rage and anger out on my mom."

"But he never hurt Calypso? Why beat the shit out of the girlfriend and never touch the wife." I hold my hand up when she begins to speak. "I'm not saying he should've ever hit your mom. I don't think that for a second, but abusive men, usually struggle controlling their temper."

She huffs a laugh, and I realize I don't know shit about her club. "Calypso was the president's daughter. Breaker inherited the club after he died in a motorcycle accident. Grinder is one of the original crew from her dad. My dad wouldn't lay a hand on Calypso because he was terrified of Grinder, even after her dad died. The 'daddies' in the porn are from the original club. Decades of power and control. Breaker had no real control, and neither does my brother."

"So he took all his frustration out on your mother?" It makes more sense now.

"Like clockwork. Calypso wasn't the kind of woman to roll over and take my dad's shit, but she hated her life. Hated that she was practically bred for the man that was going to take over the Renegades. She treated me with kindness because she knew I didn't have a choice either."

I narrow my eyes at the info. "Were you?"

She tilts her head, confused. "Was I what?"

"Promised to one of the club members?"

Her cheeks pink. "Butch."

"The VP?" I scrape a hand over the coarse hair shadowing my face. She nods. "How old is he?"

"Thirty-one, I think," she answers. "My dad never came out and said it, but he hinted at it more than once."

"And what the fuck does Butch think about it?" I don't even try to hide the anger in my voice, no clue why the proprietary lilt is there to begin with. Shadow has his own opinions about the Renegade VP, but I've always felt he was the only man in the damn club with any fucking sense.

She laughs, and it makes the hair on the back of my neck stand up.

"He's not interested in the least, and it's not been anything Scorpion has mentioned. Like I said, to my brother, it's like he forgets about me when I'm not around. He doesn't consider me at all."

"Do you think Grinder threatened him?"

"Why would he?"

I barely keep my eyes from rolling. "You said no one touches you because Grinder warned them off. Do you think Butch has kept his distance because he was threatened?"

She shakes her head. "Butch isn't intimidated by Grinder and the old guys in the club. I don't know if he's fearless or has a death wish, but he wouldn't stay away from me if he wanted me, no matter what Grinder may have said to him."

"Do you think Butch knows about the porn?"

"I doubt it," she says finishing off her coffee and walking to the sink to rinse the cup before placing it on the rack in the dishwasher. "He's not the type to let something like that continue. I mean he has his share of fuck buddies, brings more hangarounds to the club to fuck than any other member, but he's not into underage girls. They aren't really his thing."

Fuck, I hate to even ask, but I need to know if things are going to go south because Butch feels as if he has some claim on Mak. She wants out, and I plan to do everything in my power to make that happen. "What is his *thing*?"

"Other men's women. He claims they're less clingy, less of a chance they get attached. He's adamant about his free fucking. Doesn't want to be tied down, loves the variety."

I ignore the twitch of my cock at her use of foul language.

"I'm just," she says pointing down toward her room. "I think I'm going to take a nap. I didn't sleep very well last night, and we woke up early."

I swallow hard at the thought of her stripping out of her clothes and climbing back into a bed that smells of the sex we had this morning.

"Stop," I command just as her back is to me.

I smile when her shoulders slump forward, but her feet go still.

Chapter 13

Makayla

My body obeys his order even when my mind urges me to ignore him. Even when I've felt fear, I've always held tight to my free will, but that doesn't seem to matter with Dom.

"I need all the details, Mak." My back is still to him because I'm even more powerless when looking into his steel gray eyes.

"I've told you everything."

"You touched on things, Makayla. I need to know it all, every gritty detail."

My hands tremble knowing I can't go into explicit detail of the abuse I've suffered. The assaults are bad enough when they come back in vivid detail in my dreams, verbalizing them would ruin me.

"The crimes. The illegal acts you've been involved in, the things you've witnessed him do. I need to hear it all."

I turn back to him finding that he's standing from the kitchen table, food half-eaten and already forgotten. He points to the sofa in the living room.

I obey, somehow instinctively knowing he doesn't want to cause more distress.

He sits beside me, thighs touching, and just the warmth of his body makes me feel safe to disclose information I'd never speak of to anyone else, no matter what I told Grinder I'd do. For the first time in my life, I feel protected, sheltered by his determination to rescue my sister and put an end to the horrific things Grinder has been involved in for decades.

He waits patiently as I try to find a starting point to the things I've seen, things I've done at Grinder's will.

"Grinder is the Renegade's Sergeant at Arms, the enforcer. He's sick, sadistic, and takes way more joy in hurting people than anyone who's not a psychopath is capable of." I swallow and peer down at my hands. Noticing my diverted attention, Dom clasps one of his large hands over mine.

"Go on," he urges.

"Like I said earlier, he's been around since the inception of the club, which is more than thirty years. Everyone knows he's crazy, but like Scorpion has said on more than one occasion, sometimes crazy is exactly what you need to get things done." I do my best to ignore the stroke of his thumb on the back of my hand. "He has a makeshift torture chamber in the basement of the club, gets off on the pain and desperation that clings to the place long after the bodies are dragged out and disposed of."

Memories flood but I ignore the tears as they begin to streak down my face.

"He's made you watch while he hurts people?"

I nod. "I've watched him kill more people than I can count, watched him fuck club whores down there while rolling around in his victim's blood."

He stiffens beside me.

"The first time he raped me was down there after an especially brutal double murder." I shiver against the memory. "Told me after the club girl left him unsatisfied that all he could imagine was my virgin blood mixing with theirs. Called it nirvana."

He squeezes my hand too hard at my confession, only easing up when I wince.

"Sorry," he mutters.

"They call him Grinder because his favorite form of torture includes a vice around a person's head." I shake my head and swallow down the bile that's threatening in my throat.

"Jesus Christ," he snarls.

I continue, needing to get it out, so I never have to speak of it again. "He's held my hand, forcing me to pull the trigger more than once. He's forced me to turn the spindle until skulls have been crushed. I've been forced to help clean up his dungeon, bury and burn bodies."

My shoulders shake under my wracking tears and sobs.

"Enough," he commands, much the same way he did this morning when he pulled himself from my mouth. He crushes me to his chest, and I immediately hate that we're wearing clothes because I miss the heat of his skin on mine.

As fucked up as it is, the word does unexplainable things to my body. My heart rate increases, beating in an erratic rhythm while my stomach clenches, demanding I act.

I nuzzle into his neck, my lips finding the thrumming pulse below his chin.

"Don't," he urges, his voice pained at his own request. "Not like this, not after what we've been talking about."

I grip him through the denim of his jeans. "Now is exactly when it's perfect."

He pulls me away from his chest with gentle hands on my upper arms. His eyes search mine as if assessing my state of mind after such a horrific story.

"Now when I have power over it," I insist, shifting my body so I'm straddling him. His words are rejecting me, but his body is on board, much like my reaction to him when his commanding voice gives instruction.

His lip twitches, more in indecision than agitation. "Power isn't something I ever relinquish, Mak."

Ignoring him, I lean forward, my mouth searching, seeking his. I feel the warmth of his panting breaths against my lips, but he turns his head to the right, denying access to his mouth. Undeterred, I lick and nip at his throat as my hips circle, pursuing his hardness against the needy flesh inside my pajamas.

"God damn it, Mak," he grinds out. His big hands grip my hips, rendering them immobile for a few seconds before he takes over and controls my rhythm.

"Please," I beg, lifting my mouth from his neck and pulling my top over my head. "I need this. Just for a little while, I need to forget."

He shakes his head, but his eyes never leave my exposed breasts. "This isn't healthy."

"Everything that feels good, tastes good, is unhealthy, Dom." I gasp when his lips wrap around the stiff peak of my right nipple. My hands find his hair and I hold him against me, relishing the attention when his soft sucking turns to stinging nips and bites.

"Fuck it," he mumbles against my flesh. No less than a second later we're off the couch. He holds me against his body as he makes his way down the hall, muscle memory carrying us to his room.

Eyes never pulling from his ministrations on my breast, he accesses his room, the whirring of the digital lock the only sound aside from our heavy breathing.

I expect him to throw me on the bed, strip me naked, and fuck me hard, so I'm surprised when he eases me down his body and begins removing his own clothes.

"Get naked," he whispers.

My hands are pushing down my pajama bottoms before he can toss his shirt to the floor.

"Fuck you're perfect," he praises. He must be ignoring the yellowing bruises on my rib cage.

"And you're the fittest guy I've ever seen." His jaw twitches and I have an urge to tell him he's the only real man I've seen completely naked but his jeans hit the floor, and his glorious cock demands my attention.

He fists it as he kicks his jeans away. I watch, awed by the rough grip, paying close consideration to how he likes to be touched.

"Are you wet?" I nod. "Show me."

If I wasn't before, I am now. The gruff command of mandate slickens me more.

Not having a clue about seduction other than a desire to please him, I trail my finger over my breast and down my stomach, my hips jolting when the tender touch hits me in the right place. Releasing his hold on his cock, he walks toward me, my core clenching around the finger I've been using.

His own fingers walk over my flesh from my shoulder to the back of my hand, where he tugs it free. Glistening on the tip, he draws it into his mouth.

"I want your mouth," he urges around my finger. My lips tilt up, and my mouth floods at the anticipation of his mouth on mine. I take a half step closer, inching up on the tips of my toes, only for him to release my hand and press a gentle hand to the top of my head.

My movement is stunted for a long second, but I slink to the ground. Wanting a kiss but getting this instead isn't so bad. I swallow, my tongue snaking out to wet my lips. The instant the softness of his crown parts my lips my eyes flutter closed, and I suck in earnest. The hand that guided me to my knees now fists at the nape of my neck, much like it did this morning. Squirming doesn't help ease the urgency in my core, but knowing that doesn't prevent my weight from shifting. My hands find the front of his thighs as he sets a punishing pace. This is only the second time I've had my mouth on him, but he's already aware of the heights I can take him.

"Jesus, fuck," he spits. "Look at me."

I ignore the spark of pain from my hair being pulled and me fighting against his will.

"I want your eyes on mine," he insists.

I pull off of him, pushing gently on his thighs but don't look up. "I want your mouth on mine," I whisper

"I don't," he pants tracing my swollen lips with his cock. "I don't kiss, Mak. It's too intimate."

I huff a laugh. "Your cock is in my mouth, what's more intimate than that?"

"My tongue in your ass," he says without missing a beat.

I sputter around his dick when he shoves it in further. I counter by hollowing my cheeks with extreme suction until he uses the grip on my head to pull me from him. The same hand guides me to my feet while my eyes stay locked on my hand as it fists his cock.

With reigned frustration, he urges me away and reaches into his bedside table. I appraise his technique as he opens the wrapper and rolls the latex down his thick cock. His hand finds mine, and he tugs me to the bed, only he settles his back against the headboard and pulls me to straddle his lap. With one hand on my hip and the other lining himself against my entrance, I groan a long sigh when I sink down on the first few inches.

My eyes drift closed as his warm mouth finds my neck and shoulder, praying it eventually finds my mouth even if he insists it's not something that he does. My battered heart and abused body crave that connection to him.

"Your eyes, Mak." There's enough warning in his voice to make my body tremble, but I continue to deny him. It's the only control I have. I may be riding him, he may be on bottom, but he's still in ultimate control.

I tilt my head back, my mouth falling open as my hips circle hard.

"Damn, Mak," he grunts.

I shriek when I fall to my back, and he's over me. My feet are pinned against each shoulder as his hips pick up the rhythm.

"Oh God, Dom. Right there." The words leave my mouth, and he pulls out, my body clenching around nothing.

"Your eyes, Mak," he demands again. I shake my head and squeeze them tighter. "You won't come until you look at me."

"If I do, you'll get attached and won't ever want me to leave," I tease.

"Not likely," he says, the tone of his voice more serious than it should be right now. "I never do, sweetheart. My heart died seventeen years ago."

I stiffen under him, the truth in his words enough to cause pause.

I shake off his admission because the grinding of his hips paired with sweet measured strokes nearly have me on edge.

"If you don't kiss me, I won't let you come," I drawl, on a gasping breath as he hits that spot inside that is tantalizing enough to hand over my first born child just to feel it again.

"Eyes, Mak!" The growl is almost enough to snap open my eyes, but before I can I feel the pulsing of his cock deep inside of me. I turn my head away when his breath skates over my cheek to my ear. "I make the rules."

I shove at his chest, tears nearly falling. I don't know if I'm more upset about the orgasm denial or that once again I have no control over my body. He leans back on his heels, and the smirk on his face is just egotistical enough to make me scream.

Rather, I slide out from underneath him and begin to gather my clothes, only then realizing my shirt is still on the couch in the living room.

"Where are you going?" Honest confusion marks his voice. "I'm not done."

"I am," I say. "I'm so fucking done."

I pull open his bedroom door to the sound of motorcycles near the house.

"Fuck," he hisses and pulls his phone from his pocket, locating an app and tugging on his clothes simultaneously. He looks down at his phone, and my blood runs cold before he even says another word. I'd recognize those patches from miles away. "Renegades."

My eyes find his now. They plead with him, *I'll give you anything you want if you protect me.*

Chapter 14

Dominic

Pure fucking terror in her eyes. If I ever had any doubt about her honesty concerning Grinder, the truth is written on her face.

"Panic room. In my closet," I instruct. "Passcode is zero-seven-three-one."

She shakes her head violently. "You can't lock me in a room."

"It's the only thing I can do right now." I look down at the app, seeing them dismounting their bikes. "Get in the fucking room, Makayla."

Almost as if she's in shock, the only movement in her body is the darting of her eyes as the search for an alternative escape.

"Mak," I say grabbing her by the arms and shaking her. "They're fucking coming."

Her head turns to look past me, and I know she's not hearing a damn thing I say. "Mak. Baby!" She tilts her head up to me. Goddamn, she's beautiful. "Listen to me, baby. Let me get rid of them, and I'll be right back."

I all but drag her inside the closet, and I think she's going to comply, but when the door pops open after I enter the code, she turns in my arms and fights to get away.

"It's too small," she hisses trying to get away from me.

She must not hear the pounding on my front door because she struggles in earnest to get out of the closet. I grip her face in my hands, silencing her with my mouth on hers, doing my best not to get lost in her taste and the way no matter what is outside of this room, in this five seconds nothing else matters.

"Stay," I demand pulling my mouth from hers.

I shove her as gently as I can and close the door to the panic room, all sound from the inside ceasing immediately. I look up at the micro camera that looks just like another hook on the tie rack that's disguising the door to the room.

"I'll be back, baby. Settle down. No one can open the door from the outside unless the person inside allows the override. You're safe. I'll be right back."

It's a lie. The lock can be overridden, but that requires an override from Blade, former Marine and intel expert for Cerberus, but the truth remains that Renegades will never get their hands on her. They could burn this place down around that room, and she'd still be safe.

I stop by the bathroom and splash water over my hair, not giving a shit that it runs down my chest and back. The wetter I am, the easier it makes the lies to swallow. Ripping the hand towel from the rack, I make my way out of my room, stopping to grab my t-shirt from the floor, ensuring the door is closed behind me. Now two barriers protect Makayla, the second impenetrable.

The flash of color from the left catches my eye. Looking over, her bright pink pajama top is in stark contrast to the dark and neutral tones of my living room. I shove it under the couch cushion and pull my t-shirt over my head. The echo of pounding fists rings throughout the house again. I grab my keys from a table near the door and pull it open.

I channel the calm patience my mother had always told us boys to showcase rather than the angry side from my father. Even though I'm fighting against every instinct in my body, I know killing Grinder and the two 'daddies' that are standing behind him on my porch will bring too much heat, and I really like this neighborhood.

"Grinder," I bite out in my typical asshole fashion.

I may have enjoyed a couple of his club whores at parties, but there's no love lost between myself and the Renegade crew. I know now why the older guys, who are usually the most laid back in most clubs, were the ones I always got that sick vibe from. Luckily these three fuckheads didn't come to many of the private get-togethers, and have all but stayed clear of anything in the community.

"You find out anything?" he asks following me down the front steps to my bike.

I make a showing of setting the house alarm from my phone. I don't worry that they will be able to get to her if she stays put, but I sure as fuck don't want to come home to a busted front door or shattered window.

"About what?" I say playing the idiot.

"Makayla." He narrows his eyes. "You were there when I was talking to your damn brother."

I shrug. "I don't really get involved in club business. Kincaid is probably looking into it."

"How would you feel about the indifference you're showing if one of Cerberus club girls went missing?" He sneers but takes it too far when he continues. "What about if something happened to Emmalyn or Misty? Hell, even that pretty little Khloe, Kid seems to be so enamored with."

I turn on him, shoving my phone deep in my pocket so both hands are free for the ass whipping he just earned.

"Are you threatening my family?"

He has the common sense to take a step back and hold his hands up to ward me off.

"I said I don't know shit about that girl you're looking for. You spoke with Kincaid about her, so explain to me why the fuck you're at my house?"

I watch his Adam's apple bob under a rough swallow. "It's on the way into town from Durango. Just thought we'd check. Scorpion is going out of his mind."

"Really?" I huff incredulously. "If he were so concerned why isn't he down here asking for help? Hell, he hasn't even called Kincaid to find his sister."

The last part is a gamble, but one I feel confident in taking after the things Mak has told me about her relationship with her brother.

"He's upset. Like I said. He asked me to reach out while he explores other avenues closer to home."

Lying piece of shit. If anything I bet he's made up some plausible story about her taking a trip and Scorpion has no clue his sister is on the run.

"I'm heading to the clubhouse now. Feel free to follow." I look at him and the other two pieces of shit. "Better drop the accusation and disrespect before you make it over. This isn't fucking Durango."

I jump on my bike and rev it up, pulling away only keeping my eyes on them in my small rear view mirror. Thankfully they mount up and follow.

My lip twitches as we ride across town, me in the lead and them following behind me. Not officially a Cerberus MC member, I'm not even wearing a cut. It's a clear sign of power and control on my part.

Strangely, when we get to the four way stop halfway through town, Grinder and the others turn right rather than following me. I make it to the clubhouse in record time, ignoring the few guys out front while I pull out my cell phone and check on things in the house, which requires a confidential call to Blade across the country for a one-time passcode.

"The fuck do you need that for. The panic room is the only place you can't access without it?" This asshole is way too damn analytical for my taste. I ignore him, freezing him out and hoping that silence will work. It doesn't. "Fuck, man. Goddamn it, Dom. Please explain to me why a half-naked girl is hunkered down and crying in your fucking panic room?"

I remain silent.

"Tell me, brother. Have you seen the therapist since you've been home?" I snarl at him. "I'll take that as a no. Explain, man or I'm calling Kincaid on the other line."

Now is not the time to have my brother trying to talk reason to me. "Kincaid call you about the Renegades."

"He did." I hate the sound of his groan when he puts two and two together. "Fuck my life, Dom. Please tell me you didn't abduct the Renegade Princess and you're holding her hostage in your panic room."

"If you even have to ask, you sure as fuck don't know me," I growl into the phone, but have enough piece of mind to turn my back to the guys in the yard and walk up the long driveway. "I'll tell him soon. But know this fucker, she came to me looking for help. Now give me the Goddamn passcode."

He sighs but rattles off a handful of numbers that I commit to memory long enough to hang up on him and type them into my app.

I do look like a psycho when I see her curled up on the small cot in the room. Her head is down, but her shoulders shake with her sobs.

"Twice in one week," my brother's voice says behind me. I close out the app and pocket my phone. "What do we owe the pleasure?"

I needed to draw three psychopaths away from the woman I'm harboring at my house.

"Bored," I mutter as we walk back to the front of the clubhouse.

"Well, I'm glad you're here. I have a favor to ask."

I groan. "The last time you asked for a favor I ended up naked in a hotel in Tijuana with my head shaved," I deadpan. His boisterous laugh carries us through the front door of the clubhouse and all the way to the couches off to the left.

"You chose that woman, not me," he reminds me. I shudder at the memory. "I need you to go to Tennessee with Bri."

"Fuck no." I don't refuse my brother many things; call it the guilt from leaving to go into the Corps which resulted in my mother's death. Accompanying Brighton Griggs anywhere is just asking for trouble.

"Shadow would do it, but Griffin has the flu," he says.

"I was just over here the other night, that little boy is fine."

"Kids get sick really fast. Her asshole of a boyfriend refuses to move out of her condo. He needs a little persuasion to kick bricks. She's been bad mouthing the fucker for months, and I don't trust any of the other guys to stop at just scaring him and convincing him to leave."

I shake my head, still denying him. "What makes you think I won't tear him to shreds?"

He looks at me, eyebrow raised, bored with my question.

"You're the most level headed man I know. It's just one day, two max."

If he had any idea I nearly killed three Renegades on my porch in broad daylight he would reconsider his statement.

"Why the urgency?" I ask. "This situation has been going on for well over a year. Can't it hold for a couple more weeks?"

Kincaid narrows his eyes at me, trying to figure out why I'm so anxious to stay when I've never had a problem dropping everything to take care of something like this.

"Bri is all over my jock, Diego. I can't take all the fucking aggressive flirting," I explain and hope its excuse enough to keep him from wondering what is really going on.

He laughs again. "Don't fuck her if you don't want to. Simple as that. You never do anything you truly don't want to do."

Tell that to my lips that still feel the warm heat of Makayla fucking Evans'.

"Goddamn it," I grumble. He smiles, knowing I'm heading to Tennessee. "When do I leave?"

"Tomorrow."

Chapter 15

Makayla

My eyes stay focused on the door as I try to fold myself in the smallest, inconspicuous ball at the top corner of the small cot. The room is as small as jail cells I've seen on TV shows, and I'm grateful that I'm not claustrophobic, but the longer I sit here, the tighter the walls seem to close in.

I'll be right back.

His words have echoed in my head for the last hour, the same amount of time the tears have been falling down my face.

The small room is air tight. I don't hear any activity outside of the room, and rather than providing safety it freaks me out even more. The small camera screen only shows a couple of feet outside the door, so anything going on beyond that is a mystery. I wouldn't know if someone is right outside of the closet seconds away from hurting me until they come right up to the door. Even the promise that no one can get in unless I allow it doesn't provide much comfort. The stress is making every muscle in my body ache, tension thick from my neck all the way down to my calves. The room is stocked with blankets, bottled water, and vacuum sealed food, but the only thing I concern myself with is a blanket to cover my naked top half. I was only supposed to be in here for a few minutes, the amount of time it took Dominic to get the Renegade bikers to leave.

I saw three, Grinder and the two guys who're always connected at his hip. My mind flashes to Grinder torturing Dom the same way I've seen him hurt countless people and the shakes and tears start again. I don't think I could live with myself if being here is the cause that Dominic was hurt or killed. As strong and able as Dominic is, I know what Grinder is capable of.

I focus my attention on the fading bruises on my wrists, tracing them with a finger as I try to calm my thoughts enough to formulate a plan to get out of here, get Jasmine, and kill the evil man that has ruined my life. My brain, however, won't get with the program because I've had to remind myself more than once to actually breathe, so conscious planning is impossible.

The innocent blue eyes of my little sister spring to life in my head, filled with a pleading so familiar from my past. I feel defeated, as if I failed her before I even had a chance to save her. I squandered the opportunity several months ago. Jasmine's mom was too high to pick her up from school. I sat at the crossroad with her in the backseat, left back to the clubhouse with the guarantee of pure hell or right leading out of town. I sat only a moment from turning and leaving town, deep down knowing that even with no money or plans we'd be better off out of Durango. The blare of a horn behind me and instinct kicked in. I turned left and headed right back to the clubhouse.

It's not the fear of the unknown that's kept me at the clubhouse. It's the vivid memories of what Grinder is capable of that keeps me terrified of acting on my own.

I twist my hands in my lap to the point of pain as I rock back and forth. Deep breaths in through my nose, slow, measured breaths out of my mouth. It doesn't help, so I close my eyes. The trembling increases as my view of the door disappears behind my closed eyelids.

I push out thoughts of Grinder, Renegades, and for the moment, Jasmine, because the hopelessness I feel isn't helping anyone right now. The last thing I need is to hyperventilate and pass out. I'll lose every defense then.

Instinctively my fingertips go to my lips, my mind back to the brief kiss Dom used to manipulate me into this room. I knew when it was happening what his intentions were, but for the briefest of seconds, I let myself imagine that he wanted me. Not my body, not to use me for sex.

I used him too. I wanted to sleep with him just as much as he wanted me, but I can't deny that deep down I want more from him. I'm not talking marriage and children. It's more of a thirst for that connection I've never felt with a man, to feel valued and necessary. To feel wanted and desired emotionally, not just the abuse someone uses to get off on.

My dad didn't want me. He reminded me often in everyday conversation, not words he'd regret later for speaking out of turn when he was mad. At least I knew where he stood. Scorpion blames me for his mother's suicide, feels that if my *whore mother* stayed away from his dad, his mother wouldn't have done what she did.

Calypso never treated me like the bastard child of her cheating husband, even though that is exactly what I was. Too bad her son took so much after his dad and didn't end up with any of the compassion his mother had. The disdain he has for me keeps me away from him. Never one for masochism, knowing how he feels about me keeps me in my room most days, away from a brother I can't help but love and the man who hurts me every chance he gets.

I shake my hands out, a futile attempt to stop the shaking. I hate my cowardice right now, but I know it's the unknown and lack of control of my current situation that has me out of sorts. I'm normally brave, my smart mouth getting me into trouble most days.

For the first time in my life, I wish I had a line of coke. The girls at the club rave about the powdered substance. I know they use it to better deal with the horrible situation they've got themselves in, and the escape would be blissful right now.

My eyes dart open when a hushed rustling sound comes through the microphone from outside of the room. The motion activated lights that had darkened the room while I sat idle flash on when I jolt. I've stayed as still as possible since the darkness is more comforting. It allows me to imagine no one can see me, so most of my time has been spent staring at the small screen on the wall, the image the only light in the room.

I clamp a hand over my mouth, eyes glued to the screen. My heart races, praying I'll see Dom outside of the door, but he doesn't come into view. I imagine Grinder outside with his men, rummaging through Dom's things, looking for clues. He won't have to go far. The guest bedroom doesn't automatically lock when closed, and one look inside, and he'll be well aware I've been staying here.

With marked, shallow breathing I sit until the lights flicker off again. Darkness cocoons me, and my heart rate calms just a fraction. I know I can open the door from the inside, but I won't chance it. As much as I hate it in the tiny room, I know I'm safer in here than anywhere out there. So I sit in silence and wait.

Chapter 16

Dominic

"Fuck," I grumble dropping the kickstand on my bike. Acting like a child has never really been my thing, but the thought of leaving Makayla combined with the fact that I have to spend time with Bri, makes me want to pout and throw my damn toys.

I walk the perimeter of the house even though I know the Renegades never came back here. I would've gotten notifications from my security app, and not one has come through since I left. I also know that Mak is still holed up in the panic room because it hasn't pinged that she's opened the door.

I take my time, cataloging the flower beds, checking the windows, and even walking to the end of the dock for anything out of place or suspicious. I find nothing.

Shoving my phone in my pocket, I enter the house from the backside, contemplating whether or not to leave Mak in the panic room while I toss back a few fingers of whiskey. My body began to hum the second I stepped inside, as if knowing she's nearby. I hate myself for how much I want her. I fucked her the first time because I just couldn't resist, the second time because that first taste would've never been enough, but wanting her again does something to my psyche that has me questioning my entire life.

Once was too many considering I haven't had anything but quick fucks and one night stands since leaving my wife. Imagining Mak as a quick fuck makes me want to punch shit, but on the other hand, I can't picture her as anything else because it goes against the way of life I've had for the last twenty years.

Knowing she's been in that tiny fucking room long enough, I head in her direction instead of toward the bar in the den. I grab her pajama shirt from behind the pillow on the couch even though the last thing I want is for her to cover her tits up. My bedroom door is closed, and the bed covers are crumpled just as they were when I walked out of here this morning.

A few short strides later, I'm standing at the closed door.

"Mak." I don't bother knocking because the door is so thick, she'd just hear the noise through the intercom. "Open up, baby."

I have no clue when I started calling her baby, but I have no desire to stop.

I wait, giving her time to get to the door, but it never clicks open.

"Just press the red button beside the screen. It opens the door."

Nothing.

My heart starts hammering in my chest. I know she's in there. The app on my phone is military grade. It doesn't just randomly fuck up like some bullshit app you buy on your phone. Even knowing this I check the fucker again. No notifications.

I pound on the door, anxiety thick in my veins. "Open the fucking door, Mak."

An endless thirty seconds go by before I hear the mechanical click of the lock withdrawing. I tug it open a second before it's fully disengaged and have to pull a second time.

She's standing with her face in her hands in the middle of the room.

"Fuck's sake, Mak. Why did you take so long?" Instinctively, I wrap her in a hug as her shoulders shake with her sobs. "You're safe. Don't cry."

My words make no difference as she continues to cry for long minutes.

"I-I was so happy to see you on the screen that I started crying again. I didn't want you to see me acting like a baby."

I chuckle but otherwise remain silent, refusing to bring up the tantrum I wanted to throw after talking with Kincaid.

The expectant look in Bri's eyes as we discussed the flight schedule and what I needed to do to get her bum-ass boyfriend out of her house the quickest pissed me off even more.

"You were gone so long. You told me minutes," she pauses to sniffle. "I thought he killed you. I was waiting for him to come in and hurt me too."

I frown down at her. Even with red-rimmed eyes, unable to hold the tears back, she's gorgeous. I bite my tongue until the acrid taste of blood fills my mouth. With what she's gone through, I'd never be able to tell her that her tears, while she's tied to my bed and gagging around my cock, would be the most amazing sight.

Trying to ignore the twitch in my cock at the mental image, I push her hair from her face. "One, Grinder couldn't hurt me even with the posse of geriatrics he has following him around. Two, even if he got the drop on me, there's no fucking way he'd be able to access this door. If he even tried, hell like he's never known would rain down on him."

She looks confused at my response but doesn't question my words.

"I'm glad you're back," she says softly as she backs out of my embrace and wipes at her eyes with the backs of her hands.

I turn to walk out, scooping up her shirt from the floor of the closet. I hand it back to her, inwardly groaning as her breasts disappear behind the fabric.

"Thank you," she offers.

She sits back on the edge of the small cot, clearly not ready to leave the sanctity of the small room.

I join her. "I have to leave for a few days."

Might as well get the shitty news out of the way first thing.

She stiffens beside me, and her breathing grows shallow, but she doesn't speak.

"The house is fully stocked," I tell her to help calm her fears. "You won't have to leave the house for anything."

Her face tilts up, and her sad eyes find mine. "Where are you going?"

"That's not important." Cerberus business isn't something I ever talk about to people outside of the club, and even though this really isn't a Cerberus matter, Bri is Shadow's sister. As the Cerberus VP, I'm sure he wouldn't want any of this spoken outside of the clubhouse walls.

"You want me to stay here while you're gone?"

I look down at her. "Yeah. I expect you to stay here. Keep the lights off at night, stay in the house, and you'll be perfectly fine."

She shakes her head. "He'll come back. He doesn't give up easily."

I hate the tears that had finally begun to dry are renewed on her cheeks. She lowers her head, looking at her hands. I bite my lip against insisting she look me in the eyes.

Instead, I cup her chin and angle her face up to mine. "He doesn't suspect a thing. If he did, he would've doubled back after I left and went digging around."

"How do you know he didn't?"

I tap the phone in my pocket. "He didn't, Mak. You're safe here, but if you hear bikes outside, you can always come in here. I'll give you a burner phone. If you end up in here just call me on it and I can tap into the security system to see what's going on."

"Why are you helping me?" The vulnerability in her voice makes my heart clench.

"Because you asked me to." Her face softens. Damn, she's gorgeous.

"You don't even know me." She tries to pull her face from my hand, but I tighten my grasp on her chin. Not enough to hurt her, but enough to let her know I don't want her pulling away from me.

"I don't have to know you to be the type of man that wouldn't turn away a woman who really needed help. It's not in my nature to walk away from someone who needs help." I wipe away tears from her cheeks with my free hand. "I walked away once, thinking I had time."

The words stick in my throat. Blinded by my love for Karen, immaturity, and desire to be a better man than my father got my mother killed. I've never let my own emotions dictate who I help, and when I doubt my responsibility, I always err on the side of caution.

"Who?" she whispers. "Who did you walk away from?"

I shake my head, my lip twitching in agitation at the information I just openly disclosed.

"It's not important," I mutter releasing her face.

I stand from the bed and leave the closet, walking toward the kitchen. "I'm thinking about having pizza delivered is going to be our best bet—"

She's not behind me like I'd expected her to be.

I turn back and finding her still inside the panic room.

"You need to eat," I say barely hiding the annoyance in my voice. I don't want her to think she's the reason for my continued sullen mood.

Reluctantly, she stands from the bed and follows me out of the room.

"How do I get to the panic room when you're gone if your bedroom door is locked?"

"Code for the bedroom door is three-eight-two-five," I inform her as we enter the kitchen and I tug open the drawer with the takeout menus.

"Any significance?"

I shake my head. "Just a number."

I refuse to explain that the code to my bedroom spells FUCK on the phone because even after all the years I've spent alone and even though I make every woman I've ever fucked leave before the sun comes up I honestly hate sleeping alone. There's no way in hell I'll ever tell her the code to the panic room is the date my world ended when I caught my wife fucking the neighbor, knowing the next time I have to cower from someone and lock myself in that room, my world might as well be over.

Chapter 17

Makayla

"Mmm," I hum around the first bite of pizza.

Dom chuckles beside me, but there's more fire than humor in his eyes. Muscles clench low in my belly, a clear warning that my body isn't ready to give up having sex with him even though my mind knows it isn't a good idea to continue. A thirty-eight-year-old man who's known for not having any type of relationships with women isn't someone I should get tangled with, but my body doesn't understand what my heart already knows.

Men as handsome as him shouldn't be allowed to exist. Add his looks to the gentlemanly aura that surrounds him and the fire in which he's taken my body twice, and the result is a combustion too great to resist.

"Good?" he asks when my eyes flutter closed.

I point to the generic pizza box on the living room table in front of us. "Who made this? We don't have pizza like this in Durango. It's something about the sauce I think."

"It's a little hole in the wall pizzeria in town. I don't think I'd ever move away from here. I stay just for this pizza," he says with admiration.

I know that's not true. He stays because this is where his brother is. Kincaid is also expecting a baby if stories around the Renegade clubhouse have any credit. He's loyal and devoted to family, so the anticipated niece or nephew will keep him around as well.

"I guess Farmington residents can sleep well at night knowing you're around to protect them so long as the pizza place stays open." I smile sweetly at him and take another bite, the same delighted sound escaping my mouth.

"Keep moaning like that," he mutters in warning. His weight shifts and I know he's aroused. Even if I hadn't trained myself to pay attention around men as a form of self-preservation, the bulge in his jeans isn't easily ignored.

I narrow my eyes at him, assessing, trying to figure out if he's turned on from the sounds or if he has some kind of weird food fetish.

"Sorry," I tell him and turn my attention from him back to the food, cognizant of nothing but keeping my pleasure over the food silent.

He clears his throat and takes a long pull from his bottle of water. "I can take you to the clubhouse if you don't want to stay here alone."

My eyes snap to his. "Did you tell them I'm here?"

"I haven't, but I don't want you to spend several days here in fear that something will happen to you. That kind of stress isn't good for your body." He takes another bite of pizza, and my eyes fixate on the sauce piled on the corner of his mouth, muscles clenching again when his tongue sweeps out to gather it.

I shake my head, frustrated that I react so easily to such innocuous actions.

"Several days? How long will you be gone?"

He shrugs as if it's no big deal leaving some woman he barely knows alone in his house for days unsupervised, and it makes me wonder just how many women have passed through his doors over the years.

"Two nights, three tops."

"Where are you going?" He wouldn't give me any information earlier, but I hope he'll at least tell me a little more now.

"Tennessee." All of his answers are short and bordering on annoyance as if I'm some nagging spouse.

I just nod. If he doesn't want to tell me anything else, I won't ask again.

"I'd rather stay here. I don't know any of the people at your clubhouse, and that will be more stressful than worrying about Grinder sneaking in and killing me in my sleep." He frowns, but there's no point in lying to him.

"If you let me tell Kincaid, he'll send someone over here to keep you company," he offers.

I shake my head again. The last thing I need is one of those bikers in the house. The mere thought shoots gooseflesh up my arm. I place my slice of pizza on the plate in my lap and rub my arms.

"Cold?" The tone of his voice is half concern half opportunistic. I wait for him to say something like 'I'll warm you up' but he remains silent.

"I'm fine." I look up to find him gauging my expression. "I don't want anyone knowing I'm here. I've already caused enough trouble just by coming here."

I watch the ripple of his back muscles as he stretches forward and places his empty plate on the closed pizza box. Strength I've never seen outside of actors on TV is evident in the bunching and pulling of the thin fabric. Safety and virile sexuality roll off of him without him even trying. It's no surprise I succumbed to the testosterone that seeps from his pores. It's as if just by his scent and proximity I was helpless in resisting him. Not that I tried.

"Being here is a blessing," he says leaning further back on the couch. A hint of compassion and something I can't quite read fills his eyes, but he catches himself and schools his face back into impassivity. "I mean, we would've found out about Grinder's bullshit eventually. That crap doesn't stay in the dark too long. You showing up has saved who knows how many women and girls from being violated."

I take a drink of water from my bottle as an excuse to take my eyes off of him. I don't want him thinking I'm heroic because all I can think about are the things going on at the club and I'm here, helpless to do anything about it. I imagine unthinkable things happening to my sister while I sit idle in this house eating pizza and fantasizing about a future with a man I have no business even speaking with.

"You know I have to tell him eventually. We've already had this conversation. I don't know why Kincaid knowing a few days earlier makes any difference. I can have one of the girls come over and stay with you."

My lip turns up in a sneer as I look over at him. "I don't want to be babysat by a club whore either."

Stoic and aloof he leans forward, within inches of my face. The power and control radiating off of him is a physical thing in the air. "I wouldn't have a club whore in my house, Mak."

"I'm here," I whisper. "Grinder told me every day I was his whore."

His hand reaches out so fast, I don't have time to react. Anger fills his eyes, but his grasp on my chin and cheek is as gentle as I imagine he can do. "Call yourself a whore one more time, Mak and I'll tie you to my bed and whip your ass so hard you won't sit down for a week."

He speaks to my mouth, and the attention along with the violent insinuation of his threat has the opposite effect I thought my body would have. Rather than cowering in fear, the urge to beg for just that hits hard in my gut. I can't admit that to him, though, because it feels wrong and immoral. Those types of feelings are dangerous and only lead to pain and regret.

"I'm not into pain," I lie.

His tongue sneaks out wetting his lips, and he's so close to my face, I can feel the heat from it. Steel eyes rove from my lips until his gaze is burning into my own. "You'll come so hard you'll beg me for more."

Dark, risky threats.

"Go ahead and get some rest, Mak." He releases my face without fanfare, and I curl a little inside myself that he's so easily able to control his body when mine is screaming out, wanting to beg him to fulfill his promises and so much more. "I'll clean up."

He pulls the plate I'd forgotten about from my lap, gathers his plate and the near empty box and disappears into the kitchen.

I do as he instructed, shuffling down the hall and away from his rejection. We've had sex twice and haven't spoken a word about either time. Now I know what the girls at the clubhouse meant when they said he could fuck you to the point that you think he's ready to devote his life to you and then turn into a cold bastard who acts as if he's never seen you before, while kicking you out of bed so he can go to sleep.

I hold on to the knowledge that he held me in his arms last night, something I haven't heard of him doing with the women he's hooked up with from the Renegades. As I take a quick shower, I push the thoughts of his messing around with other women from my mind. I only imagine the times we've had together as I dry off and pull on a clean set of pajamas.

I know when I lay down on the bed in the guest bedroom alone that I'll never be able to fall asleep. The room is too big and empty, void of the safety I feel when Dom is in here with me. I roll over for the millionth time, planting my face in the pillow, and punching it with my fist. I hate the vulnerability, the inability to calm my nerves enough to go to sleep.

I grab my pillow from the bed and the comforter, imagining I'd be more comfortable on the couch. At least the sofa won't smell like the combination of both our bodies.

Cracking open the bedroom door, I peek out and listen for him. Not a sound can be heard, and his bedroom door is closed, so I sneak down the hall toward the living room. I startle when I see a figure walking down the pier, but my fears are quickly diminished when I recognize Dom in the stream of light lining the wooden dock.

An idea strikes since he thinks I'm in my bed. I head back down the hall, but I bypass the guest bedroom. I punch the numbers into the keypad to enter his room, close the door quietly behind me and enter the closet. The second set of numbers is accepted on the panel to the panic room, and within a minute of seeing his shadowy form outside, I'm closed away in the panic room.

What once felt like claustrophobia earlier today feels more like a cocoon tonight. My skin crawls at the thought of sleeping alone with easily accessible windows and doors in the guest room. I adjust the pillow and blanket on the cot, and within minutes I'm slipping into an exhausted sleep.

Chapter 18

Dominic

The scotch burns my throat as I swallow the last third left in the tumbler. Peacefulness surrounds me out on the dock, but the thoughts and emotions rumbling around inside me doesn't allow for the calm to seep into my core. Leaving her alone is the last thing I want to do. I need to move on Grinder and the other pieces of shit involved in hurting Mak and the other girls in the pornos they're making. I need her out of my house, longing for her is not something I anticipated or even want.

The chirp of a notification pings on my phone. I pull it from my pocket since I don't get many I check it every time I'm alerted. I'm not a social media user, so it either has to be an email, text, or a security message.

"Damn it," I groan when I look down and see the details on my phone. Makayla has to have locked herself back into the panic room. The door has been opened and closed, and the only thing she went in there with earlier was her pajama bottoms, and she was wearing them when she exited.

Apparently, the visit from Grinder this morning left her more shaken than I realized. The fact that I'm leaving for a few days probably isn't helping any either.

"I'm not her keeper," I grumble to myself as I walk back down the dock and lock myself back into the house. I take my time hand-washing my scotch tumbler and setting it in the drainer to dry. After checking all the doors and locks and activating the alarm I go to my room, smiling at her closed door. I bet she went in there thinking I wouldn't have a clue and assuming she was in her room. I check her room anyways, finding a pillow and the blanket missing from the bed.

Opting to let her sleep exactly where she wants, I strip out of my jeans and t-shirt. Five minutes of economical showering later, I'm crawling into my bed. The coolness of the sheets offer respite against my heated skin, but familiar comfort never finds me. My eyes stay locked on the closed door of my closet willing it to open.

Awareness of her only a dozen feet away refuses to let my brain calm and settle into sleep. I lay for over an hour futility agitating enough to begin to anger me. With a frustrated huff, I climb out of bed and head into the closet. She better be sleeping, if I find her upset and teary eyed like she was earlier I may lose my shit.

I press the intercom and command her to open the door. She doesn't immediately but the lock whirs and opens much faster than it did earlier.

Tired eyes and rumpled hair accompany her into the doorway. No matter how many times I see her, I can't get past how gorgeous she is. The bruising on her face and neck are almost gone, and without a speck of makeup, she's handsdown the epitome of natural beauty. She blinks her sleepy blue eyes up at me, a small smile tugging at the corners of her mouth.

"You caught me." The sleep-filled huskiness of her voice hits me hard in the chest... and dick. "I couldn't fall asleep in the guest room."

I barely keep myself from offering a couple of orgasms to help her feel better, but I somehow manage to keep my asshole attitude locked down. "You can't sleep in here, Mak. The air is recycled and isn't meant for long-term stays."

I don't share that it would take days before the air is depleted enough to become hazardous. She frowns, her bottom lip a fraction further out than the top. I picture biting it since she seems to be offering it up to me. She's so small I could dead lift her without any effort and have her pussy against my mouth in a second flat. My cock stirs, but she doesn't seem to notice as she looks from me and back to the disheveled blanket on the cot.

"Can't be very comfortable. You'd sleep better in the bed," I offer and want to slap myself.

She tilts her head to the right. "I'd rather sleep in here than in my room alone."

"Your bed is too fucking small for the both of us. I woke up with my back hurting this morning."

"Okay." It's all she says as she turns around and fixes the blanket on her makeshift bed.

The idea of inviting her into my bed makes my heart race. Not one woman has slept in my bed since I had the house built years ago. Before that, I'd stayed with friends when on leave. I don't even fuck women in this room, and other than Emmalyn, Rose, and now Makayla no one has even crossed the threshold. I refuse to picture her on her back as I fucked her this afternoon.

"You're not sleeping in this room," I hiss.

She turns, arms crossed over her chest.

Two strides and minimal effort and she's over my damn shoulder and being carried out of the panic room.

"You can sleep here," I say as I toss her on my bed. Pink hair fans out, some on her face the rest over the pillows.

She huffs but doesn't argue.

"You don't seem like the cuddling type," she snips as she settles against the pillow and pulls the blankets to her chin.

"I'm not." I climb in the other side, giving her my back.

She calms quickly, and within minutes her breaths even out and I know she's asleep. I listen to the rhythmic sounds for a long while before sleep pulls me under.

***

I may have fallen asleep on one side of the bed while Mak took over the other, but somehow we both managed to move to the middle, myself moving more than her.

The warmth and soft skin on her belly where her shirt rode up during the night is amazing. The arm around her back is pulling her closer before I even have the chance to second guess myself. The heat from her pussy is radiating against my thigh, and I wonder what it would feel like bare and finding purchase against the coarse hair on my leg.

I hate how much I actually like waking up with her wrapped around me like a second skin. Even though I'm chastely against keeping a woman in my bed, it's always been something I missed since divorcing Karen.

My already thickened cock jumps in my boxer briefs. I push it down with the heel of my hand, not needing that complication this morning. It's the last thing I should've done. The half-hearted shove has no effect other than to entice him more.

Looking down at Makayla splayed across my chest, I time the pattern of her breaths. She's still sleeping, and I'm too fucking horny to keep myself from letting her hair sift through my fingers as I grip my cock and stroke it under the covers. I pretend it's the tight grip of her pussy sliding up and down my length as I bring myself closer to the edge.

My fingers hit a tangle in her hair, and she stiffens beside me, the rhythmic sound of her breathing ceases entirely.

"I'm sorry," she mutters and shuffles back and off of my chest. "I didn't plan on laying on you again."

My deviance would have stayed hidden if the blanket wasn't wrapped around her back, but she's uncovered my stroking hand as she slides away. Her eyes shoot from the angry veins in my throbbing cock to my eyes. Pink flushes her cheeks as mirth fills her beautiful blue eyes.

Her tongue skates over her lips and I groan in response. Unapologetically, I renew the stroking, my eyes on her watching my fist work up and down. My legs shake with impatience, toes curling as my hips buck up of their own accord.

"You want help with that?"

Before the sentence is fully out of her mouth, my hand is once again tangled in her hair, and I'm gracelessly shoving her mouth on my cock. Three strokes of her hot fucking mouth are all it takes. I thicken and lengthen in her mouth before blowing down her throat with a roar forceful enough I'm surprised the windows didn't rattle in their frames.

"Fuck," I say gripping her by the hair, and only relenting when she yelps in pain. "Bottoms off," I growl.

The second the pajamas clear one ankle I pull her up, directing her to straddle my face. Her hot cunt settles on my mouth, and I devour her with an urgency I've never felt before. She's soaked, wetter than I imagined she would be after such a brief encounter with my cock, and I love how ready she is for me.

"Dom," she pants as her hips circle on my tongue. "Please."

With my mouth suctioned to her perfect, pink clit I shove two thick fingers in her, groaning against her as she bucks against me.

"Eyes," I say. I mean for it to come out as a command, but after her refusing yesterday, it ends up sounding more like a plea.

Forehead resting against the headboard, I look up to find her eyes already on me. My spent cock begins to thicken again at her attention. Lips parted, breath gusting out, and heavy-lidded eyes make her the sexiest sight I've ever seen. At least that's what I think until she shatters and the whimpering escapes her throat. I continue to suck as she pulses against my mouth, drinking in every second I can.

She tries to lift off of my face, but the orgasm must have worn her out because she unceremoniously just falls to the side, thigh still across my chest. I look down her body, watching the rapid rise and fall of her chest and the sweet smile on her face.

"That was—" My cell phone alarm blaring from the bedside table startles both of us.

I reach over to turn it off, hating that she tucks her leg under her and climbs off the bed.

When I look back over, she's tugging her pajama bottoms back on. "Umm. Thanks for that."

"You're thanking me for making you come?" I chuckle.

"I'm thanking you for *letting* me come."

Thank you, Sir is what I heard.

Full God damned erection flagging in the open air.

"I'll let you pack," she offers before bolting out of the room before I can insist she climb back up here with the promise of several more earth-shattering climaxes.

Chapter 19

Makayla

I hate goodbyes, even though I've never had the chance for many in my lifetime. My mother died of an overdose the day after accusing me of purposely catching the eye of her shithead boyfriend. My dad was shot and killed on a random Tuesday. I didn't get to say goodbye to either of them. Not that I would have if given a chance.

For some reason, though, I find myself hiding out in my room avoiding the uncomfortable 'see ya later' with Dom. It isn't until my stomach begins to growl that I'm forced out of the room in search of something quick to eat.

We nearly run into each other in the hallway. Always the gentleman, he takes a step back and lets me go ahead of him.

"Is that all you're taking?" I ask when he places a small duffel bag on one of the stools at the breakfast bar.

"I don't need much," he explains. "Men don't carry frivolous shit with them when they travel."

I turn toward the coffee pot and roll my eyes. "Well, I wouldn't know what it's like to pack for a trip. My stuff followed me from my mom's to the clubhouse in a couple of trash bags."

The sound of a clip engaging in a gun has me turning back to him.

"You know how to use one of these?" he asks palming the small pistol in his huge hand.

"I hate guns," I inform him. The only times I've used them was by force with Grinder.

"I can appreciate that." The look on his face begs to differ. "But do you *know* how to use it?"

I nod. Guns are commonplace around the clubhouse. Even some of the women carry them, more trying to look like badasses than actual protection.

"Just in case." He lays the weapon on the counter top and walks into the living room. "I want you to have this also."

I follow him and watch as he pulls open a drawer in the entertainment center. He pulls out a cell phone. Simple, cheap. A burner.

He turns it on and enters a few contacts and hands it over.

"I've put my number in there, the clubhouse, and a direct line to Kincaid." His eyes find mine. "If anything goes down lock yourself in the panic room and call him. There may not be much reception in there so a text may be better. It will continue to attempt to send it longer than a phone call, depending on signal strength."

The warning makes my heart race, as if he's anticipating a problem but leaving me here alone anyway.

He must notice the stricken look on my face because he closes the two-foot distance between us and in a very un-Dom-like move he pulls me to his chest. Unsure of how to respond, I leave my arms hanging by my sides.

"You'll be fine," he promises against the crown of my head. He inches away and chucks his finger under my chin. "Two days, three max."

I nod but notice his eyes on my lips rather than my eyes. Before I can lie and assure him I'll be fine, his lips take mine in a searing kiss. There's no danger right now, no attempt to get me under control by stroking his tongue against mine. I cherish the moment, sweeping my tongue over his. He pulls away too soon, emotion resembling confusion in his eyes.

Clearing his throat, he takes several steps backward. "Call me if you need anything. I'll activate the alarm from outside. Don't leave the house, open a window for fresh air, or answer the door if someone knocks. Keep the lights to a minimum at night."

"I won't," I promise.

"I'd rather you sleep in my bed than lock yourself in the panic room. The door is lined and reinforced with steel. It would take someone with brute strength or a battering ram to breach it." His lips dart to mine one last time before he walks away, grabs his bag, and leaves the house.

The second the roar of his motorcycle fades into the distance, I wander the house and close every one of the blinds and curtains, cloaking the house in darkness. He must really enjoy his privacy because not one stray beam of sunshine makes it into the living room.

Even though I hate guns, I carry the handgun and cell phone with me everywhere I go, including the restroom. I've left the door to his bedroom, and the panic room open on the chance I may have to run in there.

I'm bored out of mind four hours in. I've been binge watching The Tudors on Netflix, but it's not the same with the sound turned off, and I can't risk not hearing someone if they drive up. I'm on edge, jumping at the sound of ducks quacking out on the water. I nearly pissed myself when the mailman stopped outside of the house and took his sweet ass time sitting in the driveway sorting through his next batch of deliveries before turning around and heading back out. I wonder if Dom has ever regretted building a house on a dead end street.

My finger twitches against my leg with my feet propped up on the coffee table. I hate being idle. It drives me up the wall. Toss in the fear of being alone, and I'm a ball of anxiety. So I do what comes naturally: I snoop, not giving a damn about the cameras he's admitted to having all over the house. Knowing he could be watching me right now makes me want to strip naked and finger myself to orgasm.

I jump up off of the couch, gather the phone and gun and wander. First stop is the drawer he pulled the burner from. I find several more in there. After looking around, now wishing I wasn't being watched, I slip an extra into the waistband of my jeans, turning around to face the room as if I wasn't stealing shit from him. Even though I feel guilty, it doesn't stop me from walking down the hall and closing myself in the guest bedroom.

I dial Jasmine's mom's phone from memory and listen to it ring. If anyone other than my sister answers the phone, I'll hang up and destroy the burner. Thankfully, my sister's young, sweet voice comes over the line.

"Hello?"

Tears burn my eyes at the sound. "Jas. Don't say my name."

"I miss you," she whispers in the phone. "When are you coming home? I haven't been able to go to school the last couple of days because mommy is too tired to get out of bed to take me."

"Where is your mommy?" I ask hoping she's not in the room with her listening to her daughter talk on the phone. Jasmine answers this phone all the time because her mother leaves it everywhere and is fucked up on drugs more often than not.

"She's asleep in her bed. Hold on, and I'll go hide in the bathroom," she says conspiratorially. After half a minute she says, "I'm back."

"Are you safe? Has anyone hurt you since I've been gone?" I literally cross my fingers in front of my face. Bad news will have me out of this house and headed to Durango in a heartbeat, and I know that's not good for anyone involved.

"Other than missing school, almost everything is normal. Grinder's not in a very good mood. He's been yelling more than normal, and it's upsetting some of the other guys."

"And how are you handling that?"

"I stay in my room just like you tell me to. We still have enough of the food you brought last week." I can hear her soft cries through the line, and it breaks my heart. "I miss you."

"I miss you too, sweet girl. Give me just a little longer, and I'll be back."

I can't tell her the plan. She's too young to understand, and telling her I'm taking her from her mother would be hard on her. Just as I did at that age, she loves her mother, no matter how neglected she is. She internalizes the blame her mother has been spewing at her all her life.

"Don't tell anyone I called, Jas," I urge.

"I won't, Poison. I promise." I end the call with tears streaking down my face, and I'm near sobbing when I bust the phone into pieces and let the water from the sink run over it.

I can't leave it operational because I don't know if it can be tracked, but her not having a way to get a hold of me strikes fear in my heart.

After throwing the ruined phone in the small trash can in the restroom, I make my way to Dom's room, closing the door behind me before climbing into his bed.

I sob into his pillow, missing him as his scent surrounds me. It seems like forever before the crying stops entirely. With wet cheeks and a snotty nose, I open the bedside drawer looking for a tissue, too tired to actually get up and walk into the bathroom.

The only thing inside the drawer is a small, weathered photo album. Without a second thought, I pull it into my lap and open it.

A much younger Dom peers down at a beautiful woman as she looks into the camera. I turn the pages and find him exactly like the first. He's always watching her, love evident in the way he holds her to his chest and smiles when she smiles, as if his happiness is dependent on hers. The last two pages stop my breathing. The first one is of him and the same woman from the entire album posing for the camera holding a marriage license, the gold ring on Dom's finger catching the light from the flash. The last picture is of him holding her as her legs wind around his waist. Their lips are locked as the picture was taken. I close the album, feeling like an interloper on his happy times.

My heart died twenty years ago.

My hand shoots to my mouth as I remember his words from yesterday. If his wife passed away, it would explain why he's never let another woman in. The light in his eyes and smile on his face in those pictures, there's no denying how much he loved her. It's as if it flowed off of the pages. I know without a doubt he'd never love another woman as much as he loved his wife.

Chapter 20

Dominic

"You seem agitated," Bri says as we stand and wait for her three suitcases to show on the conveyor belt at the Nashville airport.

I ignore her as best I can as I pull up the security app on my phone. I roll my bottom lip between my teeth to keep from smiling when the picture pulls up to Makayla sitting on the couch watching TV. I feel Bri inch forward, almost in my personal space. I close out the app before she can tilt her head enough to see what's on my phone.

I huff, shove my phone in my pocket, and cross my arms over my chest.

"You could've flown in first class with me," she whines when I don't make eye contact with her. "The upgrade wasn't that expensive."

"The cost wasn't the issue, Bri." If she only knew how the Marines transported us in and out of the desert, she'd understand that riding coach is more than enough.

"Are you going to act like an irritated child the whole trip?" I quirk an eyebrow considering the concept. "I was hoping we would get to know each other better."

I see her first suitcase slide down the belt and step past her to grab it. Tugging it to her side, I watch for the next one to appear.

"You were late. You can't be mad we missed the first plane."

Now I look over my shoulder at her. "You weren't even packed when I got to the clubhouse, Bri. You were the one who packed all sorts of shit you knew they wouldn't let you carry on. You were the reason we had to wait in line at security again after checking your carry on."

"Sorry," she mumbles. "We only had to wait an hour for the next one."

Her second and third bags come out at the same time, and I thank whatever cosmic alignment that's at work for it.

After shifting the strap to the small duffel on my bag, I get hers situated where I can carry them for her. The chivalry is ingrained from being raised by an amazing mother, not that Bri even offered to help.

Another hour later, long after the sun has painted the western sky pinks, oranges, and purples, we're in the rental car heading in the direction of her condo.

"What's this asshole's name," I say, speaking for the first time since leaving the airport. The GPS says we only have another five minutes before arriving.

She huffed when I typed the directions in, insisting she could've told me the directions. I'm grateful for the navigation because it keeps me from having to listen to her voice. Each time she speaks, she reminds me more of Karen, and that's the last woman I want on my mind any day of the week.

"Trey," she offers. "Twenty-nine, gorgeous, but lazy as all hell. Spends all of his time sitting in front of the TV playing online video games with other lazy idiots around the world."

"And you've asked him to leave?"

I see her nod from the corner of my eye. "Yep. About a dozen times. Last time I told him to leave he said we'd discuss things when I got back. I've been avoiding coming home."

We pull into the subterranean garage and park in the empty spot designated for her condo number. I look over at her. "You haven't been home once?" She shakes her head. "You've been at the clubhouse for over a year."

"I know," she says with a quick shrug. "I like it there."

"Are you even sure he's still here?"

She points out her window to a faded red truck. "His truck."

"Looks broken down. Sure he didn't just leave it?" If I flew all the way to Tennessee and his ass isn't even here, I'm going to be pissed. Actually, I won't. I'll turn right back around, catch the first flight back to New Mexico, and crawl into the bed with Makayla.

"He called me from the condo landline yesterday," she says with a frown. "He's still here. I have no clue how he's paying the bills. I had the electricity and water turned off. The condo is paid for, except for yearly dues."

"Is he the violent type?"

She smiles wide. "Are you afraid of a little scuffle?"

I sigh, the frustration from earlier coming back full force.

"He's indifferent, not violent. I could've come back and eventually convinced him to leave, but I don't want to be away from the clubhouse any longer than I have to. Em's about to have the babies, and I want to be there to help when she gets out of the hospital."

I cough to keep from laughing at the ridiculousness of her words. She doesn't know shit about kids and has no honest desire to learn, but I can appreciate the friendship she's formed with my sister-in-law.

"Let's go," I say getting out of the SUV. "Leave the bags. We'll come down and get them later."

The elevator ride hints at how nice her condo is going to be. "What do you do for a living?"

"Real estate," she answers. "But the business isn't as lucrative in New Mexico."

"I imagine not," I say as the elevator dings announcing we've arrived at her floor.

She pulls the key from her purse and plugs it into the lock. Stale air and arguing hit us the second we walk in. I follow Bri into the living room, stepping over clutter on our way.

I clear the threshold into the room just as Bri does. The young guy, who I assume is Trey, is kicked back on one of those game system rocking chairs made for adolescent boys.

"Hey babe," he says with a quick smile before turning his eyes back to the screen for a full three minutes before exiting out of the game and setting the controller down. "I knew you'd come ho—"

His eyes land on me for the first time and his smile fades. I don't even hide the scrunch of my nose at his wrinkled, dirty clothes. Did she say he was handsome? He doesn't look like he's bathed or shaved in weeks.

"Who is this," he asks with an edge to his voice that makes my hackles rise.

"Dom," she answers. "The Enforcer for the Cerberus MC back in New Mexico."

The corner of his mouth twitches. "Dom? Like on *The Fast and the Furious*?"

He offers a hand that I ignore. "Believe me, kid, I was around long before Vin Diesel even considered acting was a good idea."

Bri stands off to the side, enjoying our interaction a little more than she should be. Her eyes squint, and her teeth scrape her bottom lip as if she's picturing me covered in grease and bald.

Five minutes in this trashed condo and I'm ready to leave.

"Did you say enforcer?" He turns back to Bri who straightens from her fantasy and looks at him. "You brought fucking muscle from New Mexico or is this the guy you're fucking now?"

She doesn't say a word, letting him believe what he wants. I want to clear up any confusion, but Bri needs to have the upper hand here. He's already been staying here after being repeatedly asked to leave. I don't, however, appreciate the tone he's taken with her. She claimed he's not abusive, but a lot can change over the course of a year.

"You need to pack your things and leave," Bri says with boredom in her voice. She's not concerned he'll get violent, so I allow my adrenaline to calm marginally.

"I'm not going any damn place, Bri. This is my Goddamned condo, too!"

I look up at her, and she gives her head a slight shake. Things would be a little different if he had some claim to the property.

"I paid this condo off two years before we even met. No part of it is yours." She points to the childish rocker. "I even bought that stupid thing and the Nintendo you play all damned day."

He laughs, and I have the urge to laugh right along with him. She's showing her age and lack of game system knowledge. I don't play the stupid shit, but even I know that he's playing a newer Xbox.

"Nintendo?" he sputters while taking a menacing step toward her. "You're old and fucking stupid."

I clamp a hand on his shoulder digging the tips of my fingers into the sensitive flesh behind his collar bone.

"Time to go, buddy."

Like the pussy that he is, he backs down immediately as if catching himself in the middle of his anger.

"I need time to pack," he mutters.

I don't let him go but guide him by my grip to the door Bri points out for me.

"Grab what you need for the night, and I'll make sure she leaves the rest of your shit downstairs for you to pick up first thing in the morning. If it's not gone by noon it's going in the trash."

He glares at me, looking down at the clothes strewn all over the floor and back down the hallway toward the living room. He lifts the collar of his shirt to his nose. Deeming it clean enough, he sits down on the edge of the bed and pulls a pair of Chucks on his bare feet. Forgoing everything in the room, he walks back down the hall, grabs an empty grocery store bag and begins unplugging his game system. This guy's priorities are all kinds of fucked up.

We watch in silence as he bags his Xbox, Bri and I giving him space. He stands and shoves the last cord into the bag and looks around the room. With the bag hanging from his wrist he clutches the back of the gaming chair and drags it toward the door.

I step past him and pull it open for him. Once out in the hall, he looks back at Bri like a lost child. "You don't even care where I go?"

I don't give her time to answer. "Nope," I tell him and close the door in his face.

Watching him through the peephole, I follow him until he gets on the elevator without a backward glance.

"That was almost too easy," I tell her when I turn back in her direction. "Think he'll be back?"

She shrugs. "Maybe after a few days when friends get tired of smelling him. The place will be empty by then."

I look around the room, finally realizing the extreme mess of the entire place. "I'm not staying in this shit tonight."

I may turn down first class over coach, having known much worse, but sleeping in filth is something I've always avoided.

"Me either," she says with a seductive edge to her voice.

I open the door again and cross a hand in front of me indicating for her to walk out first. She switches the light off before I close the door.

"The cleaning company is going to make a killing," she mutters as we make our way down in the elevator and back out to the SUV.

We make it out of the elevator in time to see Trey pulling away in his truck.

"Sad fucker," I mutter. I shake my head at the ridiculousness of the whole generation. "No wonder the world has gone to shit."

I open Bri's door for her, something I was an asshole about and didn't do at the rental company. I climb in and take her directions to a hotel a few blocks away. After parking, I pay for two rooms in the overpriced hotel, much to Bri's dismay. She insisted she needed all three suitcases but actually offered to handle the one she was denied as a carry-on at the airport.

"You could've saved quite a bit of money and shared a room with me," she purrs leaning in a little too close on our elevator ride up to the floor we will be sharing.

The glint in her eyes makes me wonder if she picked this expensive ass hotel because she was hoping I'd balk at the price and offer to stay in the same room with her.

I shake my head and take a step away from her. "Bri, I know you have some sort of crush on me, but it isn't going to go anywhere. I'm not trying to be mean, but you're wasting your time."

"Is there someone else," she prods as we step off of the elevator and head in the direction of the room indicated on the key cards we were provided.

Makayla flashes in my mind, but it makes no difference. I never would've touched Bri even before she showed up on my doorstep. But now? The thought of touching another woman seems abhorrent to me, and that causes more concern than I feel like dealing with.

Bri looks up from the two sets of cards in her hands. "Looks like we're neighbors. Which one do you want, left or right?"

"I'll take whichever one you don't want."

She picks the room on the left and offers the other set to me. I hold up her suitcases to indicate I can't take them from her just yet. She unlocks her door with a small laugh and flicks on the lights once she's inside.

"We're neighbors with connecting doors." She points to the door on my right and turns the deadbolt until it unlocks. She winks at me. "Just in case you change your mind."

I place her suitcases near the dresser and hold my hand for my set of keys.

"Goodnight, Bri," I mutter as I leave her room and close the door behind me, locking it for good measure.

I toss my duffel on the bed in my room and head right back out, the bar on the ground level calling my name.

Chapter 21

Makayla

I scrub at my eyes as I leave Dom's bedroom. Even the comforting smell of his body on the sheets all night didn't bring me the sleep I'm so desperately missing this morning. I lay in bed for two hours after waking up from another nightmare. They didn't happen when I was in bed with him, and I hate feeling like I need him next to me just to get some rest.

"Who are you?" a young voice says as I walk into the room.

Startled, I fumble the cell phone and the gun in my hands, dropping them both on the floor.

Like a wild animal caught in unfamiliar headlights on a dark, deserted road, I freeze and stare at her. Auburn hair surrounds her youthful face, and wide hazel eyes stare right back at me.

"You're Makayla," she finally says.

Alarm rings in my ears, forcing me into action. I squat and reach down for the gun.

"Please don't," she begs. "I'm Khloe."

The name is familiar, but I can't recall where I've heard it before.

"Kid's girl," she offers as my trembling hands lift the gun from the floor at my feet.

"Cerberus?" She nods. The fear and pure shock at seeing me here make me believe she means me no harm. She had no clue she'd find me here today.

Keeping the gun pointed in her general direction, I reach down one more time to grab the phone. I glance at the screen and realize it's busted. That makes two phones I'll have to pay Dom back for.

"What are you doing here?" She looks absurd with her hands up like she's the cashier behind the counter in a robbery. "You can put your hands down. I won't shoot unless you make a move toward me."

"You're scaring me," she whispers, her chin trembling.

I lower the gun and tuck it under my arm. "Why are you here?"

Hands still up she points into the living room. "It's my turn to water the plants. I swear Dom thinks they stay alive by sheer magic. Kincaid usually sends Em over, but her feet are really swollen, and he's keeping her under watchful eye since the doctor told her the babies could come any day."

"Babies?"

She nods, and a small smile plays on her lips. "She's having two little girls."

Two nieces for Dom. I bet he's scared shitless.

"How do you know who I am?" Anger washes over me, warming my cheeks at the thought of Dom going behind my back and telling any of the guys at the Cerberus clubhouse that I'm here when I specifically asked him not to.

"Kid asked me yesterday if I'd seen you. Described your pink hair." The index finger on her raised right hand points in the direction of my hair.

"Not very conspicuous is it?" I hadn't even thought of changing the color or cutting it since I haven't left this house in days.

"It's gorgeous, but yeah, you kind of stand out." She smiles in earnest this time.

"Put your hands down," I say again with a chuckle. "Did Kid explain why he asked you?"

She finally lowers her hands when I pull the gun from under my arm and place it on the counter.

"He said you went missing from your clubhouse. Said some scary guys from there were looking for you. Didn't say much else. Just warned me to stay away from anyone on a motorcycle that isn't wearing a Cerberus patch."

I watch as she heads back into the kitchen, pulling two gallons of water from the pantry. After adding some Miracle Grow she retrieved from under the sink, she leans against the counter and gently shakes the jug until the powder dissolves and turns the water bluish-green.

"He didn't have to even warn me, though. Most of those Renegade guys are really freaking scary, so I always hide out when they're around."

You have no idea.

"How old are you?" I ask more for verification before I drop my guard completely. I now remember where I heard the name.

"Nineteen," she answers. "I've been with Kid almost two years. My birthday is in a couple of months. How old are you?"

"Twenty-four. You go to college?" I always wanted to go to school, but it was never in the cards for me.

She nods. "I took my GED in what was supposed to be my senior year. Never thought I'd go. Kid persuaded me. I only had one class this morning. Was just stopping by on my way home. Dom doesn't like many visitors, so we take turns taking care of the plants when he leaves."

"Why not just get rid of the plants?" I ask making my way to the coffee pot. Khloe slides over to give me room to get water from the tap.

She laughs. "I asked Kid the same thing. He told me Kincaid said it's the only other living thing in the house, that Dom needs things to remind him that life goes on."

"That's kinda fucking sad," I say.

"I'm honestly surprised to see you here. He doesn't ever have anyone over when he's here. I think the guys come over every so often, but he usually ends up at the club."

Of course he does. That's where the easy pussy is.

I wait in silence, keeping my eyes on the coffee pot as it begins to trickle the life force of my day into the carafe.

"I'm going to water the plants," she says when I don't offer up any more information or questions.

"Want me to make you a cup?" I offer as she begins to walk away.

"That would be wonderful," she praises. "A little sugar and tons of milk, please. I was up late last night."

By the time she is finished breathing life back into Dom's flagging plants, I have the coffee waiting for both of us on the coffee table in the living room.

Mindlessly, I point the remote at the TV and start the next episode of *The Tudors*.

Gracelessly, Khloe flops down beside me, scoops up her coffee, and mimics me by kicking off her shoes and putting her feet up on the table beside mine.

I laugh at her free spirit. "You don't mind if I hang out for a while, do you?"

I'm not going to turn down the company. "Did you lock the front door and turn the alarm back on?"

"Always," she answers. "I think it's silly since this is one of the safest neighborhoods in Farmington, but Kid insists on it. I don't like him having to worry about me."

"Over protective?" I would ask her if he's possessive, but I imagine all men who really care about their women are to a point.

She smiles wide. "Just the right amount of protectiveness."

I turn my eyes back to the TV as the beginning credits finally end on the screen and the show begins. "Turn the volume up," she says. "I can't hear anything."

I turn it up, for some reason feeling safe with her here, even if it's a false sense of security.

"Henry the eighth was an asshole. I wonder if this show would have been as successful if Jonathan Rhys Meyers was replaced with someone less handsome."

I grin at her assumption. "He loves hard and then moves on pretty quick doesn't he?"

She sighs. "Poor Anne Boleyn never stood a chance."

"Some men draw you in, and even though you know it's only going to end in tragedy you still can't resist falling for them." I take another long sip of coffee. Now is not the time to reflect on my current living situation and impending homelessness after Dom takes care of Grinder.

"He doesn't want her," she offers. "If you're worried about him messing around with Bri."

"Bri?"

She nods. "He went to Tennessee to help get rid of the mooch of an ex that wouldn't move out of her house. He barely tolerates her when he's around. I don't think he'll mess around on you."

"What?" I sputter into my cup. "Dom and I aren't together. I'm just staying here until he can help me out with some things."

She has the tact to look mortified. "I just assumed. I saw you coming out of his room. I know no one is allowed in there. I figured if he gave you permission you were like *his*."

His. Oh, God. How I wished.

"I'm not going into why I'm here, but he gave me access to his room in case of an emergency." It's all I will offer her. No matter how much I can see us being friends, we're not. Trust no one has been ingrained in my head from the day I was born, and a young girl who seems innocent isn't going to make me change that now.

She nods, not seeming upset with my vagueness. "The panic room. I get it."

I turn my eyes from her and back to the TV, effectively ending the conversation. As much as I want to ask her more about this woman he escorted across the country, I keep my mouth shut, only opening it to finish my coffee.

We watch four episodes of King Henry cheating on and killing off his wives before Khloe stands to leave.

"You sure you don't want to come back to the clubhouse with me? We can hang out. The spare room is probably not as comfortable as it is here, but you won't be by yourself."

She's sweet to offer, but there's no way I'm going against Dom's orders to stay in the house. I've already sort of broken his 'don't open the door if anyone knocks.' He didn't bother to inform me that random women show up to take care of his house plants.

"He texted earlier," I lie. "I want to be here when he comes home tomorrow."

She tells me the code to reset the alarm, and we say our goodbyes.

"Hope to see you around sometime." She looks like she wants to hug me, but that's not really my thing. We end up with an awkward handshake.

"Maybe." I smile at her, but shut the door the second she's outside.

It only takes a few minutes before the silence surrounds me and makes my skin itch. After checking all the doors and windows again, I head to the back of the house, taking liberties in Dom's shower. Getting clean or the perception of clean always makes me feel better. I have no idea when Dom will be home, but I pray it's tomorrow, just like the lie I told Khloe.

Chapter 22

Dominic

Thankfully, Bri stayed behind in Tennessee to get her condo in order. All day yesterday was spent getting the cleaning service and exterminator lined up. I jump on my bike outside of the clubhouse the second I park the SUV we drove to Albuquerque and fire it to life. Even the hour-long layover in Dallas didn't put a damper on my mood since I didn't have to listen to pettiness or deflect Bri's attempts at seduction.

Itchy waves to me from the front door, having heard my bike crank up. I can tell he wants me to chat with him, but he can use the phone like every other person in the world. Two nights being away has been way too long. For the first time since calling Farmington home, I'm actually excited to open the front door of my house. Anticipation of seeing the pink haired woman who hasn't left my thoughts in the last forty-eight hours fuels me to drive faster than I normally would through my quiet neighborhood. My phone died on the last leg of the flight and not being able to check in and see her watching TV or doing dishes is making me antsy.

I gave firm instructions for her not to open the door, and she didn't, but I've texted her a few times, and she didn't mention her visitor. I knew one of the girls would show up at the house. If they think I don't know they show up each time I leave to water the damn plants I give no shits about and clean old food out of the fridge they must not know me very well. I knew she needed the company. It's the remaining silent about it that has me eager to punish her for it. My fingers twitch with the need to tug her hair and spank her ass for the lie of omission.

Frustration washes over me as I round the last curve near my house. Three familiar bikes sit lined up in my driveway. This was bound to happen. I risked the knowledge of her being here when I didn't stop Khloe from showing up. I figured if either she or Misty showed, the secret would be out. Those two women tell their men everything. It's mildly deceptive, but not a blatant betrayal of her trust.

Narrowing my eyes at the sight of my brother sitting on my front porch like he owns the place, I pull in and park by the other bikes.

"Brother," I say coming up on the front porch, agitated that I have to deal with him before I can see Makayla.

He doesn't look at me, only stares off into the distance like I'm not worthy of his full attention. That rankles, too.

"You need something?" I play it cool, forcing him to bring her up.

"Em kicked me out of the clubhouse. My own fucking clubhouse has been taken over by a dozen women with bags and bags of pink shit." I chuckle while he turns his head and sneers at me. "The fuck am I going to do with two girls, man?"

I shrug. "Couldn't tell you. Lock them up and never let them leave your sight?"

"I said that exact thing to Em. She called me a barbarian." He pulls his eyes away once again.

My pulse thrums, needing to go inside and find Mak. From the bikes out front, I know Kid and Snatch are inside, so I'm not worried about her safety, but she's probably scared out of her fucking mind. She doesn't know any of the men at Cerberus, and her experience with bikers has been less than pleasant.

"Speaking of pink things." He leans forward, elbows on his knees. "You got something to tell me?"

"Bri's ex is a petulant child, but we had no complications. He left without much argument. She's staying behind for a couple of days to get shit together so she can move down here for good."

He ignores my briefing on Tennessee. I watch his jaw muscles tense. I wait for the explosion, but I'm already preparing my defense. "You haven't let a woman come between us in a long time, Dom."

I'm the older brother, but I sit on the porch with Kincaid feeling thoroughly chastised. I'd expected him to be pissed at the secret not hurt.

"No one is coming between us. I just... fuck." I, too, begin to stare at nothing across the yard, unable to watch the disappointment play out on his face. "She needed my help."

Silence seems to drag on forever. "Just saying it's not like you. Is there some sort of love connection?"

I huff.

"Has to be something, brother, because she left her MC to run to you. The club is looking everywhere for her, worried something bad has happened and you have her here."

"She didn't run *to* me, Diego. She was running *from* Grinder."

His head turns to me at the confession, eyebrow raised and waiting for more information.

I stand from the chair beside his. "I figured she would've told you what was going on when you arrived."

He shakes his head and stands along with me. "She hightailed it, gone before we came through the door. Left a burner on the table and a handgun I recognize as yours."

"Are you sure she's here?" My heart is racing, unfamiliar panic rushing through my veins as I push the front door open.

I've seen her more than once on the video feed walking through the house. That gun is always in her hands. Poor Khloe nearly got shot, and I'm sure to catch shit from Kid for it. I wouldn't be surprised if he punches me in the face for putting his girl in danger.

"Coffee on the table still had steam coming off of it when we came in. Door to the panic room is closed, figure she's in there."

My eyes dart from Kid and Snatch sitting on the couch watching ESPN down the hall in the direction of my bedroom.

"I pressed the button to the intercom and tried to speak with her, but she wouldn't speak back or open the door," Kincaid continues. "Even called Blaze to get him to look inside. He told me there was no danger and if I wanted information I needed to call you."

"You should've called me to begin with," I mutter, inching my way further down the hall.

"I tried, asshole," Snatch pipes in from the couch. "Went straight to fucking voicemail."

Snatch is usually laid back, the comedian, if you can call him that, of the club. Although he looks sinister as hell because he's covered practically from head to toe in tattoos and body piercings, he is the softest member of the club. I figure the ink and metal are his way of shielding himself from the world since not many people will approach him.

I take a step toward Snatch, in no mood for attitude in my own fucking house. Kincaid shoots his arm out in front of my chest, stopping me from taking my irritation out on a guy I'd normally consider a friend.

"Leave it," Kincaid says.

"What crawled up his ass?" I grumble.

Kid snorts, earning him a hard backhand to the middle of his chest from Snatch.

Kid looks over at me, eyes narrowing in warning. Jesus, how much more can I fuck up this situation. I knew not telling them right away wasn't the perfect plan, but this shit has spiraled out of control. I'll hear from Kid later about the Khloe situation, but I can't focus on that right now.

I turn my attention away from the delinquents on my couch and begin to head down the hall to the panic room.

"Are you going to tell me what the fuck is going on?" Kincaid asks to my back as I walk away.

Halfway down the hall I turn back around and face him. "If she won't, I will, but it's not my story to really tell."

Kincaid sighs and runs his hand over his head. "It's that fucking bad, huh?"

"It's up there with some of the craziest shit we've dealt with. You remember Malaysia?" He nods.

I pop an eyebrow at him. "Fuck," he mutters.

"Yeah," I tell him and venture back down the hall toward my room.

I make sure to close my door behind me, a false sense of security for Mak. I trust all three guys down the hall with my life, so suffice it to say they each have the code to get in my room.

My once sterile looking room looks... lived in for the first time. The bed isn't made, one of the books from the shelf in the living room is on the bedside table, and the photo album I kept from my time with Karen is peeking out from under it. I bite my lips, not really upset but filing it away for a later time when I can spank her ass for it.

At just the thought, my palm grows warm and my cock begins to fill with blood. I've desired women before, so the reaction isn't a new one. What I haven't done in a very long time is *yearn* for a woman over the actual act of sex. Which makes me want to edge her for hours, not letting her come for getting under my skin the way she has.

I will away the thoughts because fucking her while my brother and two of his men wait for answers in the living room is not how to get back in their good graces. I almost ignore the sensible side of me because she's going to be pissed. Pissed that I didn't tell her about one of the girls coming over. Pissed that three bikers she doesn't know have forced her back into the panic room. I want nothing more than to fuck her until she's too spent to argue with me. Angry sex isn't something I've done in a while, opting to walk away from women who have too much attitude, but damned if I don't want to fuck the 'pissed off' right out of her.

Chapter 23

Makayla

Light flashing across the small video screen catches my eye. It's been black dark since a man I know as Kincaid tried to get me to come out. He must've closed the closet door leading into the bedroom completely.

Dom's face comes into view, and I nearly squeal at the sight of him. I'm so grateful he's only been gone two days rather than the three he projected.

The intercom crackles, his husky, beyond sexy voice filling the room. "Open the door, baby."

There's a hint of need to his voice. Something so dire I almost forget how mad I am at him. Almost.

I haven't used the intercom before, but it's very similar to the one in the living room, so I figure it out with ease.

"I'm fine where I am," I say with more bravado than I feel. He's told me I can trust Cerberus, and I know he wouldn't let anything happen to me while he's here, but I wasn't going to chance facing Kincaid without Dominic present.

He had to have known Khloe was going to come over. I didn't think to ask her not to tell Kid about me being here. I figured she'd assume since no one knew that it was a secret. I'm agitated, but can't be mad she didn't lie to her man. It just proves her character, and also where her loyalties lie, even though I don't expect that from her either after a couple hours of girl time on the couch.

"Makayla." One simple word with an edge as sharp as a surgeon's scalpel.

It makes me picture sheet-clawing sex. It makes my mind wander to the duffel bag of toys I found while bored and snooping through shit in his closet. The muscles in my thighs tighten as I try to ward off the incessant thrumming at my center.

"And if I refuse?" I watch the screen and wait for his reaction.

His steel gray eyes look up, directly into the camera and it's like he's seeping into my soul. The maniacal look on his face and the twitch in his jaw on any other man would terrify me to the point of begging. This look on Dominic Anderson also makes me want to beg just with a ton of *please, Oh God*, and *harder* attached to it.

"God damn it, Mak," he growls into the camera. "This isn't the way to test me."

I straighten the pajamas on my body. I've been in here for several hours. After having stayed in bed late again, I didn't make it to any level of functioning until after eleven. The roar of motorcycles drove me in here before I could get my second cup of coffee drank.

I attempt to fingercomb my hair, but I'm met with the resistance of tangles I don't have time to work out.

The second I open the door, Dom is on me, pressing me against the cold wall. Hot, mint-scented breath washes over my face and his thick erection presses against my stomach as the sound of the door closing us in echoes around the room.

I whimper more out of need than actual fear.

The tip of his nose trails the length of my neck. Uninhibited, I tilt my head giving him access to the throbbing pulse point just under my ear.

"I should fuck you against the wall," he threatens. "No one would hear you scream as you beg me to stop, beg me for *more*."

Even with my history and the rapey menace in his voice, my body demands that it comes to fruition. "Yes, please."

"Fuck you," he spits, but his words hold no malice as he rips my pajama top open and his mouth finds the hardened tip of my breast.

"Oh shit," I moan at the attention.

I reach for the waist of his jeans, needing him inside of me, but I'm pressed so hard against the wall there's no room for my hands between us.

In a flash, both of my hands are pinned above my head by only one strong arm of his. In the next breath, my legs are lifted, anchored on his as he rips the seam of my pajama bottoms at the crotch. Even as wound up as he is, he doesn't fumble once with his belt or the zipper of his jeans. I keep my eyes on his, knowing he'll demand them if I don't as massive fingers slide my panties to the side and probe my cleft, undoubtedly checking for readiness. He finds me soaked, and approval fills his eyes like he knows some secret I'm not privy to.

I cry out, just as he promised I would when he pierces me without warning. He reaches up, I assume to cover my mouth even though I know he wants to hear my screams, but his fist latches around my throat. A split second of panic runs cold through my body, but his mouth is on mine in the next second, and all other worries fade away.

Relentless hips drive in and out, the trim hairs at the base of his working cock brushing against my fevered clit. Sensation bombards me from every direction, the rough bite of his teeth on my bottom lip, the firm hold of his hand against the arms pinned above my head, even the stinging rasp of his open zipper against my ass sets fire to my blood.

"Harder," I beg even though I don't know how that's possible. If it weren't for the fabric of my shirt, I'd have scrapes and scratches all over my back from the texture of the wall.

Somehow, against physics and all logic, his hips gain strength, his cock tunneling deeper. A haze clouds the periphery of my vision, both from the impending orgasm and the tightening hand at my throat. The only thing I can see is his face and the open pant of his mouth.

"Come for me," he commands. The tingle in my spine obeys and rockets to my swollen clit. I pulse around him, my vision losing all focus as every nerve in my body relents to the demand at the apex of my thighs.

"Oh fuck," he hisses, pulling from me and jetting hot ropes of come on my stomach.

His forehead meets mine as he catches his breath. I wiggle, needing fresh air. He loosens his grip around my throat but doesn't release me entirely.

"This wasn't my intention when I walked into the closet." There's a vulnerability in his voice that I've never felt before. My heart aches at the urge to beg him to take me to his bed and hold me against his chest.

He doesn't want to hear that, though. So I do my best to keep it casual. "I missed your cock," I whisper. "Seems like he missed me, too."

He frowns and it's clear I missed the mark with my words. Releasing my hands and the grip on my neck, he makes sure I have my bearings, and my feet are safely on the floor before he steps away.

His eyes are zeroed in on my neck, and I can tell without even looking in the mirror that the fading marks from Grinder's hatred have been replaced with bruises from a fist filled with passion instead of rage.

I touch the warmth left by his hand with a delicate finger and confess, "I like it."

Remorse flips into renewed hunger at my words, but he turns his back on me to zip up and wipe his mouth with the back of his hand. He grabs a pack of wet wipes from the supply shelf and offers them without turning around.

"Get cleaned up. My brother is waiting to talk to you."

It's almost like he's angry at himself for feeding his body's needs, and I deserve the brunt of that irritation. I snatch the package from his hands, attitude the only defense I have for the tears I can feel burning the back of my eyes. The rough sex, command, and control he has when he fucks me isn't the problem. The indifference afterward is what makes me feel like a used up whore. I hate how similar the reaction is to the way I feel after Grinder has taken me without permission.

I wipe the semen off of my stomach and remind myself that Dom is nothing like the evil man I'm hiding from. Dom may act like an asshole, but he also holds me when I'm scared and keeps me safe when he can turn me away at any time.

He looks over at my ruined clothes, a hole ripped in my pajama bottoms and the buttons missing from my shirt.

"I'm going to get a quick shower. The ride in from Albuquerque was extra gritty today. Get dressed," he insists before opening the door to the panic room. He stops short. "I'll grab some clothes from your room."

I bite my lip, unsure how the next few minutes are going to go. "I moved my things into here."

His shoulders stiffen, but he doesn't say a word about me taking over part of his personal space.

"Wear a bra," he directs. "I don't want Snatch staring at your tits."

He closes himself in the bathroom before I can quip about his possessiveness. My eyes land on the corner of the photo album showing under a book I tried to read last night. It reminds me that he's not possessive, just an angry asshole who can no longer have the real woman he loves.

Chapter 24

Dominic

"I don't think I can do this," Mak whispers when I step out of the bathroom after my quick shower.

She's piling her hair on top of her head in a loose knot, no regard to the fresh bruises around her neck. I look away giving more attention to toweling off my body than required. I can't even explain to her how my marks on her makes my blood boil in heated arousal. How do you illustrate such things to a victimized woman?

"Leave it down," I tell her. Even though my brother, Kid, and Snatch are well aware of my sexual proclivities, I don't feel the need to explain myself to them, especially after she shares her story with them.

Grabbing clothes out of my dresser, I turn to lay them on the bed so I can search for socks. Her eyes are glued to my cock. Even nearly flaccid, it hangs with an impressive weight between my legs.

I ignore her attention and in turn the now less than deflated member. I tug on boxer briefs and then jeans restricting myself to the point of pain behind denim. After pulling a t-shirt over my head, I once again give her my attention.

"Might as well get it out of the way," I urge knowing I won't force her to do anything she legitimately doesn't want to do. "They're not going to hurt you. I'll be right beside you."

She watches my eyes, and the scrutiny of her gaze unsettles something in me.

"I can tell them everything I know, Mak, but it's your story to tell, not mine."

"Okay," she finally agrees, even though her eyes dart to the door with nervous energy.

Her willingness to walk out of this room and face three bikers she doesn't know just because I'm there with her says a lot about her faith in me. After what I did to her in the panic room, she should hate me. I do my best not to think about the repercussions since she doesn't seem to.

I resist holding her hand as we make our way out of the bedroom to join the three impatient men in the living room. Her change in demeanor as she inches closer is evident in the slight raise of her chin and the way her shoulders straighten. She may not be fearless, but she's good at looking like she has balls of steel. Pride winds itself around me, both in her strength facing my brother and her ability to be vulnerable when we're alone.

Her steps stutter slightly when she sees the hulking men as all of their eyes are turned in our direction when we make our entrance. Without thought, I place my hand at the small of her back, and I'm rewarded with a weak smile from her lips. I almost smile back, but catch myself. Turning back to the guys situated around my living room I discover all three of them giving me the same dumbfounded look.

I guide her to the unoccupied love seat and sit beside her.

Kincaid speaks first, and I'm certain that's because Snatch is gawking at her and unable to speak. His attention makes me want to throat punch him.

"We thought you had a lot of people worried about you, scared for your safety, but Dom hinted that it's more likely that you're scared of those looking for you." His face is a mask of concern. I've seen him like this many times. Clarity and compassion in the face of evil has been a skill many of us have perfected over years of helping women in abusive situations.

"Grinder," she begins but pauses to look over at me.

I don't know if she's seeking comfort or permission, but her approval check doesn't go unnoticed by Kincaid. Almost imperceptible to anyone who doesn't know him, the half second twitch at the right corner of his mouth tells me he's not only amused at her response to me, but a little confused at the reaction.

She clears her throat, looking back at my brother. "He's hurt me." Shame pinks her cheeks as she looks down, and as much as I love her submission, right now is not when she needs to show it. "A lot. He's hurt me a lot for a number of years."

"You're safe now," Kincaid consoles. He looks at me. "We'll tell Scorpion that she's safe. Wait. Does your brother know his SAA is hurting you?"

Her head is still down, but he gives me a look as if he's planning the murder of the entire MC if they're allowing that shit to go on over there. The exact same thoughts I had before she told me her whole story.

Mak shakes her head. "Scorpion doesn't give a shit about me, but he'd never let someone do to me the things that Grinder has done."

"So we let your club know that you're done." Kincaid slaps his legs.

I know he's in a rush to get back and check on Em. He looks over at Kid and Snatch who looked even more annoyed that they've wasted hours for a situation that they deem resolved too early.

"We'll discuss what happens to Grinder at another time." Kincaid doesn't want to speak about the things he wants to plan for Grinder's demise in front of Mak. The other Cerberus members perk up at the promise of fucking someone up.

"Kincaid," I say with my hand out to stop him from standing. "That's not even the tip of the iceberg."

I feel Mak's eyes burn into my face who would've been happy just to let the guys leave.

I look over at her, and my heart breaks at the sight of the tear cresting and falling down her cheek and the quiver in her chin.

"I can't," she whispers. Realizing her moment of weakness her spine stiffens, and she sweeps her hair off of her shoulder, so it's lying in a mess of waves down her back.

"Shit," Kid hisses.

"The fuck?" That comes from Snatch along with a low whistle.

Kincaid's eyes dart to mine. Rather leave shit alone because he can tell how fresh the bruises are and knows she's been here for days, he presses her. I just hope the reminder of our time in the panic room not long ago is a pleasant one and pulls her from this emotional slump.

"Grinder give you those bruises on your neck?"

Her eyes dart from mine to my brother as her tiny hand comes up to her neck. This time her cheeks turn red from embarrassment, as if the marks are a neon sign describing in detail the rough sex we had.

"He's bruised me before, but umm..." her eyes dart to mine again. "These aren't from him."

Kincaid's lip twitches again.

"My man," Snatch whispers loud enough for Kid to punch him in the shoulder. Snatch isn't a stranger to rough, deviant sex either. He prefers multiples, but it's never been my thing, so I haven't seen him in action.

I clear my throat, throw the best chastising look I can manage at Snatch, and then turn my attention back to Makayla.

"How about I tell him the rest, and you let me know if I leave anything out?" She nods her approval.

Two hours later the Cerberus members leave motivated enough to take down an entire MC if their Prez gives them the go ahead. I was very detailed to the guys, and Mak only chimed in when she demanded that she is kept in the loop and wanted to be a part of whatever we had planned to take down. The guys were gracious enough not to laugh at her, and Kincaid placated her as best he could.

"That went better than I thought it was going to," she confesses as we finish the dishes from the quick sandwiches we made before bed.

I won't tell her I told her so; she doesn't need to hear it. I'm honestly glad she feels like she can invest even a little bit of trust into my brother's club.

We head back to my bedroom, which forces a tired smile on my face that she just assumes I'm going to let her sleep in my bed like she did before I left and while I was away. Of course, I'm not going to tell her any different. I wouldn't ask her to stay if she made a move to go back to the guest bedroom, but I sure as fuck won't ask her to leave.

I watch as she strips out of her clothes and disappears into my walk in closet. I hold my breath while she's in there, praying I don't hear the snap of the panic room door.

A couple minutes later she peeks her head around the door. Her cheeks are the reddest I've ever seen them, and the roll of her lip between her teeth forces a smile to tug at her mouth. I can tell she wants to speak, but for some reason, she's trying to build the courage to get the words out.

"So umm…" she finally says and clears herself of the door.

It's not her naked body, although incredible as it is, that cause the thickness between my legs but the length of rope and blindfold hanging from her fingertips.

Chapter 25

Makayla

"No," he says immediately, but it's pained as if his mouth is contradicting his brain.

A smile spans my face when I see his legs shift under the sheet. His head shakes as I take a step toward him.

"No, Mak." Rather than sounding weaker, his voice has gained some strength. I falter on my next step. "Put it away and let's get some sleep."

I swallow, the urge to obey thick in my throat.

"You sure?" I taunt swinging the rope just enough to catch his eyes like a hypnotizing pendulum.

"It's been a long day. I'm tired." His eyes never leave the implements in my hand. If I'm not mistaken a light sheen of sweat is forming on his brow.

"Is it your age?" I pout prettily. "Can't handle sex twice in one day?"

Now I'm just talking shit because the first two times we slept together was within twelve hours of each other.

His eyes snap from the rope and pierce mine with enough heat to stop me in my tracks.

"I was already too rough with you today." His words are measured, deliberate, and leave no room for argument. "Covering your eyes and tying you to the bed after what you've been through is too much, and I'm not taking advantage of you."

My shoulders slump forward, heavy with disappointment and rejection.

"If you continue to provoke me like a petulant child, I will treat you as such and bend you over my knee."

Arousal zings through me, the shiver racing goosebumps over every inch of my flesh. His eyes heat noticing the furl of my nipples. I've been hurt, kicked, beaten, and assaulted on numerous times, but not once have I been spanked. The parents I was graced with couldn't be bothered enough to issue any type of corporal punishment. Even without a working knowledge, my body is in agreement with his promise.

"Yes, please." I repeat the words that pushed him into action earlier in the panic room.

Crawling up the foot of the bed, I lay the length of rope across his torso. Panting breaths rush out of his mouth, and I see his finger grip the sheets by his sides.

"I want this," I confess.

He shakes his head. "I can't." His gray eyes bore into me. "I won't."

"You're the only man I trust to do this. My body wants it. I *need* it."

He remains motionless. He doesn't respond. Not when I kiss the quivering muscle below his belly button. Not when I tug the sheet from his fists and lick the thin line of hair leading down. Not when I wrap my lips around the throbbing head of his engorged cock.

It isn't until I reach up with both hands and score his flesh with my fingernails that he opens his eyes to find mine as I take him to the back of my throat. His hips buck off of the bed, driving himself deeper. I moan and my eyes water as he buries himself inside my mouth.

The rope and blindfold are in his hands, and I'm flipped on my back before my mind can register the movement.

"You want this?" He asks holding the items only a couple of inches from my face.

I lick my swollen lips and nod.

"You think you're in control?" I shake my head no, but he reads the glint of success in my eyes.

He yanks, first my right then my left arm above my head. The ropes cut into my skin enough to know I'm now captive, but not enough to hurt or cut off circulation.

He teases me with the blindfold, trailing it down my nose and over my breasts. The rasp of the silk tickles and sets fire to my skin at the same time.

I watch with disappointment as he tosses it to the floor.

"I want your eyes," he explains. "Tell me to stop if it becomes too much."

I nod.

Fast as lightning his hand slaps my breast. I cry out, the sting ricocheting in my clit.

"Use your fucking words, Makayla."

"I'll tell you to stop," I groan.

He leans forward, and the scorching heat of his mouth wraps around the injured flesh. The ropes tying my arms to the headboard have enough slack in them that I can almost reach his head. He notices the mistake but corrects it by shifting his weight and tugging my legs, so I'm further down on the bed. The taut rope stings ever so slightly.

"Fuck, I love your tits," he praises as he pulls his head back. Calloused fingers tug at the wet flesh, and my body responds with an unsatisfied roll of my hips.

"You've been tempting me with this body for days." His teeth nip at the sensitive skin on my abdomen before he flips me over on my stomach. His hot mouth continues down my spine "Showing me your pussy the day after you arrived. Teasing me with your amazing tits."

He bites my shoulder blade hard enough it's sure to leave a mark. I twist under him, but the weight of his knees bracketing my thighs makes it impossible to turn back over.

"Each time I wanted to spank your sweet ass for wanting you." His hand crashes against my flesh right at the juncture of my thighs. "But nothing made me want it as much as watching you finger yourself in my bed last night."

I stiffen under him, both loving and hating him for making my fantasy come true.

"Y-you watched that?" I squeak.

His breath is in my ear. "We came at the same time," he says. "What were you thinking about, baby?"

"You," I admit. "This."

"Finding that bag in my closet turned you on?"

"I couldn't wait to get my fingers inside of me." I moan as his thick fingers find my wet pussy.

"You didn't cover up. I watched you lay back on my bed and spread your legs wide."

"Oh God," I pant. The pressure of a third finger joining the two already inside of me is delicious ecstasy.

"You wanted me to see you."

"Yes."

"I zoomed in on that sweet, pink pussy. No matter how tight I gripped my dick, I couldn't get it as tight as your pussy." His fingers move with precision, not slow but not quite fast enough.

The heat of his body leaves my back.

"I needed to heat your ass with my hand for making my mouth water." Two blows land, one on each cheek and I shriek. "For making me ache for your pussy."

His fingers are yanked from me, my hips are lifted, and the overwhelming sensation of his mouth seers my pussy. I tremble through the fastest orgasm I've ever had.

He smacks me again as his tongue slides through my cleft. "Didn't give you permission to come."

It sets off another mini release, and I'm boneless under his mouth and hands. His fingers dig into the flesh of my ass, pulling the cheeks apart. A whimper escapes when the hot breath of his mouth transitions to the gentle lapping of his tongue against my asshole. The brief, dark touch is gone too soon.

"Some other time," he chuckles when my hips shift back seeking his mouth again.

The bedside drawer opens, and he sheathes his cock in record speed. My leg muscles, unable to hold my weight any longer, give out and I slink to the bed.

"Perfect," his whispers as his knees settle on either side of my hips.

No warning, no 'here it comes.' Dom slams into me pulling a cry from my lips. No amount of attention could prepare me for the intrusion.

He smacks my ass when I try to wiggle away, and grips a handful of my hair to hold me in place. My neck is elongated, strangled moans escaping my throat as he fucks me with abandon.

"Fuck, Mak," he pants. "I'll never get enough."

My heart sings at his words. I explode, coming in a torrent of bliss that makes spots raid my vision.

"No," he hisses as he pulls from me. I'm flipped over once again. Gray eyes have turned dark, almost demonic, possessed. "You don't listen very well."

Both hands smack my tits twice in quick succession as he rams into me again. My feet are plastered to his chest as he folds me nearly in half, driving so deep I feel him behind my belly button. His fingers twist my nipples almost to the verge of unbearable pain, but my core responds by clenching him further.

"Fuck you," he spits when my body squeezes around him. I can tell he's angry, wanting to last longer than the clutch of my body is going to allow.

"Sorry," I pant a second before another orgasm sneaks up and manifests itself.

A large hand, the same one that gripped my neck in the panic room closes around my throat. Only this time there's no easing into it. My airway is blocked, my eyes roll back, and the wave of release wracking my body intensifies tenfold. I don't see spots like I did earlier, however.

My vision goes black. I can hear his curses, feel the pulse of his cock as he pounds out his own orgasm, but I see nothing. My body is floating even though I'm being held down by Dom's weight. My skin tingles as if covered by a static current.

"Hey," he whispers as his mouth nears mine. Lips brush mine, and I crane my neck, seeking until he obliges with a kiss so sweet I almost imagine he's been replaced by another man.

My vision begins to refocus just as he's reaching up to untie my hands.

"That was... I've never... Can't explain."

He chuckles and rolls me against his chest. "I know."

It's not long before I begin to shiver and a headache knocks behind my eyes. I don't have to say a word. He reaches down and pulls the sheet over our bodies.

"Subspace is pretty fucking awesome, but the drop can be rough." His finger tickles the skin on my back, but the sensation for some reason is less than comforting. I push his hand away expecting him to be upset, but he replaces it with a harder, more comforting pressure. "I never imagined you'd respond like that. I can't wait to take you to the edge."

I pull my head from his chest and glare at him.

"The edge? I think I crashed over it."

"No, baby. You didn't even get close." He chuckles when my eyes widen at his words.

Chapter 26

Dominic

"Are you okay?" Her head only shifts an inch or so on my chest. "Use the words, Mak."

"My whole body is humming. I've never felt anything like it." I feel her lips spread into a smile. "I didn't know it could be like this."

It's usually not. I keep the thought locked tight in my head.

"Baby? Is that something you call all of us girls?" My body doesn't respond, but my brain is scrambling for the right thing to say.

I haven't called anyone that in almost two decades. I have no idea why it comes so easy with you.

"Yeah," I lie. "Just easier some days."

Her demeanor changes, only marginally and the subtlety of it makes me hate myself. The finger tracing the ridges on my stomach stills, her breathing hitches, and after a long moment of silence, I feel a tear roll down my side.

"Easier than remembering our names, I guess." The distant tone of her voice guts me, but rather than comfort her like my mind is telling me to do, I ignore the statement. "I understand."

"You don't, trust me." She wouldn't have a clue.

"I found your photo album. I know I can't be her, the wife you loved that died."

I stiffen, even after the betrayal and the heartache, I'd never wish death on Karen, my heart wouldn't allow for it. "She's not dead," I mutter. "We divorced."

"Divorced?" Disbelief fills her voice, and I know why. Those pictures are filled with happiness and ignorant bliss. "Why do you keep it?"

I ponder that for a long minute. I hate what needs to be said, but that doesn't keep them inside. "It's a reminder that true love doesn't exist. It cautions me against falling for anyone's bullshit."

Karen was my first everything until she decided it wasn't enough. That's not on Makayla, it's on me, but the warning is always there.

She remains silent, letting my words sink in and how they correlate in our current situation. I hope she understands. I'd rather her read between the lines than actually having to say the words out loud. My brain, mouth, and body are all on different wavelengths, and I know I'll fuck that conversation up. Eventually, I shift her off of my chest, check to make sure she's okay one last time and disappear into the bathroom.

She's getting too attached. Fuck, I'm getting too attached. Even knowing that and knowing I need to put an end to whatever this is that's building between us, I'm still agitated when I open the door into the bedroom and find my bed empty.

Crawling into bed without bothering to put on clothes, I lay, wide awake and staring into the darkness long after I realize she isn't just in the guest bedroom getting cleaned up. I spend countless hours tossing and turning in a bed I'd found comfort in just last week. I only sleep in bursts, much like I did in Tennessee.

Kincaid, Kid, and Snatch left before discussing or making solid plans about what needs to happen with the bullshit going on with Grinder and the Renegades. I know he wants to do that without Mak around. I make mental plans to head over there first thing in the morning. The sooner we can get to the bottom of that mess, the sooner I can get her on her way.

***

I wince when I roll over in bed, finding the sun barely shining around the black-out curtains in my room. I haven't had a worse night of sleep in as long as I can remember, but I refuse to examine it for what it actually is.

After another long shower, letting the hot water attempt to work out the soreness in my muscles, I head to the kitchen to make coffee. In my own house, I walk as quietly as possible as to not bother Makayla, when in actuality I want to bang on her door, so she'll join me in the kitchen. I also have a pressing urge to apologize for last night, to explain that I do things with her I haven't felt comfortable doing to anyone in a long time, including using a pet name and letting her sleep on my chest. Those confessions, however, will come with a slew of questions I don't know that I'll ever be able to answer, at least not with the response she probably wants to hear.

She never shows her gorgeous face, so I disappear outside and down the dock. The ducks ignore me just like they do every morning. I don't feed them often because it's a bitch to drag the water hose all the way down here to spray off the shit they leave behind after they've been congregating. I had Kid down here shortly after I discharged after finding out the reason I had such a mess was because he and Khloe had been hanging out down here. He lugged that heavy ass hose all the way down and back with a smile on his face.

I remember those days. The ones that were never long enough, never enough touching, kissing, promising. Not a thing in the world I wouldn't do for Karen. All she had to do was ask or even hint at needing something, and if it was in my power, it was hers. It wasn't until after a few nights of binge drinking and deep reflection that I realized just how one sided the relationship had always been. I was blind to it until my eyes met the sight of her fucking another man in my house.

Eventually, as the sun is rising in the sky, I head back into the house. Passing by the hallway into the kitchen, I see her coming out of my bedroom.

"Looking for me?" She stiffens, and I notice the way her clothes are disheveled and her hair is a mess. Before she even says a word I know what happened last night.

"I, umm." She points over her shoulder at my closed bedroom door.

"You slept in the panic room again." She nods softly.

She had to have gone in there while I was in the shower. Knowing she didn't have time to shower before locking herself in makes my cock grow in my jeans. I resist the need to pull her against me and drink in the smell of me still on her skin. I turn and walk my coffee cup back to the kitchen.

I hear her follow behind, keeping her distance, giving me what I told her in context clues last night. My fingers ache in my gripped fists at her obeying so well. It makes me want to reward her with orgasms while at the same time punishing her with a series of slaps on the ass for not clinging to me the second she saw me.

I hate not being in control, and she's challenged every bit of mine since the day she arrived.

"I'm heading to the clubhouse," I tell her shifting away from the counter as she reaches for the coffee pot. "I want you to go. I think you'll be safer there."

"You want me to stay there?"

"Yes." *I need you out of my house, out of arm's reach.*

"Will you be staying there also?"

"No. They have some renovations going on and only one empty room."

"I want to be where you are," she confesses.

Fuck, why does hearing that make my heart pound harder?

"Can you stay there with me?" Her blue eyes find mine, once again filled with the same fear that was in them when I left to help Bri.

"That's not such a good idea," I say turning my attention from her piercing gaze to the sink to rinse my coffee cup.

"Listen," she says turning her body so one hip is leaning against the counter and she's facing me. "I don't have any grandiose ideas about what's going on between us. I'm fully aware we're just having a little fun until Grinder is dealt with."

Hearing it from her mouth, the words I've been struggling to say myself, sit heavy between us. Her face is emotionless, showing none of the emotions I must have read wrong. She wants to be protected, kept safe, not loved like most girls her age dream of, not the way I'd misinterpreted the way she clung to me last night.

She sighs when I don't respond.

"Even if we're both there, it doesn't mean the sex has to continue, Dom." She turns again to make her cup of coffee. "I'm sure there are other girls there you want to get to since I've kept you away so long."

Just the thought of choosing one of the club girls over Makayla makes me sick to my stomach. You don't settle for sherbet when you can have the option of the creamiest, most delicious ice cream in the world.

The mental reminder of how sweet her pussy is sets my mouth to watering, as if I'm in the desert again and the only thing that will quench my thirst is the delicate honey between her thighs.

"Get packed," I grumble. "I'll do the same."

I may like to engage in mild forms of torture with the women at the end of a crop, but masochism isn't my thing. Staying here and needing to be inside of her, knowing she's miles away seems like it would be the worst kind of agony.

Chapter 27

Makayla

I feel weird trailing behind him to his room. He turns with a questioning look when I cross over the threshold into his room a few seconds behind him.

Full of embarrassment, I open the bottom drawer of his dresser and pull out the clothes he bought for me. I set the arm-full on the bed, and before I can ask, he pulls a small suitcase out of the closet and sets it down beside them. I pack what I'm not going to wear today and begin to pull my t-shirt over my head.

"Change in the bathroom," he insists. "I don't have time to fuck you before we leave."

Without a word, I carry my clothes into the bathroom, eyeing the shower with the longing of a girl who's never used one with that many jets before.

Instead of changing, I strip naked and turn on the shower. I may never have a chance like this again, and there's no way I'm walking out of here without this experience again.

My head rolls on my shoulders as glorious hot water pounds my back from the jets on the wall.

"Fuck, that's good," I moan.

I take as long as possible, only soaping up and washing after my fingers have begun to prune, hoping he'll join me and fuck me against the wall. Sadly, he stays gone. I dry off, twisting my wet hair into a pile on the top of my head and get dressed.

I smile into the mirror, the bright bulbs highlight each and every bruise on my neck. I want him to see them. I want him to remember giving them to me. For the first time in my life, I wear my marks with pride, knowing they were earned through passion and not malice.

My suitcase is gone from the bed. I carry my dirty clothes with me and find Dom standing near the door leading into the garage, eyes focused on his phone. I'm reminded for the first time since he came home yesterday that I haven't bothered to think of the burner phone and the handgun since.

I turn back around, heading to the panic room to retrieve them.

"What have you forgotten?" he asks. "You were in the shower for over an hour, Mak. We need to hit the road."

"The phone. The gun," I answer wondering what in the hell is so urgent that we need to rush getting out of here. I push down the thought that he's eager to get to the clubhouse for the reprieve from me and the company of the other women there.

"You don't need them. Let's go." He never makes eye contact with me as he opens the door, holding it open for me to pass through it.

I don't argue about leaving them here. If he's going to stay at the clubhouse, I won't need them because he's there to protect me.

Opening the back door of a dark tinted SUV, he waves me inside. "Take your hair down before we get there," he orders.

I nod knowing I'm not going to listen to him. He doesn't get to fuck me against the wall of the panic room within a minute of laying his eyes on me, choke me to orgasm, and then turn around and pretend it didn't happen.

"I'm not worried about Renegades lurking around, but I don't want to take any chances." His eyes find mine in the rear view mirror ten minutes later as we drive through town.

I acknowledge him with a quick nod.

"I don't want any trouble there," he continues unprompted. "Not with Griffin and Em about to have two more babies there."

I want to be petty and childish and ask him to just forget about helping me. Tell him to drop me off at the nearest bus station. I'm afraid he'd actually do it and then I'd have to ask him for money for a bus ticket.

Once on the Cerberus property, we pull into one of the buildings beside the clubhouse, not getting out until the garage door has sealed us inside.

He doesn't look at my neck again until we empty through another door inside the clubhouse after walking down the long tunnel. Before he can give further direction about it that I'd only ignore, Khloe and Kid walk up to us like some impromptu welcoming committee.

"Hey," Khloe says. "Great to see you again."

I should be mad at her, but for some reason, the girl just exudes warmth and kindness. It's not her fault for being honest with Kid when he happened to ask the right questions.

"Oh gosh," she gasps, eyes zeroed in on the marks I've put on display. "Makayla, what happened? Those weren't there the other day."

Dom likes to choke me when we fuck.

Kid grabs her hands and pulls her against him whispering something in her ear, while Dom shifts uncomfortably beside me. Her eyes trail over my neck again, only this time her gaze is heated. I don't know what Kid is telling her, but the look on her face is making me hot.

Khloe nods, and in a flash both of them are gone, disappearing into a room down the hall.

"I told you to take your hair down," Dom hisses before another woman comes sauntering up.

It's clear she only has eyes for Dom with the way she's running her tongue over her bottom lip as she approaches. Funnily, Dom takes a step closer to me, his hand settling on my lower back. It's only then that she notices me standing beside him. Her face falls, eyes wrinkle at the corners for a split second before she catches herself.

"Hey, Dom." She's beautiful, closer to Dominic's age, and full of self-confidence I can only hope for in this lifetime. I'm intimidated immediately.

"Bri," he replies with curtness.

Bri? The one he spent two days with in Tennessee?

Forget intimidated, now I just feel hopeless.

"She's young," she whispers purposefully loud enough for me to hear as she walks by and closes herself into another room.

"She wasn't supposed to be here," he mutters as he directs us to a room down the other end of the hall.

I try, I really do, but I can't keep my mouth closed.

"Guess I know where you'll be tonight," I say without looking in his direction.

I hear my suitcase and the duffel bag he carried drop to the ground, and in the next breath, I'm pinned against the wall with his hard thigh between my legs.

"I'll be wherever the fuck I want to be." His hot breath ghosts over my face and neck as he leans in closer to my ear. "And that's going to be buried in that sweet little pussy of yours."

I'm gasping, aching, and reaching for him when he takes a step back. I follow his eyes to the open door to see a very pregnant woman standing there gawking at us like we're aliens.

"I heard a crash," she explains.

Dom doesn't say a word, just gives her a quick kiss on the cheek and walks out of the room.

"I'm Emmalyn," she says offering her hand. "Em."

I shake it. "Makayla. Mak."

She takes a step back and bends to get the duffel and suitcase off the floor.

I stop her. "Let me get that."

"I'm pregnant, not helpless."

I grin at her fiery personality. "Don't need your water breaking on the floor. I hear this is the only open room."

"It is," she answers. "I had to come meet the girl Kincaid believes has finally seeped inside of Dominic."

I shake my head, rejecting her words. "It's nothing like that."

"Is he planning to sleep in here with you?" The sparkle in her eye tells me she already knows the answer.

I shrug. "I guess since it's the only room." I open the suitcase Dom provided for me on the bed and start taking clothes out and putting them in the small dresser. "He could also be down the hall with Bri."

Her laugh startles me, and I drop the socks and panties from the top of my clothing pile. "Yeah, that's not going to happen."

"I'm not jealous or anything," I tell her taking the pile of Dom's clothes from her hands. "She can have him."

I know how vindictive club girls can be, and I have no interest in getting in between that gorgeous woman and a man I've known less than a week.

"He doesn't want her." I put his clothes in a different drawer and reach back to her for his zipped leather bathroom bag. "I think he has his sights set on someone else, anyway."

I ignore her words even though they make me wish and hope for things I have no business even imagining.

"Come on," she says from the doorway. "Everybody is in the living room."

Instinct tells me to stay in the room, but Dom is out there, and he's the one I want to be around, the one I feel safest with. I follow her out of the room, back down the hall and turn left. Talking, laughing, and all around cheer greets us when we walk into the room.

Kincaid is off of the couch and in front of Em before she can sit down on her own. He guides her to the spot he'd just vacated and helps her lower to the couch. She rolls her eyes but takes his help. I can only imagine he's been hovering for a while. With a protective hand on her stomach, he begins nuzzling against her neck, bringing a smile so sweet to her face I look away feeling as if I'm intruding on a private moment.

I don't see Kid and Khloe in the living room, but I didn't expect to see them so soon with the heated look in Khloe's eyes as she stared at my neck.

I sit down on an unoccupied chair, grateful that it's not too close to anyone. Unfortunately, it's directly across from Dom who happens to be right beside Bri. She looks possessive, and he looks more than a little uncomfortable. She's angled her body his direction, and it's then that I can see how uncomfortable he is. Stiff shoulders, darting eyes, and the hardness of his mouth are only a few clues.

I'd expected to be grilled and interrogated when I came out here, but everyone talks and jokes, including me at times. I've never felt this welcome some place new. Hell, I don't feel this welcome at the Renegade clubhouse. I smile when appropriate, keeping my eyes away from Dom even though I can feel his burning a hole through me.

Chapter 28

Dominic

The air shifts the minute she walks into the room. An electric charge drags my eyes from the tight fit of her jeans to the mess of hair piled on her head, the hair I instructed her to take down to hide the marks I've left on her neck. She refused, and it made my cock harder than it's ever gotten for another woman.

Two available spots left in the living room and she picks the one that's not beside me. I'm both proud she feels comfortable enough here that she doesn't cling to me, but at the same time the distance between us, albeit only a few feet, makes me feel cold, empty.

Bri sat down beside me within minutes of me entering the room, and I know Mak seeing her beside me is part of the reason she's keeping her distance. Jealousy looks incredible on her. It isn't until half an hour later, after Kid and Khloe join us that I realize she's not jealous, just indifferent. I don't feel her eyes on me, even when I get distracted by others in the room, even when I know she can feel my eyes burning into her.

She has Snatch's undivided attention, although Kid and Khloe are also part of the conversation. He hasn't reached out to touch her, and I can't hear every word they're saying, but it doesn't seem sexual or explicit. It still niggles that she's laughing and smiling with another man, annoying me to the point I feel the tips of my ears heat from my blood pressure increasing.

Bri is in my ear squawking about nothing like usual. I pick her hand up from my thigh and place it back into her lap, again. She's been drinking and seems to have forgotten our conversation in Tennessee.

I interrupt her mid-sentence. "I thought you were going to stay back home for a few days to get things straightened out."

With lazy eyes of inebriation, she glances over at Mak and back. "I wanted to get back. Make sure everything was okay."

Translation: She got wind of Makayla at my house, and she's here to get in my business or try to keep herself in the running for my attention.

The couch shifts beside me, and I can't even hide the sigh that rushes from my lips.

"Hey, Dom," the redhead whispers on my left.

"Snapper," I say.

She doesn't touch me other than the light rub of her thigh against mine. She knows better. Snapper and I fucked once, years ago, long before she turned into a sneaky, conniving bitch. I wouldn't touch her today with Snatch's dick. Hell, I don't think he'd touch her with his either.

She's pulled way too much shit in the clubhouse, and I have no fucking clue why she's even still allowed to hang around. If I were running things, she would've been gone at the first sign of trouble. I haven't heard of her pulling anything other than jealous, possessive banter since she fucked Kid when he had amnesia.

"You looking for some company tonight?" Snapper purrs in my ear

I huff, not even bothering to look over at her ridiculous offer.

"Are you kidding me right now, slut?" Bri leans forward to make eye contact with her. Her hand is on my thigh again, but I don't attempt to remove it. The anger rolling off of Bri right now annoys the fuck out of me, but at least she'll keep Snapper away.

I look over to see Mak with her eyes pointed in my direction. She's not looking at me, but shifting between the women on either side of me. A slight frown pulls down the corners of her mouth before she looks away, turning her attention back to the cluster of people she's sitting with.

Almost every eye in the room shifts when Kincaid walks back into the room after helping Emmalyn to bed. I use it as my opportunity to get out from between the bickering women.

Bri's hand tightens on my leg. I look from it to her face in warning, but she doesn't read me the right way, alcohol making it impossible.

"At least he's fucked me," Snapper hisses when Bri smirks at her. "He wouldn't give you his dick once."

Shadow's sister's eyes widen in disbelief, not that I fucked Snapper once upon a time because that's not news to anyone here, except Makayla. I watch, angered when Mak's head snaps over at Snapper's loud confession. Disappointment clouded with an air of resolve cover her gorgeous face, as if she suspected as much and confirmation changes her opinion of me. She's looking at me as if I'm every other man in her life, assholish and unable to think without his dick.

"Fuck this," I mutter standing from the couch.

I turn back to both girls who have the gall to turn expectant eyes up at me, like it's time for me to make a choice between the two of them.

"How about you women fight over someone who you actually have a chance with."

Bri's face falls, tears pooling in the corners, but Snapper sits back, arms crossed over her chest, bitchy as usual. She's getting pretty used to the guys at the club turning her down. I wouldn't be surprised if she doesn't move on to another club soon.

I don't give a fuck about Snapper's feelings, but I hate the crestfallen look in Bri's eyes. I walk away before I apologize to her, knowing she'll just see that as another chance. Hopefully being a dick tonight will get her to move on and give up on the notion that we'll ever be more than friends.

Standing attracted Kincaid's attention, so I walk to him, slap him on the back, and head to the front door. He follows just like I knew he would.

He's laughing by the time we hit the front steps and close the door behind us.

"Don't start," I bite out.

"Two," he says holding his fingers up for emphasis. "You have two drunken women fighting over you and the only woman in the room your cock gets hard for is chatting it up with Snatch."

"Story of my life," I mutter with more vulnerability than I want to show.

"You don't have to concern yourself with Snatch, brother. He knows not to push up on her." As if I need the reassurance, he slaps me on the back with camaraderie I don't feel right now.

Maybe it's the glint in his eye or the minor quirk of his lip, but I get the sensation he's taking too much joy in fucking with me right now.

"Fuck off," I say shrugging his arm from my back.

"Come on," he chides. "Don't be like that. You want to talk about it? Get some advice on how to keep a woman after she's already seen your tiny dick."

I could junk punch him right now.

"It's all in the tongue, big brother." He smiles from one side of his face to the other, and I picture what he'll look like after I knock out a couple of his front teeth. Em getting mad at me is the only reason why I don't.

"Give me a ride back to my house," I mutter as we walk across the gravel in front of the clubhouse.

"You just going to leave her in there without even telling her you're going back home?" He says the words but never stops walking toward the truck parked out front.

"I need my bike, but I need the Tahoe here in case something happens and I have to get her out of here in a rush."

"Makes sense," he offers with a shrug as he climbs inside.

Pulling off of the property, he glances at me several times before he speaks. I keep my eyes on the darkness out of my side window, hoping he'll just keep his damn mouth shut, but knowing my brother enough that he won't.

"She's not Karen," he says after ten minutes of blessed silence.

I grunt. We've never had this conversation. Diego was a kid when I went into the service, and by the time I took my next leave after finding my wife with another man, I was already divorced, and our mother was dead. We had a billion other things to talk about, and dozens more to pretend didn't exist than my cheating wife.

I was willing to discharge from the Marines then to be responsible for Diego, but he wanted to live with our aunt, uncle, and cousin Kaleb. He got years to live in a fully functioning family, time to be raised by a real man who knew how to treat a woman. He didn't have a serious relationship until Emmalyn, but he knew how to treat women right.

"I know she's not Karen," I mutter as we pull into my driveway. I finally pull my eyes away from the nothing I've been staring into and over at him. "She's a lot like mom. Brave even when her chin is quivering, and she wants to cry. She's resilient and compassionate even after the shit hand she's been dealt."

Kincaid smiles. "I know exactly what you mean, man. Em is the same way."

We sit in silence for a long moment, both reflecting on the woman who raised us as best she could and the ones that currently have us so tangled up.

"You have a beautiful family, little brother, and it's only going to be better when those angels get here."

He nods, accepting my praise but the look on his face says he's thinking much deeper than this very moment.

"I don't want to be like dad," he whispers, eyes pointed through the front windshield.

"You're nothing like that motherfucker," I assure him. "You're not the one choking a rape victim and watching her eyes roll in the back of her head as she comes, fully aware of the cycle of violence. If anyone has to be worried about ending up like that fucker, it's me."

He tries to stop me, but I climb out of the truck. Walking past my bike, I head around the house and down to the dock. Nothing like a reflective conversation with your brother to bring out all of the faults, concerns, and worries you're having about a woman, one I'm not even sure will be around this time next month.

Chapter 29

Makayla

Kid and Khloe are unlike any couple I've ever seen. The proof of his love is evident in the way he watches her, touches her for no other reason than to feel her skin against his. It's in the brush of his fingertips on her forehead when her hair falls into her eyes, the smile on his face when she whispers something in his ear.

Their attentiveness isn't something I'm used to. At the Renegade clubhouse, everything is brash and dirty. The men are getting sucked off in the middle of a conversation, the girl choking on dick while the guy rests his beer on the back of her neck and slaps her across the face if she jerks up when he chokes her, and she causes it to spill. The women serve the men and then know to stay out of the way unless they're needed to sexually please one of the men. The women here are valued and treated with respect, involved in the conversation. They seem to be part of the family.

I do my best to keep my attention on Snatch, unnerved by the passion and comfort of the couple in our small cluster. There are at least a dozen people in the room, grouped together carrying on numerous conversations, and I'm thankful that the three people are taking the time to speak to me and make me feel welcome.

My eyes drift more than once over to Dom who is now sandwiched between Bri and an attractive redhead. I feel his eyes on me, feel the burn of them on my face, the exposed skin on my arms, but I keep my attention on my present company.

I may have been lying about wanting to keep things casual, but I refuse to let him in on that little secret. Acting like a crazy, jealous woman just isn't something I'm going to do. If he wants those women, he can have them.

"Really?" Snatch says bringing my attention back to the conversation. "I would've never guessed. You seem pretty fucking smart to me."

Khloe glares at the side of his head. "Just because you struggle in school doesn't mean you're stupid."

I nod in agreement. "I had a lot of family shit, club shit going on. I couldn't concentrate on the work, missed a lot of days. I'm just glad I graduated. Not that it means anything now."

"You can always go to college," Khloe says with encouragement.

"Khloe got her GED and is doing great in school." Kid punches Snatch in the shoulder. I wait for them to start brawling which is what would happen back home, but Snatch just grins over at him. "My girl isn't stupid either, asshole. She had other shit going on too."

Snatch holds his hands up in mock surrender, a playful smile on his tattooed face. "Fuck, sorry. I didn't mean anyone was stupid. I can't say shit. I didn't really graduate either."

Kid scoffs. "You were in the Marines idiot. You had to have finished school in some fashion."

"I had a couple of chicks who did all of my work, took my tests even. I got in so much trouble in school the teachers threw a party after I walked across the shitty stage at graduation."

"At least he fucked me!" We all look over at Dom and the two women who seem to be competing for his company.

"Here we go again," Khloe mutters.

I watch Dom stand from the two women as they face off against each other. The arguing and women fighting over each other is what I'm used to. The unfamiliar sight is Dom standing up, facing them and speaking to them in a voice only they can hear and walking away. A Renegade would have sat back and let them fight over him, and the one who won would've been the first one to deep throat his dick while the other had to wait for her turn.

The sneer on Khloe's face when she turns back to our conversation has a story of its own. Kid leans in and whispers in her ear, and some of the anger melts from her eyes. I'm a pretty smart girl, so I can tell something happened between Kid and the redhead, something Khloe is not happy about at all, but whatever it is that Kid tells her appeases her for the moment.

He holds her closer, her head resting on his shoulder the same time the slam of the front door rings through the clubhouse. Conversations start up again as if a club girl didn't just voice her history with the man I've been sleeping with. A quick glance back in that direction shows that Bri has gotten up and left. The redhead sits alone, running her eyes over everyone else in the room, planning and plotting out her next attempt to get in someone's bed tonight.

I fake a yawn and make my excuses before leaving the room. I only wanted to be out there because that's where Dom was. He walked out and has been gone for some time, so I don't bother staying. I take a shower and climb into bed with wet hair and still damp body. Soft silky sheets wrap around me as I bury deeper on the opposite side from where Dom sleeps in his own home.

I have no false illusions. I know he may not get in this bed tonight. I may hardly ever see him while we're here, but at least I have Khloe and Em seems really nice and welcoming. It isn't until I'm straining to hear what's going on outside of the room that I realize it's very quiet and peaceful, another contradiction to the Renegade Clubhouse. There, you're lucky if you get only a couple of hours of sleep. People normally party until they pass out and no one is on the same schedule, so it's chaos all the time.

I'm on the cusp, the part of sleep where you're awake but still miss chunks of time when the bed shifts behind my back. His familiar scent hits my nose before the warmth of his chest hits my naked back. Still inches from me, the safety he provides calms nerves I didn't know were still on high alert at being in a foreign place.

"Those other women," I whisper. "You really aren't getting attached to me are you?"

I feel his weight shift, and I wait for his arm to wrap around me. The air between our bodies turns cold at the lack of contact.

He clears his throat like he hasn't used his voice in a while. "I told you. I don't work that way."

When I think he's going to face the wall, turning further from me, I feel his arm wrap around my waist. The heat of his chest against my back is welcoming but sets me on edge as well.

"I won't fuck you on the same night you fucked someone else," I mutter and try to pull away.

He responds by holding me tighter but doesn't say a word.

"Maybe if there's someone else you want to pair up with and we all get started together," I offer only as a test. I don't fault people for doing that sort of thing, but I truly have no interest.

"Threesomes aren't my thing, Makayla. When we fuck, it's only going to be you and me."

"Okay," I whisper because honestly, I can't think of anything else to say.

I settle into his embrace, allowing my muscles to relax against his hold. I don't want him to let me go, and I know how dangerous those feelings are.

"I want to spank your ass for not sitting beside me in the living room earlier," he confesses in my ear. I smile in response. "I feel territorial over you, and I don't know why."

I give him the answer I know he wants to hear. "Lock that shit down."

He sighs, his warm breath rushing over my bare shoulder and cheek before he pulls away. "I'm trying to."

I feel him roll over and face away from me, the distance allowing me to think straight once more.

I know I'm getting emotionally involved. He's on my mind all the time. I wonder what I can do to please him or how I can anger him, so he fucks me with relentless abandon. In the days he was gone to Tennessee, I let myself imagine he was mine and only gone on a business trip. I pictured him coming home to a clean house and a woman who missed him so much she was waiting on her knees ready to act out all of his dirtiest fantasies.

It's dangerous, deadly. False hope and a worthless sense of security are not only unhealthy but also unsafe. More to my heart than my physical well-being.

Chapter 30

Dominic

Her warm breath is tickling the hair on my chest as I wake. I don't question the forces that pulled us together in the night. I knew it would happen when I laid down on the bed. I knew, no matter what position we were in when we fell asleep, we'd be just as we are, her halfway laying across my chest with both of my arms wrapped around her. I can't be angry about it, so I don't even try. Holding her while she sleeps, even though my mind argues against it, has become one of the few things I look forward to each day.

One hand running through her gorgeous hair, the other gently cupping her full breast, no immediate concerns that need our attention. Perfection. Cock hard against the side of her hip, ready, willing, and able to fuck her into next week, but content to just touch her warm skin.

I lean over, pressing my lips against her forehead, wanting to crawl inside of her, wanting her to carry a piece of me with her for the rest of her life, and cursing Karen for fucking my head up so badly. My emotions are all twisted together, so much I can't unravel them any longer. I can no longer tell if I just want her or if I've crossed over into needing her.

The intoxicating scent of her skin, different from the way it smelled when she used my soap at home fills my nose. My neglected cock jumps at her hip, eager to slide inside of her. My eyes rove from her face down every delicious curve of her naked flesh, stopping on the glistening tip of my weeping cock. The thought of her wrapping her talented lips around the crown nearly makes me moan.

The urge to fuck, to take, to conquer is so strong, I can't remember the last time I wanted to sink inside of pussy so often. I've slept with more women than I'm proud of, sometimes often enough on leave to make my cock raw, but it was always to stock up before spending months surrounded by other men in the desert. Never before have I craved the same woman, repeatedly needing to be inside of her like I do with Makayla Evans. I can chalk it up to good pussy, but I'm not one to lie to myself.

Her eyes flutter open, and for a second she looks up and gives me a soft smile. Then, as if remembering herself, she stiffens against my chest and tries to pull away.

I grip her tighter and move my mouth over hers, groaning when the light brush of her tongue mixes with mine. I only wanted to hold her a little longer, feel her against my skin before words were spoken, and things grew more complicated, but her hips circle as she grinds herself against my legs. The heat of her skin on mine is intoxicating, and like an addict, I need more.

Shifting my weight until she's on her back and I'm nestled between her legs, I nip at her bottom lip, our panting breaths mingling.

"Dom," she whispers but I swallow her pleas.

Her wandering hands skate over the bare flesh of my back and still lower to my ass. I need the feel of her nails digging into my flesh, marking me, claiming me. Craving it so much, I understand just how perilous the urgency is. I lift her arms over her head, pinning them with one of mine as I kiss my way down her neck.

The heat of her cleft pulls more of my attention than I can handle. With a skilled shift of my hips, I'm lined up with her entrance and begging for access. Rotating her hips as much as she can, I slip the first amazing inch inside of her, relishing the feel of her pussy as it squeezes the head and begs for more.

"Dom," she whimpers again. "Please."

Ignoring the urgency in my balls, I slide into her inexorably slow until she's wrapped around me and clinging to the base of my cock with desperate clenching flesh. I feel every tiny internal muscle rippling up and down my shaft, quivering as if confused by the delicate intrusion, but needing more.

With my free arm, I raise her leg, resting it in the crook of my arm, not increasing the speed of my hips but being able to sink deeper. Her eyes flutter, rolling up.

"Look at me," I beg, too far gone to even make it sound like a command.

Unfocused eyes peer up at me as my hips pump with almost sluggish determination. Ignoring the necessity, both in her eyes and my own body, I keep the languid pace. Soft push forward, rotate my hips brushing against her needy clit, slow withdrawal. Over and over until she's liquid fire under me, trembling, so close to the edge but unable to spill over.

"Please," she begs. "Faster."

I shake my head and take her mouth again. Her warm breath over my skin heats me to the point of combustion, but I stave off the demand and fuck her slow and sensual. Another thing Mak deceives my body to do that I'd never experience with another woman.

"Dom," she gasps again. "Faster, please."

I know the slow build, the controlled climax isn't what she's used to. The times we've been together before have been rough, hard, and bordering on violent. It's not what I'm offering this morning, and her senses don't know what to do with the change.

"Take it," I pant. Fuck she feels so good. "Take what I give you."

She whimpers again, and the pressure at the base of my spine builds. Squeezing my eyes shut for a second I stave off the need to come. When I open them again, I find her eyes pooled with unshed tears. Her head is turned to the side, and she's focusing on something other than me, other than our coupling, almost as if she's lost in her own head, as if willing the orgasm to take hold.

I read it wrong until she hiccups and begins to cry, the soft whimpers shaking her shoulders with the same violence she displayed after her nightmare back at my house.

I push back on my heels immediately, a reluctant withdraw from her tight, warm body and release the grip on her arms confused by her reaction.

"Mak?"

She's trembling, a full body shake as she raises both of her hands to cover her face.

"Mak?" I say again. "Baby, what's wrong?"

She doesn't answer me, only shifts her hips, a sign that she wants me to move. I oblige, unsure of just what the fuck is going on.

"Damn it," I mutter. "I was going to let you come. I only wanted slow with an edge of desperation."

She shakes her head almost violently.

"Grinder," she sobs. "*Take it*, that's what he always said to me when he…. He…"

She can't even get the words out, but I know exactly what she's recalling.

She climbs out of bed, and all I can do is watch her retreating back as she closes the bathroom door. Prior images in my head of ending Grinder have never been as violent and brutal as they are right now. I want to cut away bits and pieces of his body while he begs me for a quick death.

Flopping on my back on the still warm bed, frustrated hands tug at my hair. Words that felt right at the moment and received the wrong way have fucked everything up. I argue with myself over what to do next. Do I force myself into the bathroom, show her that I'm not Grinder, prove to her that I'd never hurt her? I can't make that promise, though. The pain

I want to inflict, the way I need to hear her moan and beg for more when I hit her, choke her, is what we both need.

It's not the same.

My mind chants the mantra over and over until I begin to believe it myself.

She needs it as much as you do.

It bounces around in my head, fueling me, powering me.

My body aches for her, and not just in a sexual way. The pain I've felt at my wife's betrayal, the voice in my head that tells me not to trust anyone with a pair of tits grows quiet around her. The silence in my head when I'm inside of her is something I crave, something I need, something I can't ever recall happening before.

She calms me and sets my blood on fire in the same breath, healing me and ripping open old wounds simultaneously.

Unable to lay down a second longer while her sobs filter through the door, I climb off the bed. I don't reach for the door knob immediately, rather press my ear to the door, analyzing what's going on inside.

Muffled cries and the sound of the shower running greet me.

I know if I step into that bathroom, if I become what she needs, holding her and reassuring her that everything will be okay, I strengthen her connection to me, which will be extremely messy later.

I huff. "Messy. Shit's already as fucking messy as it can be."

Talking to myself is a new low.

I don't love her, of that I'm certain, but I'm sure as fuck not done with her. It's the consideration that I may never be done with her that has me taking additional pause outside of the bathroom door.

Chapter 31

Makayla

Feeling like a freak of nature, I close myself into the bathroom, immediately turning on the shower. Memories I need to scrub free of my body and soul flash in my head. I'm confused, ashamed, and embarrassed from walking out on him, leaving him in the bed bewildered at my quick retreat.

I don't understand how choking me, smacking my ass until it feels like I've been burned, is okay, but making love to me, slowly rocking in and out combined with the wrong couple of words turns my world upside down. His steel-gray eyes turned muddy brown, the soft enraptured face became scarred, mouth twisted up into a demented snarl. He became Grinder.

I'm beyond fucked up, my body needing things I never would've imagined, my soul wanting to cling to a man who's made it clear that fucking me is the only thing he wants.

The water burns my skin as I step into the cramped shower. I revel in the way it forces me to focus on the pain on the outside of my body, pulling my attention away from the broken places inside.

It can't be longer than ten minutes before the shower curtain is pulled back and Dom steps inside with me. I look away, sure that my face is a red blotchy mess. Without a word spoken, he lathers up his hands with the lavender scented body wash and begins to run his hands over my shoulders, down my back as he pulls me against his solid chest. The crying begins anew.

"I know you're nothing like him," I explain unable to look him in the eye. "I don't know why I reacted that way. You've never hurt me in a way I didn't enjoy."

His hands still, one on my lower back the other gripping my hip with a softness I'd never attribute to him.

"It's a trigger," he says into the crown of my head. "It may go away with time."

"I hate him," I mutter.

"I know, baby. I do too."

I shift my weight from one foot to the other and feel his straining erection pinned between us at my lower belly. On instinct, I reach for him.

"You didn't come," I say taking him in my hand. "Let me take care of that."

His hand covers mine, stopping it as I stroke upward.

"Mak, that's not important right now."

He pulls my hand free but soothes the rejection with the sweep of his lips against the knuckles. This is the part I hate, the Dom that doesn't make sense. The man in here with me right now is sensitive, protective, and so fucking easy to love. The man wrapped around me right now is the most dangerous predator I've ever met.

Like the swaying head of a cobra, entrancing you to the point of stupidity before it strikes and leaves you bleeding, in pain, and full of a poison you're never able to get rid of. His touches, the passion and empathy in his voice bury deep and encapsulate you in a burn so slow, you don't realize you're past the point of turning back until the damage has left you a smoldering pile of ash.

I can't help but wonder if the only reason I'm having these intense feelings for him is because he's the only man I've encountered that has treated me with respect, the only man to hold me when I cry. These are things a dad should be the first ever to provide for their daughter. My father didn't get the memo, effectively breaking my heart long before a man ever had the chance to.

"You'll feel better when he's dead," Dom assures me. I look up at him. "When you know he can no longer hurt you, you'll be able to finally heal."

I shake my head, unable to imagine a time when the thought of Grinder won't make me cringe and shudder.

"I'm not saying it's going to be immediate, but it'll get easier." His eyes cloud as if thinking of his own demons.

"I've got to get my sister out of there," I offer, changing the subject before he's lost to his own troubles. My pain I can deal with; I've been doing it for years. The thought that he's struggling with his own darkness is more than I can handle.

"We'll get her, baby. I promise." Tender fingers reach up and push a wet lock of hair from my face. "Is her mother on board?"

The thought of Jasmine's piece of crap mother makes my blood boil. "She sees Jasmine as a weight, a burden. She complains incessantly that my sister drags her down, but she knows Jasmine's unspoken paternity is the only reason she's allowed to stay."

His eyes dart between both of mine, trying to read my thoughts. It's unnerving because if he could, he'd know I never want him to let me go. I can't picture a future with him. Hell, I can't picture a future at all, but one including an amazing man isn't something I'd ever let myself wish for.

"What happens when we get her out? Do you plan on raising her on your own?" His eyes stay locked on mine.

"Why wouldn't I? Family takes care of family." His thumb brushes my cheek, and I lean into the soft touch before thinking about it.

"It won't be easy," he whispers. "Taking care of a kid."

"Nothing about my life has been easy. All I know is struggle and difficulty. If Jasmine is safe, the least I can do is make sacrifices for her." My eyes begin to pool with tears once again, and I'm grateful for the water pouring over us as it masks the wetness flowing down my cheeks. "No one bothered to protect me, to love me. She doesn't need to grow up like that. The last thing I want is for her to be as fucked up as I am."

I turn my head from him then, looking at the shower wall, concentrating on the mist covering it. I hate the vulnerability he pulls from me. The words I've never spoken, the feelings I've tried my whole life not to feel just pour out like a broken water main when I'm in his presence.

He refuses to allow the diversion, hooking a finger under my chin he tilts my face back up to his.

"You are not fucked up," he insists. "You have some shit to work through, baby, that's all."

I huff a laugh as he pulls me against his chest. He doesn't make promises, doesn't assure me everything is going to be okay, but he holds me against his hard body as if letting me go is the last thing he wants.

"You're one of the strongest women I've ever met. I know you'll give that little girl everything she'll ever need. She's lucky to have you." My heart sings at his words, allowing just a little of the doubt in my inability to be replaced with confidence.

My mouth finds his just as the rough skin of his fingertips meet the furled flesh of my nipple. We groan in unison, feasting on each other's mouths. The kiss isn't fast but has an edge of desperation to it. This time the need isn't one-sided, but a tangible thing rolling off of both of us.

His arms sweep under my thighs, crooking the backs of my knees into his elbows. He enters me the second my back touches the cool shower wall. I whimper in his mouth, needing more, needing less. I just *need*.

The banging on the bedroom door startles me enough to make me screech. Thoughts of Grinder busting in immediately come to mind. Dom, unaffected looks over his shoulder.

"This better be fucking important," he bellows.

"Sorry, man." Snatch's voice not the demonic voice of my perpetrator. "Em's gone into labor, and Kincaid is freaking the fuck out.

He says it's too early. They're already headed to the hospital. Thought you'd like to know. I'm heading out if you want to ride with me."

Dom pulls out of me, unsatisfied for the second time today.

"Give me five," he answers Snatch before turning back and lowering my legs to the shower floor. "I'm going to fuck you stupid when I get back."

His dark promise makes my smile grow and my cheeks heat.

I climb out of the shower right behind him, taking my time to towel off. I'm mesmerized by the efficiency that he dries his own body. My eyes trail him into the other room, drinking in every bunch and ripple of his muscles as he dresses. It isn't until he sits on the bed to lace up his boots that he notices my perusal.

"You look hungry, baby," he teases. After he's laced up, he walks to me and plants a sweet kiss on my forehead. "Stay that way."

I turn around and hit the shower again, needing to cool off. I know I'll spend the next however long waiting, anticipating his return.

Chapter 32

Dominic

Snatch's incessant leg bouncing is about to drive me up the wall. We've been waiting for what seems like forever. Kincaid has texted a few times, so we know everything is going fine. His earlier freak out wasn't warranted, but I can't blame him.

"Would you calm the fuck down?" I hiss at him.

"Sorry," he mutters. "I'm nervous."

"You're nervous?" I shouldn't chide. Everyone in the waiting room is strung tight with anxious energy. Kincaid has been so distressed since Em was told to take it easy, that it's got everyone else just as concerned.

"You didn't see the fear in his eyes, man. I've never seen Kincaid that worried. Not even that time in Bangladesh when he had that AK pointed at his fucking head." Snatch raises the fingernail he's been chewing on to his lips and speaks around it. "He was freaking out because of how early it is. If he loses those babies, or if something happens to Em…. Fuck, man. I can't even think about it."

"Idiot." I smack the hand away from his mouth. "One, that's nasty. Keep your hands out of your mouth. What are you three? Two, she only had four weeks left. That's pretty damn good for twins. Diego says they're fine. Chill out. You're driving me nuts."

His eyes narrow, but rather than saying anything, he looks across the room. His eyes land on the only open seat in the room, the one beside Itchy. I can see the wariness on Snatch's face and the challenge in Itchy's eyes as they look at each other.

Making his choice, Snatch turns his body, so his back is to me instead of going and sitting by the guy that was once his best friend. Some stupid shit is going on because they've somehow been cordial, but invisible to each other for the better part of a year. Things got weird around the same time that Darby chick from Vegas left, which is weird because they've shared women for years and not one of the chicks they banged was able to come between them. I'm sure Kid has more of a grasp on what the fuck is going on, but bikers don't really go around talking about their feelings and shit, so no one has bothered to ask.

I look around the room, filled with every member of the club. Almost everyone in this room, I'd gladly take a bullet for, a few I'd lay down my life without question. We're an unlikely family, clinging to each other to fill voids our own families never did. I couldn't ask for a better group of people in my life. It isn't until my eyes land on each and every person there that I realize my mistake.

"Snake, Itchy, and Ace," I snap. Each one looks over at me. "Back to the clubhouse."

Snake and Ace nod, one standing from his chair and the other pushing off of the wall near Snapper. Itchy, being the petulant child that he is frowns. "The babies will be here soon."

"Look around, fucker," I hiss. "Doc's out of town. That leaves Rose and Makayla alone in the clubhouse."

Itchy's eyes scan over the large group.

"Do we leave our women alone?" He shakes his head. "Double time."

They're out the door not a minute later.

I realize my mistake when I catch Bri's disappointed look from across the room. Sitting beside her, Khloe, grins from ear to ear, approval glinting in her eyes.

Our women. Fuck my life.

I rest my elbows on my knees and my head in my hands. This is going to be one long ass day.

***

"Sorry you had to wait so long," Kincaid says with a slap on my back when I walk into the dimly lit room. "We just wanted a little time to ourselves before everyone started filing in."

"I understand." And I do. I know what it's like to need time away from the other club members. I wouldn't trade them for the world, but sometimes you just need to take a step away and breathe.

Em looks up from her pink-wrapped bundles and smiles. She's clearly tired, exhaustion evident in the paleness of her skin and the stray hairs sticking out on her head, but her eyes are lit with a world of love as she holds her miracles.

I clear my throat more than once, yet I'm still unable to clear the lump that formed the second I saw the sheer happiness on my brother's face.

"They're beautiful," I whisper looking down at the two girls that just stole my heart at first glance. I can't imagine what my brother is feeling right now.

I hate Karen more now than ever before for taking moments like this from me. She said she wanted kids. We were going to start a family the second I discharged from the Marines. I found out years later that she got her wish, only the babies we were supposed to have together were given to another man.

Overwhelmed with emotion and a jealousy for my brother's life that I have no business feeling, I sit down in the chair beside the bed.

Em looks over at me, reading the emotion I'm too exhausted to hide. "You want to hold them?"

"Please." My voice cracks pulling a tear from Em's eye.

Diego coos softly to his daughter as he switches her from his wife's arms to mine.

"Georgia Leigh, Gigi for short," he says with pride and reaches for the other. "And this is Genevieve Layne. We're going to call her Ivy."

The burn behind my eyes is too much to ignore as I look down into the perfect sleeping faces of my nieces. I look up from them into the face of my brother. He doesn't bother to wipe the tears streaming down his face. Pride has no place in this room. I blink, allowing the very first tear in as long as I can remember to roll down my cheek. Em is full on sobbing at this point.

The unspoken words pass between Diego and me. We nod at the same time.

Mom should be here for this.

I lower my eyes back down to the babies, my tears making dark circles on their pale pink blankets.

"You did good, little brother." My voice is deep, causing one of the girls to startle in my arms.

"They're bald," Em says with a chuckle easing the seriousness of the moment. I'm grateful to her for that.

"They're perfect," I argue.

I sense Em shifting in bed, wincing as she moves. Kincaid is by her side immediately. I watch as he whispers in her ear, comforting her. We were two boys fucked up by what their father did to their mother for years. At least one of us turned into a man she would be proud of.

For just a moment, I picture myself younger. I'm holding my own babies in my arms. I let go of the bitterness that I'm too fucking old to start a family now. I'll have these sweet angels to spoil and protect, and that has to be enough.

Closing my eyes, I hum to them, soft and low, so even my brother and his amazing wife can't hear.

My mind pictures coming home to my pregnant wife, wrapping my arms around her and sweeping my nose up her neck. I smell the lavender from Mak's skin, see a flash of her pink hair, and for a moment I just let the daydream continue letting my mind wander to all of the things I know I'm too selfish to even ask for.

The sharp whimper of one of the girls snaps my eyes open. I find Diego nearly on top of me at the second long distress of his daughter. Emmalyn chuckles behind him.

"Those girls don't stand a chance. I won't be surprised if he wraps them in bubble wrap for the ride home." Her smile is wide as daddy takes the wiggling baby from my arms.

"I've already strapped the car seat to the back of my bike," I tease.

My brother's fiery eyes meet mine. "Over my dead fucking body," he hisses.

"See what I mean. He can't even take a joke anymore," Em giggles.

"I think she's hungry," Kincaid says turning toward his wife. He looks over his shoulder at me. "I love you, brother, but Em's trying to breastfeed and if you see her tits, I'll have to fucking kill you."

I hold my hands up in mock surrender as I stand from the chair. I grin over his shoulder at Em, who's shaking her head at her over-protective husband. I clasp Kincaid's hand in mine and pull him against my chest for a hug. After tears and a near emotional breakdown on my part, it just feels like the right thing to do. I slap him on the back.

"Heading back to the clubhouse. Gonna relieve the guys so they can come up and check out those princesses." He gives me a knowing look when I pull away. He knows going back has more to do with the pink haired woman staying there than the three idiots protecting her.

Chapter 33

Makayla

"You seem a little on edge," Khloe says from across one of the dining room tables. "He's not messing around with any of the other girls."

I raise a disbelieving eyebrow at her.

"You'd know," she insists. "The only women left here for him to sleep with would rub it in your face."

I hear what she's saying, but I have a hard time believing it.

It's been two weeks since the babies were born. Two weeks since he touched me in the shower after my freak out. I ached for him the entire time he was gone to the hospital, but he has all but ignored me since he got back. If I walk into a room and he's there alone, he makes a hasty retreat. He's been showering and sleeping somewhere else since the hospital as well.

I haven't pushed him, haven't questioned where he's been, whose bed he's keeping warm, whose pussy he's fucking. The man was insatiable around me, so I know he has to be sinking inside of someone. A man as needy as Dominic Anderson doesn't stop fucking, he just moves on to the next willing thing. Our time fizzled out. It hurts more than I should've ever let it.

"He's been spending a lot of time with Kincaid and the girls," she continues.

I nod my head. How can I be mad at that? Everyone in the clubhouse has gone all soft over those two little girls, and they should. Babies are amazing little miracles and should be treated as such, but it doesn't ease the burn I have for him or the pain in my heart for needing him.

I stand from the table, and Khloe follows. I wonder if she's been instructed to keep me company, fill my time with watching TV and chatting, so I won't bother Dom.

"I'm going to take a nap," I mutter.

"Still not sleeping well?"

I shake my head and walk out of the room. The nightmares have returned, only this time I wake and comfort myself. Dom doesn't come into the room and hold me in his arms any longer. He doesn't promise me I'm safe and that he won't let anything hurt me. I believed it when he would whisper the words in my ear. I tried the same thing the first time it happened and he wasn't around. I found out very quickly that I don't believe a fucking word coming out of my own mouth. I don't have faith in my ability to stay safe on my own.

I can rest during the daylight hours. I can fall into a somewhat peaceful sleep while others are awake. I know they'd never let anyone breach the front doors because there are three children here that every one of the members and even the club girls would protect with their lives. It's only when the darkness creeps in, and the sun sets that the fear becomes unbearable. It's then that I picture Grinder turning to smoke and slithering by the sleeping members, only to materialize in my room to finally carry out the threats he's been telling me for years.

Bone weary, I collapse on the bed, but sleep doesn't find me. The agitation has been building, and the conversation with Khloe must have tipped it over the edge.

Not one conversation has happened about the Renegades. Not a single word spoken about getting my sister out of that horrific place. The arrival of Ivy and Gigi has put that issue on the back burner or made it disappear altogether.

It's then that a thought strikes me. Is he ignoring me, refusing to speak of my problems a way for him to force me to leave? Is he hoping I'll just disappear?

"Sounds like a perfect idea," I mutter climbing off of the bed and pulling the suitcase out from under it.

I should leave all of the shit he bought for me, but I have nothing else and walking away without it would be foolish. Pulling open the dresser drawer, I scoop my clothes out and begin stuffing them into the open case on my bed.

"What the fuck do you think you're doing?" The gravel in the familiar voice makes the hair on my arms stand on end.

I don't even turn around to face him. Just as I'm about to leave he shows up? After I've given up on waiting, he wants to come in and dictate what I do? Fat fucking chance.

"Look at me, Makayla." The command in his voice is unmistakable. My body wants to obey, but obeying has gotten me nothing but heartache, and wasted time that could've been used to save Jasmine.

I grab a stray sock from the mattress and stuff it into the suitcase before zipping it up and turning to face him. He looks as tired as I feel. Dark rings circle his cloudy gray eyes.

"Where are you going?" It's nearly a growl, but his anger no longer scares me. I know he'd never hurt me, not intentionally anyway.

"Someone has to do something, Dom. If Cerberus isn't going to help get my sister away from the Renegades, then I'll have to figure out a way to do it my damn self." I straighten my spine, and I don't miss the spark in his eyes.

I've learned that defying him turns him on, but that isn't my objective today. Right now I just want him to move aside so I can leave.

"What makes you think we haven't been doing anything, Mak? I told you we'd take care of it and we are." He crosses his massive arms over his chest, effectively making himself wider and blocking the exit even more.

"No one has said anything to me," I argue. "I haven't heard one fucking word from you or anyone else in this God damned clubhouse. It's like you just fucking forgot about me."

"That is completely inaccurate," he hisses.

"I'm forgettable. I get that, but I can't forget about Jasmine." Tears sting my eyes, and it only serves to piss me off even more.

He tilts his head back and fucking laughs at me. I see red. My hand trembles on the handle of the suitcase, and I picture myself lifting it and slamming it against his beautiful laughing face.

"So glad you find it funny," I spit.

The abrupt end of his laughter fills the room with eerie silence. He takes a step forward. Instinctively, I take a step back. My knees hit the mattress forcing me to sit on the end of the bed.

"I wish forgetting you were that easy," he hisses. "God knows I've fucking tried."

My gut twists, pain filling my entire body. His words hurt more than Grinder's fists ever did. I hang my head, feeling like an idiot for ever thinking he was different than every other man in my life. If anything he's more dangerous because he got me to trust in him, believe in his chivalry.

"Just let me leave," I beg. If he doesn't want me here, I don't understand trying to keep me from leaving. I can walk out of here, and he'd never have to think of me again.

"I don't want you hurt," he says only a few feet from me now.

"My safety is no longer your obligation, Dom."

"That couldn't be any farther from the truth," he says.

I finally raise my head and meet his eyes. "You haven't touched me since you got back from the hospital when the twins were born. You're sleeping in someone else's room! Why do you even fucking care right now?"

I jump up and face off with him. It's ridiculous since I have to look up and hold absolutely no intimidation power against this hulk of a man.

"You freaked out the last fucking time I touched you."

"I was calm when you left," I argue.

He turns away and paces, his huge hands sweeping in frustration over his head. "I'm trying to work through some shit. The last thing I wanted was to bring you down."

I huff. "Work through some shit? Is that code for needing to fuck other women?"

Why in the hell did I bring that shit up? I sound like a fucking possessive psycho club whore.

"I've been sleeping on the fucking couch," he seethes. "I told you I didn't want any of the girls here."

"And what, I'm just supposed to take you at your word?" I glare at him until he faces me again. "You think I'm able to believe a word that has ever been spoken by a man before?"

He growls and closes the distance between us, only this time I stand firm, refusing to back away from him.

"Sounds like you got some shit to work through, also." His breath is warm and minty on my face.

"That's a fucking understatement," I murmur.

He watches me, the scrutiny of his gaze making me grow warm in all of the places I've been trying to force into understanding they'll never be touched by him again. His eyes dart to my lips and stay there.

"I didn't mean to freak out on you. You were all soft and sweet, and the last thing I wanted was you making love to me. Then those words," I pause. "I just couldn't handle it."

"That shit is a hundred percent on me, Mak. I watched your eyes that day. You wanted exactly what you were getting. My control of your body is exactly what you need, what you crave. You know I'll keep you safe. You know you can open up to me, and I won't judge you." He speaks to my mouth, unable to pull his eyes from them.

"It was too much," I whisper shaking my head. "It was too much."

"It wasn't enough," he growls.

Chapter 34

Dominic

Her legs are around my waist, and my mouth is on hers before she can deny me. The calm I haven't been able to find the last two weeks is immediate. Even with my pulse pounding in my head and my cock fighting to get out of my jeans, I have more control now than when I've been away from her.

I lick into her mouth, tease her covered nipple with my thumb, and she moans against my lips, straining her neck to close the distance when I start to pull away. She's as open to this as I'd hoped.

The tearing noise as I rip her leggings apart mingles with our panting breaths. Holding her like this, without the aid of the wall, isn't easy and my hands, needing to carry her weight, don't have as much mobility, but it's something I'll work around.

"Take me out," I mutter against her mouth and shift, so there are a few inches between us.

Her hands scramble, fighting first my belt and then the button and zipper on my jeans but not once does she reject me. I close my eyes, rejoicing in the touch of her hand on my heated flesh.

"Are you wet?" I groan.

"Fuck yes," she answers.

"Put me in," I command as one hand holds onto her back, and the other reaches up to her neck.

Her blue eyes fill with intense longing as my thumb presses against the raging pulse point. Her heart is pounding just as fast as mine is. I can barely keep it together as she sweeps the head of my cock through her arousal, wetting me with it before placing me at her entrance.

"I'm gonna fuck you hard, Mak," I warn. "Tell me if it's too much."

Her cries fill the room when my hips thrust, and I fill her in one solid lunge. The resistance of her core the second before her pussy accepts all of me is the most incredible feeling, one I know I'll long for many times after she's gone.

"Fucking perfect," I praise and shift my hips back only to slam forward again.

Glass-like eyes watch mine. With her head against mine and never breaking the connection, I fuck her just how I want, how she needs. Her nails dig into the back of my neck, exactly how I like it.

The familiar zing of release knocks in warning low in my spine.

It's too soon.

"You need to come, Mak," I grunt. "Been too long, baby."

She bites her lip and pulls one of her hands from my neck only to trail it down my chest and press down on her clit. Her eyes roll, but she manages to keep them open and on mine, pleasing me, doing exactly what she knows I demand of her.

"Come with me," I pant already feeling the pulse in my sac. She nods, whimpers one last time, and detonates around my throbbing erection. This time, my own eyes flutter as my body jerks and fills her with every scorching drop my body has to offer.

"Fuck, I needed that." Her head nods against mine, and a small smile plays on her lips.

"Me too," she whispers. "I need to get cleaned up so I can go."

The fuck?

I hold her tighter, even though I know I can't keep her. I lose a piece of myself every time I sink into her. I'd told myself one last time was all I was going to allow. I came in here seeking just that, praying she'd welcome me, let me feel her around me one last time. The lead up wasn't what I was planning, but seeing her packing that fucking suitcase pissed me off.

"A meeting is scheduled later this afternoon," I share.

Her eyes widen, and I feel her hold on just a little tighter.

"Figured you'd want to be there," I add.

She nods, and I finally release her, knowing she won't leave. At least not until the meeting is over, and then only if she doesn't feel like we're all on the same page and heading in the direction of the outcome she needs.

"Let's shower," I offer. "As much as I'd like to walk around smelling like you all day, we got pretty fucking messy."

I follow her as she leads the way into the bathroom.

"Where have you been showering?" She tries for nonchalant, but I can still hear the edge of accusation in it.

"I go home every day," I answer.

She looks over her shoulder after pulling her t-shirt and bra off. I miss the sight of her tits and fight the urge to turn her around so I can feast on them.

"But then you come back here?" I nod "To sleep on the couch?" I nod again. "Why not just stay home and sleep comfortably in your own bed?"

"You're not there," I answer truthfully.

***

"He didn't think it was weird for you to call a meeting?" Mak asks Kincaid after he explains Scorpion has been informed Cerberus needs to speak with him.

"He didn't question it," Kincaid answers.

"He didn't seem concerned that you asked to meet him on neutral territory rather than one club or the other?"

"He seems distracted," my brother supplies.

"He's been that way for months. Disappears for days while Grinder and the other miscreants run his club. My father would turn over in his grave." Her voice tapers off.

"I didn't hint what the meeting was about, and he didn't ask a single question."

"How exactly is this going to go down?" She seems like she doesn't want to ask the question because she's afraid of the answer she's going to get.

I step forward, hoping if I explain it to her it will be received easier.

"We plan to meet with Scorpion and lay out all that we know." Her eyes narrow, doubting the plan already and I want to spank her ass for it. "You told us he doesn't know a thing about what Grinder and the other two members are doing."

"I've known Scorpion for a long time. I'm not ignorant to the illegal things that he does, but the man I know wouldn't be okay with the shit that's going on," Kincaid interrupts.

"My brother and I don't exactly see eye to eye, but I don't want him caught in the crossfire when shit goes down with Grinder." Her eyes find mine, pleading for a different answer. "Can't you just take out Grinder and his sidekicks?"

"If we do that," Kincaid says before I can answer her. "We'll have a war on our hands. We can't take out three members of an MC and not expect retaliation."

"I like her idea better," Kid mutters from the other side of the table.

My lip twitches because I agree with him. It's the first time in my life I want revenge, domestic laws be damned.

"That's not how we work," Kincaid chastises. "We don't go around killing people without trying to figure out a legal way to end the conflict. We'll tell Scorpion all the gory details and go from there."

I see the tremble in Mak's hands just as Kid opens his mouth again.

"Myanmar," he mutters as if Kincaid needs a reminder of the shit that went down there a few years ago.

The snap of the President's eyes in his direction shuts him up before he can argue further.

"You'll leave him alive?" Mak asks not even trying to hide the fear in her voice. "We're as good as dead."

I close the distance between us and wrap my arms around her shoulder. She faces my brother and doesn't even sink into the embrace I'm offering. It stings more than it should.

"He's not fucking walking away," I whisper in her ear. "No matter what fucking goes down, he won't walk away from that meeting alive."

Her eyes find mine, and she reads the sincerity of my promise. A tear tips over her lashes and rolls down her cheek, and if I'm not mistaken it has nothing to do with her earlier fear, but somehow is because of the compassion I've shown to her. My heart clenches wanting to hold onto that sentiment forever, even though I know she'll be gone within a week, two tops.

"Is there any chance your brother will take a meeting and not have his SAA there?" Shadow asks, speaking for the first time since the meeting commenced. He looks as tired as I do, having lost sleep while Griffin was sick with the flu.

"Normally, I'd say no, but I think he trusts you guys so I can't be sure." Mak answers.

"He's suspicious, at least enough not to stay away. He had a feeling that Mak ran to New Mexico or he wouldn't have shown up hunting her." I explain. "It's been weeks, and he hasn't made a move on us, but that doesn't mean that he doesn't have eyes out. I bet he's feeling pretty bold right now since nothing has come of her in weeks."

Mak nods her head and turns to face Kincaid again. "He's probably gearing up for his next *Grinding Daddies* shoot."

Kid groans at the words and Snatch makes a puking noise.

"Sick fuckers," Itchy mutters.

"I have Blade already working on taking down the site," Shadow explains. "He's been able to take over, but somehow making it still available to Grinder's IP address, so it looks like it's still business as usual. He's intercepting all of the reports of the site being down. He's filtered money in as if the damn thing is still working, so Grinder and those other sick fucks don't have a clue the site has been off the internet for weeks."

"Wow," Mak says. "That's pretty high tech."

Shadow laughs. "Not really. Those old fucking idiots don't know a damned thing about technology. Blade was pretty disappointed in how easy it was. He was looking forward to a challenge."

"Full disclosure, Makayla," Kincaid begins. She looks in his direction. "We've got his off-shore account numbers, and we have every intention of seizing those."

Her back stiffens under my arm.

"Do you want the money?" I offer.

She shakes her head violently. "I don't want a penny of that dirty money."

"Atta girl," Snatch praises.

"Dirty or not, we'll use it to benefit others." I know my brother isn't comfortable with how Cerberus obtains some of its money, but he rests easy at night knowing that he turns it around and uses it for moral things. Some money filters into rescue services, battered women's shelters, and even relocation and new identity expenses. Helping people is costly, and we take all the help we can get.

"When is this meeting happening?" She asks just above a whisper.

"Next Tuesday," Kincaid answers.

"I'll be ready," she replies before turning and leaving the room.

Chapter 35

Makayla

For the first time since arriving three weeks ago, I'm leaving the Cerberus clubhouse. Only this time I'm not being secreted somewhere with promises of safety; I'm heading into the pits of hell, finally facing the devil himself. Dom insisted I leave all of my things in the room, but I have an eerie feeling I won't need to return to retrieve them. A calm I have no right to feel has settled over my body. No matter the outcome of tonight, it will be over, either by Grinder's death or my own.

The familiar roar of bikes around the SUV driven by Dom and co-piloted by Snatch serves only to heighten the anticipation. The longer we drive, the closer we get to the undisclosed location, the weaker the calm I felt earlier grows. My stomach turns, sour with the prospect that things may not go as I want them to.

I relish the fact that Grinder may have gotten meaner in his old age, but as nature has taken hold, he's also grown slower, sluggish some days depending on the severity of his arthritis. The other members are still terrified of him, but he got that bluff in decades ago, and no one has questioned it since. They don't see him the way I do. He no longer retrieves his victims himself, opting to use the brute force of other patched members. His fun begins after they're already tied up and easily managed.

"You're quiet back there," Dom says meeting my eyes in the rearview mirror.

I glare at him in no mood to make small talk. "You want to talk about dinner plans or something? What do you want me to say?"

Snatch chuckles but keeps his head turned, so he's looking out his passenger side window.

Tension fills the cab of the SUV as we continue to drive, so thick that it begins to make Snatch shift uncomfortably in his seat.

After ten minutes of glaring at each other in the rearview mirror, Snatch speaks again.

"Do we need to pull over so you guys can bang it out? Relieve a little stress?" Dom pulls his eyes from mine and looks over at the tattooed idiot. "The last thing we need is the mess between you two when we get there to cause problems."

One final time, Dom's eyes meet mine, but this time when he pulls them away to meet the road in front of us, he doesn't look up again. Sitting in an SUV with two big bikers, I've never felt more alone in my life.

Another fifteen minutes of driving and we're pulling off Highway 140 on the left, parking directly behind Kincaid and five other bikers. Knowing each one of them is armed makes me nervous because I know everyone standing in front of them, arriving earlier than us are heavily armed as well. This situation has the potential to be a gruesome blood bath. Jasmine is the only reason I care which direction this goes.

"Calm down brother," Snatch says pulling me from my morose thoughts. "You'll get your chance."

I wonder then if Kincaid actually believes the meeting we're having today is going to end up with contacting the proper authorities. Seems everyone else in the club is well aware of how things are going to go down.

The headlights of the SUV filter around Kincaid's back as he climbs off of his bike directly in front of my brother. My eyes sweep to the left of him and sure as the sunset, Grinder is there, sneering into the SUV. Even with heavily tinted windows, it's as if he can penetrate the darkness and pierce me right in the heart.

"Baby?" My eyes cut to Dom and I can tell by the look on his face that he's tried more than once to get my attention. "You can stay here if you want. I know this can't be easy."

I shake my head, refusing to allow my fear to keep me inside, not when this is my only chance to face my attacker.

"That's my girl," he says with a hint of awe in his voice.

My girl? I can only dream.

My hands shake uncontrollably as I reach for the door handle. It takes three tries before I manage to pull it open, and by the time I do, Dom is standing outside of the vehicle waiting for me to climb down. I step free of the door, and it closes with a soft thud that echoes in my head.

"You're so fucking strong," Dom says with a kiss to my temples.

My eyes dart in the direction of the Renegades, and I don't miss the death glare Grinder is shooting our direction. I see the menacing ownership in his eyes, the black cloud of his anger as another man touches what he deems his possession.

Dom's gentle hand brushes down my spine, resting on my lower back just above my ass as he guides me toward the cluster of leather-clad men.

Feeling empowered, I lift my chin and face the group that was once my family, as fucked up as they are. As strong as I feel, I still avoid Grinder's eyes, sweeping first over Scorpion who looks annoyed to even be standing here, as if he has something better to do. No change there. Butch's eyes find mine. As the only man with any decency, I know I'm going to miss him the most.

"Poison," my brother says, the aloof tone of his voice barely registering in my ears. I hate the club name that he gave me years ago before I was even old enough to drive.

I focus instead on the bugs chirping and the slow roll of the La Plata River in the distance. Dom's fingers flex on my back giving me the strength I need to face tonight.

"Scorpion," I return.

Lazy eyes turn to Kincaid, deferring to him as the club's president. "What's this meeting about?"

From the look in his eyes when I walked up, I'm not certain my brother even knows I've been gone from the clubhouse for almost a month. It lets me know I won't be missed, not that I assumed any different.

"We're here," Kincaid begins, "to discuss some things that have been going on around your club."

My eyes then lift to Grinder's. The twitch in his jaw lets me know he's well aware where the direction of this conversation is going, and he's barely keeping his rage in check.

"You don't need to concern yourself with my club, Kincaid. You never have before and you sure as fuck don't need to now." The slow drawl of my brother's voice, the indifference in his tone doesn't match the warning in his words.

"You don't think so?" Scorpion shakes his head in answer. "You wouldn't want to be made aware that your Sergeant at Arms has been raping your little sister for the last eight years?"

I tense at the bluntness of Kincaid's words and watch my brother's face.

Fire lights his eyes as his eyelids narrow, showing his first reaction since we arrived. His eyes shoot to mine, as if looking for confirmation. He finds the truth in my tears as they wash down my cheeks.

"You wouldn't want to know," Kincaid continues, "that Grinder and two of your other club members have been running an illegal, underage porn site from your club?"

His eyes snap back to the man speaking, pissed that anyone under his command would compromise his club in such a way.

My brother's body shifts, so he's facing Grinder more but cognizant not to turn his back to the opposing club. "This true?"

"Is it true?" he seethes.

Grinder laughs like a psychopath. "Who you gonna believe, Prez? I was in this club long before your daddy squirted you out of his big dick."

I can feel the threat in his words. Scorpion may be the president, but Grinder has always felt like the gavel should've been passed down to him rather than my brother. Until this moment, I'd often wondered if Scorpion hadn't felt the same. It's the first time I've seen my brother stand up to him.

Grinder's scarred lip twitches in challenge. "She fucking begged for it, Prez. Wanted my cock so bad some days she couldn't keep her hands off of it."

Bile fills my throat as my brother turns back to face me. His blank expression is more than I can bare. He believes the filthy things his SAA has just spewed. He sees me the same as he saw my mother, a disgusting whore who ruins everything she touches.

"Yeah, bitch," Grinder says as his hand pulls his gun free.

The moonlight glints off of the tip. As if in slow motion, my eyes flutter closed, a delicate whisper of butterfly wings against my cheeks. The pop of the gun going off doesn't startle me as it should, but at this moment I find serenity. Peace coursing through my veins. But the burn of being hit doesn't register.

My eyes open with barely lucid awareness to find my brother still looking at me, his arm raised to the left, and Grinder dead on the ground.

Rage rolls off of Dom to the point I can feel him shaking beside me as his opportunity to avenge me is stolen in a matter of seconds.

"Who else has hurt you," Scorpion says with a calmness no one else feels in this intense situation.

"Just him," I answer honestly.

He looks at Kincaid. "Who else is in on the site?"

"Chains and Smokey," Kincaid responds.

My brother turns with lightning speed, gun trained on Chains' forehead. A scuffling sound pulls my attention, and I see Smokey leaning forward, trying to pull a gun from his boot.

Butch is on him in a second. "Sorry, old man."

Smokey stands to his full height, defiance etched into his wrinkled face. Butch twitches his gun, an indication for him to move closer to Chains. We all watch as Scorpion stares down the two oldest remaining members of his club.

"You like to fuck little girls on camera?"

Neither one of them respond.

"Take off your cuts." It isn't until this moment that Smokey seems affected by the confrontation.

"Never," he seethes.

"You can take it off on your own," my brother spits. "Or I can burn it off of your body."

Chains removes his immediately, always the one with more cowardice. Smokey once again tests the boundaries but must see something in my brother's eyes that forces him into action, and he too pulls his cut from his body.

"Knees," Scorpion hisses as the two discarded leathers hit the ground.

They both stand stock still until Butch and Bear kick the backs of their legs, and they collapse on the ground. I feel nothing when the tears roll out of Chains' eyes. Feel nothing when Smokey looks past my brother and meets my gaze. The devilish look in his eyes tells me he's known all along what Grinder has been doing to me and did nothing to end it.

"Both of you die civilians for betraying the club," Scorpion says with more calm than any man should feel as he's about to take two lives. The betrayal not being the years of violation of my body, but bringing the possibility of heat down on the club.

I don't flinch with the first pop of the gun. I keep my eyes on Smokey as his weight shifts when Chains crumples against him. I smile when Smokey dies with the second blast of Scorpion's gun. His eyes never leave mine as he tilts left and collapses, his life's blood swallowed up by the New Mexico dirt.

My brother turns back, holstering his weapon. "Problem solved," he says his affect returning to indifference once again. He looks at Kincaid. "We good?"

Kincaid nods, his face impassive to the violence he's just witnessed.

"I want Jasmine," I say stepping forward and out of the heat of Dom's embrace.

"Good," my brother says with a smile. "Butch found Foxy dead from an OD this morning. The last thing I need is some orphan child at my clubhouse. Didn't work out so well for you did it?"

Dom steps up beside me again, a low growl rumbling from deep in his throat. He's not fond of the callousness my brother approaches me with, but I'm used to it by now.

"I'll make the arrangements," he assures me before turning back to his VP. "Clean this shit up."

We all watch, unmoving, as Scorpion and a couple of their guys climb on their bikes and ride off into the darkness.

I look at Grinder's body one last time before climbing back into the SUV. Certain he's dead, I can finally breathe again.

Chapter 36

Dominic

Hate isn't an emotion I give into very often. It's a type of poison that will eat you from the inside out. It gives power to the person the feeling is directed at, allows them space in your head as you seethe over it.

Hate is exactly what I feel for Scorpion. Before tonight, you could say I only disliked him and every shitty thing his club stood for, but after he ripped my chance of killing Grinder from my hands tonight, the hate I'd had for that piece of shit transferred to his president.

My hands hurt from gripping the steering wheel by the time we make it to the clubhouse to drop Snatch off. I press the child locks before Mak has the chance to pull her door open. I anticipate her insisting she be allowed out and inside of the club where her belongings are, but she just sighs, exhausted from the night and keeps her eyes facing outside of the vehicle.

The entire ride back to my house is spent in silence, fraught with the heaviness of what the evening entailed. I hope, as I unlock the front door and let her pass, that his death and knowing her sister will be with her soon will ease the burden she's had on her shoulders for so long.

As silent as she was on the ride here, she walks past me. I hear the soft click of the guest bedroom door while I'm setting the house alarm.

I make my way into the kitchen. She has to be starving. She refused lunch at the clubhouse, claiming she wasn't hungry. I throw sandwiches together, wishing for once in my life I'd paid attention when my mother tried to teach me to cook. Comfort food is what she needs, but peanut butter and jelly is all I have to offer.

I look up from the meager offerings to the clock, deciding maybe a pizza from the place we ordered from weeks ago would be better. It's after midnight, and I know they close at eleven on weeknights.

Placing the plates on the dining room table, I head down the hall to her door. I don't have a problem with her eating in the room, but I'd prefer she come out and not sit alone.

My knuckles rap softly on the door, but it goes unanswered. I knock harder to no avail. I can't imagine what she's going through, and I know she needs space to run through everything in her head, but knowing that doesn't make it sting any less.

I walk away from her door, back to the kitchen to wrap up the food and place it in the fridge. I pace through the house, wasting time even though I know she won't leave that room. If there's one trait that describes Makayla Evans without fail it's that she's beyond stubborn.

My pacing leads to my room, which eventually has me gravitating toward the shower. Hope renews while I soap up my body that maybe she was in the shower when I knocked and that's the reason the door went unanswered. I rush through my shower and barely dry my hair to once again stand and knock on the closed door.

"Makayla, please open the door."

No answer, no sound from within. Sighing, I leave her with the distance she's demanding, hating every fucking second of it.

Four hours later, when I know she has to be asleep, I climb out of my bed, grab the key to her room, and let myself in. She doesn't move when I lift the covers and crawl underneath. When she doesn't flinch as I wrap my arm around her and pull her against my chest, I know she's not asleep.

Normally she would shift her weight, snuggle her soft curves into the hardness of mine, but tonight she lays silent, almost lifeless.

"Mak," I whisper even though I have no idea what to say to her.

"If you want to fuck, let's get it over with. I want to be alone." Deadpan, no inflection one way or the other.

Just fucking, nothing more. My words choose now to come back and haunt me. She uses them in the one moment the lie I've told her more than once will burn the most, and it does. Contradicting myself now will only seem like a placation, especially when my own thoughts and feelings are in a battle of epic proportions.

"Mak," I whisper against her neck. "That's not... I didn't come in here for that."

A lifetime goes by in silence.

"Then I don't understand why you're in here." She hasn't relaxed into me, and I hate the stiffness of her back.

"You almost died today. If Scorpion hadn't acted so fast. Fuck, baby, I can't even think about it." Every word spoken is the truth, but I can't bring myself to speak all of the other truths that are on the tip of my tongue. I can't say them out loud. I'm not only scared of putting them out there, verbalizing them, but now the possibility of rejection seems like too real of a thing.

"It's not the first time someone has tried to shoot me," she informs with no emotion. "I've been shot at before."

The fuck?

"You shouldn't have to live that way, baby."

I'm close enough that I feel her breathing change, hiccupping slightly.

"I've broken ties with the Renegades. I don't have anything to worry about now. I can take Jasmine and live a normal life without fear of violence."

Tell her to stay, my heart insists. *It won't make any difference*, my brain interrupts.

I hold her tighter, but she pulls away.

"I want to be alone," she repeats.

"I want to hold you," I insist.

"That's not what this is," she counters immediately. I hear her words, but I also feel the hitch in her shoulders as she tries not to cry.

It can be, I want to say, but I keep my mouth shut as I climb out of bed. I look back at her one final time before locking the door from the inside and closing it quietly behind me.

I know laying back down in my empty bed will be fruitless, so I don't even bother. I opt instead, for a tumbler of whiskey and a four in the morning walk down to the dock. I'm aware of the cold New Mexico air as it bites through my t-shirt, but I'm so lost in my own head that it barely registers.

My mind only has room for one thing, and it's the pink haired woman who showed up less than a month ago and turned my world upside down. I can't put my finger on what makes her different from the other women that have filtered through my life the last seventeen years, but she's managed to infiltrate parts of my being no one else ever has.

Her rebuff wounds me more than I thought it ever could. So many times she's felt like she's needed me, needed my comfort, my arms around me, my body inside of hers. Leave it to my fucked up karma to have her reject me the one night I believe she needs me the most, the one night I need *her* the most.

I drain the whiskey before making it down to the end of the pier, trying to dull the pain and at the same time figure out a way to make her stay, make her *want* to stay.

I've used sex numerous times to control her, to get her to act in a certain way, knowing it's what she required at the time. It won't work now, and I have no other recourse to change our situation, no ideas or words to make her see that my house, my heart is where she needs to be.

The gentle breeze ripples across the top of the lake, distorting the beams of the moon as I stare into nothing, feeling empty inside. No, not empty, deprived. She feels lost to me already even though she's inside, alone, comforting herself.

Chapter 37

Makayla

Even though I'm the one who asked Dom to leave me alone last night, I can admit that waking up alone, knowing that he's near, sucks. I have, however, gotten used to it. Back at the clubhouse, even after he fucked me standing in the middle of the room, even after admitting he sleeps on the couch because I was there and not at his house, he continued to leave me alone in that bed.

He didn't need me then, so I know last night was a fluke. He wanted to hold me? He has to know that another night in his arms would make walking away from him that much harder. Asking him to leave was almost as hard as facing my demons last night.

I take longer than usual to shower and get ready for the day, hoping he has obligations that will take him away so I can continue to be alone. I don't get my wish though because he's sitting on the couch, tumbler of golden liquid in his hands when I finally make it into the kitchen for coffee. Ten in the morning and he's already drinking. Not an unusual sight, having grown up in an MC clubhouse where the guys never stop partying, but out of character for Dom.

Even though I want to, I don't question the odd behavior. I remain quiet as I pour coffee and stand in the kitchen just out of his line of sight while I drink it. I want to say a million things, but my throat grows dry and scratchy at just the thought of mentioning my feelings or desires.

Hurt before you get hurt; shoot first ask questions later, that's what I've been raised with. It's how I have to be right now, even though I know there's no hurting Dom. He's been very clear from the beginning about what we were. It's not his fault I've changed the rules by having feelings for him. This is now my mess to deal with.

Rinsing my cup to put it in the dishwasher, I look out over the lake. From this angle, it's almost as if the pool flows right into it. I'll miss this house, the comfort and security. I won't be able to find the same level of luxury where ever Jasmine and I end up, but at least we'll be safe.

The doorbell startles me, nearly causing me to drop the wet cup in my hands. Thankfully, I catch it before it shatters in the stainless steel sink. I dry my hands after positioning the cup in the top rack of the dishwasher and peek around the wall to the front door.

My depressed mood changes to one of elation when I see my little sister standing in the doorway with my brother. He looks as if he's ready to bolt and run, which is the opposite of Jasmine's smiling face.

The second she sees me, she squeals and runs into my arms, almost before I can crouch down to scoop her up. Tears flow immediately, both of us so happy to see each other neither one of us can hold them back.

The tension, as thick as lava, is heavy enough to pull my attention from Jasmine long enough to look over at Dom and my brother who seem to be in a standoff on the front porch.

"Not going to invite me in?" my brother asks with an edge to his voice I don't often hear.

"You're not welcome in my home, Renegade," Dom returns instantly.

"You think I'm a threat?" Dom doesn't answer. "I wouldn't hurt either one of my sisters."

"You've been hurting Makayla for years," Dom counters, his voice filled with so much derision it warms my heart and pains me at the same time.

"I've never laid a hand on that girl," Scorpion says with an aggressive half step toward Dom.

"Not all pain is physical." Dom's big arms close over his chest, and his mouth turns up in a sneer. I know he's been drinking and it seems he's itching for a fight. With my brother's temper, he won't have to push much farther to satisfy that need.

Trying to ignore my shock at Scorpion's confession concerning Jasmine's relation to us, I set her down. "Go look out the window." I point in the direction of the back patio door. "There's a lake back there."

She smiles from ear to ear and all but runs to look. I grin, my heart filled with happiness at seeing her carefree with her nose to the glass.

I turn my attention back to the men about to beat the shit out of each other. Jasmine may be accustomed to men fighting to solve their problems, but I've vowed to myself that once I have her, she'll never witness such a thing again.

I walk out onto the porch, running my hand up Dom's back. I almost get lost in the warmth radiating from his skin. The tension in his muscles eases slightly at my touch, and I do my best not to read anything into it.

"Thank you for bringing her," I tell Scorpion holding out my hand for Jasmine's bags resting at his feet.

"Planning on living here?" He asks as he hands them over. His wary eyes go back to Dom. I'm not even worth five minutes of his undivided attention.

"No," I whisper.

"Good," he says, but it feels more like a jab at the huge man standing beside me than approval at my decision. "Everything you girls need is in those bags."

Without another word, my brother turns his back on me, gets into the truck he drove from Colorado, and drives away.

"What an asshole," Dom mutters keeping his eyes on the departing truck until it disappears from sight.

"Did more than I expected," I say holding the bags up a little higher.

I knew it was more likely that Scorpion would've shown up empty handed with Jasmine on the back of a motorcycle. I'd also anticipated her being shoved off on one of the other members.

"Let me help you with those," he offers.

I grip the handle on the heavy bags tighter and step past him, heading back into the house. "Thanks, but I got it."

Jasmine, ever obedient, still has her nose to the window. I make a mental note to clean her fingerprints off of the glass before we leave. I don't want Dominic to have to clean up after us after we're gone. I'll make it as if I was never here, and he can glide right back into his life.

"Hey, sweet girl. Let's get you a bath and into some fresh clothes."

I hold out my hand to her, and she clasps it immediately, circumspect eyes stay on Dom until we turn the corner down the hall.

I lock the door as we enter the room, for her peace of mind, not my own. I know Dom won't bother us and will knock if he needs to get my attention.

"Is he a good man?" she asks softly as I run a bubble bath for her.

My heart clenches. "One of the best men I've ever met."

Even at eight years old, she loves a bubble bath, so I indulge her. Most of the rooms at the clubhouse only have stand up showers, which are efficient enough but not much fun for a child.

"I'm going to grab you some clothes," I tell her. "Have fun but don't splash too much."

She grins back at me and piles two handfuls of bubbles on her head.

I'm laughing at her antics when I unzip one of the duffel bags, but the humor turns into a gasp. Just under the first couple of inches of clothes are stacks of money, passports that have mine and Jasmine's pictures but not our real identity, records she'll need to start school, and two handguns. My brother has literally provided me with everything he feels is necessary to start a real life.

I grab a change of clothes from the bag and zip it up tight. The money is more than enough to get started on, but I also have to think about the long term because it's not enough for forever.

I walk back into the bathroom to find Jasmine in a different mood than I left her. I know she has to be upset, and she's doing just as I did as a little girl, pretending to be someone else when she's around others. I was always the little girl with a smile on my face, knowing angry and upset wasn't what the adults in my life wanted to deal with, so I gave them what they expected. Even though it killed me inside, all of my tears were cried in private. I hate seeing that trait in my sister right now.

She notices me in the doorway and tries to turn her lips up, but her grief is just too much.

"My mother died," she says quietly keeping her eyes on the bubbles covering her legs.

"I know sweetheart," I say as I drop to my knees on the mat beside the tub and place a gentle hand on her back. "If it's any consolation, you have me."

Teary eyed and filled with sadness she looks up at me before speaking. "You're going to be my momma now?"

I want to explain to her that I will be that and everything her mother wasn't but I settle for, "if that's okay? I'd love for you to live with me."

"Will that man out there be my daddy?" Hope fills her eyes at the prospect of having two loving parents.

"He's just a friend, Jas. But I promise to be everything you need."

She nods her head, satisfied with my answer.

"I think that's perfect," she says softly.

Half an hour later, she's asleep, her tiny body taking up only a fraction of the bed. I leave her to rest and go to find Dom. I need to thank him for helping me and ask for one last favor.

Chapter 38

Dominic

"You pitiful motherfucker," I mumble before tossing back a mouthful of whiskey.

I don't think it's even noon, yet here I sit, drunker than I recall being since before I retired from the Marine Corps. The sight of that little girl, arms wrapped around Mak, both of them crying at their long-awaited reunion, fucked me up. It hit me in the chest as hard as holding Gigi and Ivy in my arms at the hospital. Only this time it wasn't about missing out on something but wanting exactly what I had in front of me.

Mine, my heart screamed as I watched them.

My eyes swim, clouded by the alcohol, but I swear the woman that has stepped into my line of sight is the angel I didn't know I've been waiting for all my life. She's the healing balm to every wound opened up by my enemies and the woman I thought I'd spend my forever with.

"Makayla," I whisper, even though she's frowning down at the empty glass in my hands.

"May I?" she asks motioning to my glass.

I hand it over willingly, knowing I'd give her anything she asks for. Hell, I'd offer her my entire world for her to feel just an ounce of what I feel for her.

She takes the proffered glass and fills it half full from the bottle on the coffee table. With a soft huff, she sits beside me on the couch. Even drunk, I don't miss the purposeful four inches that separate us. I hate the distance, hate how easily she can just move on from what we've been building the last month.

"I set your suitcase outside of the door," I inform her. Kid dropped it off earlier, and I knew she had everything she owns packed in it.

"Thank you," she whispers. "I didn't bother unpacking it because I know we'll be leaving tomorrow."

The news hits me in the chest like a ten ton weight.

"How is Jasmine?"

"She's asleep," Mak says. "I don't think she's had a very good night's sleep in a long time."

I want to tell her I haven't either, that sleep has been elusive for weeks now, but I remain quiet. Guilting her into giving me what I need goes against everything I am.

"We'll be out of your hair first thing in the morning," she says looking down into the amber liquid in the tumbler. "I was hoping you could give us a ride to the bus station."

"I can't," I answer before her request is even fully out of her mouth.

She nods. "Thought I'd ask. I understand if you have other things going on. It's rude of me to ask for more after you've done so much."

"I want you to stay," I confess. "Both of you. I want you to stay here."

"For how long?" Her voice is strained, filled with emotion she's not trying to show.

"Forever," I offer.

She shakes her head making me want to grab her by the chin, force her to look me in the eye so she can see the sincerity in my proposition.

"I've burdened you enough," she says, voice so low I can barely hear her. "The last thing you need is me and a little girl cramping your style any longer."

"I want you here." I can hear the plea in my voice, and I wonder if she can too.

"You helped me when I needed it most, Dom. For that, I'll always be grateful, but you don't need to offer your home out of some sense of chivalry or obligation." She takes a breath as if it pains her to be saying the words. "We'll be fine on our own."

She's just not getting it. I'm the drunk one, and she's oblivious to everything. Maybe I'm not explaining myself in a way she understands.

"I love you, Mak." She stiffens beside me. Now she's picking up what I'm throwing down. "I don't know when it happened, but there it is."

She huffs a quick laugh. "Please don't," she begs. "You need to stop."

"Stop? Like what, Makayla? Just unlove you?" I laugh trying to bring some levity to the conversation.

My hands are sweaty, and regardless of all of the liquid I've been drinking since she made me leave her bed last night, my mouth is strangely dry.

"It doesn't work that way, baby." I reach for her, wanting her warm skin against mine, but she skirts the contact and stands from the couch. "Does it scare you? I'll be honest. It scares the shit out of me, but I can't stop it and I sure as fuck don't want to."

"Don't," she pleads again, this time lifting her hands to her head, the words I thought every woman wanted to hear seeming to cause her actual physical pain. "Don't try to manipulate me. I get it. You're protective. You doubt that I can make it on my own, but I'll be fine without you."

I have no doubt that she can make it on her own, but the thought of her having to does something to me. Loving her and knowing she's out alone in the world, taking on the obligation of raising a child, kills me inside.

"Are you kidding me?" My voice is low, but keeping all of the anger that's beginning to build at bay is damn near impossible.

"I won't raise Jasmine in an unstable home, Dom. You may think this is what you want, and I'm betting your unprovoked admission has more to do with the liquor you've been draining from that bottle and less to do with truth." She points at the near empty bottle for emphasis. "I will not let her get comfortable here only for you to change your damn mind when you get tired of me and my baggage."

"You've got it all wrong." I rake my hands through my head when I really want to flip the coffee table over and pin her to the wall until she believes the truth spewing from my lips.

"They really fucked you up didn't they? You can't even see a good thing when it's right in front of your damn face."

I look up to find her pissed, chest heaving up and down, hands clenched at her sides. "Throw that shit in my face, asshole. Real gentlemanly of you."

I reach for her a second time. For the second time, she rejects my touch.

"I need you here with me, Mak."

She shakes her head again.

"I love you."

"Until you don't. Until the girls at the clubhouse seem like a better idea than coming home to the ready-made family you've decided was more to take on than you imagined it would be the night you got drunk and spewed shit you didn't mean."

Is she right? The words didn't want to seep out until right now, until I let myself understand that if I didn't do something she was going to leave.

"I can already see the indecision on your face, Dominic. Just go with those thoughts." She turns to leave. "I'll have a cab take us to the bus station in the morning. Thank you for your hospitality."

If we were alone in this house, if her eight-year-old little sister wasn't in the other room, I'd chase her down the hallway and make her listen to reason. I'd tie her to my bed and rock in and out of her until she panted those three little words in my ear.

But that's not possible because Jasmine is in the house and tomorrow they will be gone. Tomorrow Makayla Evans will walk away from my home and away from New Mexico fully aware that she's carrying my heart with her. She's not aware of my past. Yeah, I told her that I kept the old photo album to remind me that love doesn't really exist that happiness is a fairy tale that never lives up to the hype. Surely she also knows that I'm an idiot and an asshole and I was covering for the pain and shitty hand I was dealt with my first love.

I can't persuade her of that now, though. She's locked in her bedroom, a room I'd never invade with her sister in there. I'm drunk, but still not drunk enough to deal with the sting her dismissal has caused all the way to my battered soul. I scoop up the nearly empty bottle. I debate on just turning it up until I spot the glass. Settling back on the couch, I pour the whiskey into the tumbler, not because I'm refined and it's rude to drink from the bottle but because that's where her mouth was only minutes ago. I get the feeling this is as close to her lips as I'll ever get again.

Chapter 39

Makayla

I stretch in the bed, still exhausted from a fitful sleep, my mind still turns over the dream that was on repeat in my mind last night. I walked away from Dom each time, leaving him at my back, begging me to stay. Today I will do it for real, the dream only preparing me in the worst way, only giving me foresight into how much it's going to hurt.

I shriek when I open my eyes to find Jasmine sitting Indian style on the corner of the bed, watching me sleep. It's unsettling, but I know exactly why she's doing it. I had to do the same thing as a child with my own mother who insisted I leave her alone until she woke. If I didn't, I knew the whole day would be bad, filled with yelling and agitation.

"Why didn't you wake me?" I ask.

She frowns, as if I already know the answer and I'm somehow testing her.

I reach my arms out to her and cuddle her to my chest. "You can wake me, Jasmine. If you're hungry or want to talk. You don't have to be afraid."

I feel her smile against my neck, and even in my sadness over what the day will bring, I smile, too.

"I saw the pool outside," she whispers. "Think I can go for a swim?"

I laugh. "It is way too cold for that, but how about when we get to where we're going I find a hotel with an indoor pool and you can swim as much as you want."

She pulls her face from mine and peers down at me. "I'd like that a lot."

"We need to get packed."

She shifts away from me and sits back on her heels, biting at the cuticle of one of her fingers.

I pull her hand from her mouth, knowing it's her tell. She wants to say something, but she's wary of my response.

"You can speak your mind, sweetheart." I hold her hand in mine and can feel it twitch with the urge to raise it back to her mouth.

"I can wait until it's warm," she begins. "I mean if we stay here, I don't mind waiting."

I try to hide my sigh. I feel like I'm disappointing her already.

"I like it here," she whispers.

"I do too, but this isn't our house. We'll find a new house, and you'll love it there just as much. I promise."

She nods, but I can tell she realizes that the home we find will be nothing of this caliber. I wish I could find a way to explain to her that a nice house isn't everything and I want her to be in a home filled with love and patience. I'm not certain that this house will stay that way. It's better for us to cut our losses and find a house for just the two of us. My gut clenches at the idea of leaving New Mexico, leaving Dominic.

I sit up and toss the blankets back. "I could use your help getting packed."

She smiles at being needed. "Can we get a puppy?"

I love that she's able to let go of disappointment and look into the future. "You think you're responsible enough to take care of an animal? Maybe we should start with a hamster or something?"

"A dog will be able to protect me," she offers.

She's breaking my heart. "You don't have to worry about that anymore, Jasmine. We'll be safe."

"I feel safe here," she offers.

"Me too," I whisper as I pull the suitcase, still packed from the clubhouse out from under the bed.

"Where are we going?"

I have no clue kiddo. "Where would you like to go?"

"I get to pick?" Her smile spans her face and eyes sparkle with being part of the decision-making. "Well, if we can't stay here, I think we'd do good in Ireland."

I laugh at her dream destination. I'd love to live there myself.

"We may need to pick something in the United States first," I counter.

Packing takes all of five minutes as we continue to discuss where we may end up. She's leaning toward Wyoming, but the thought of traveling through Colorado to get there makes my skin crawl. I explain we may need to try something a little further east, maybe Ohio. She isn't very interested in that but is willing to settle on Florida.

"We wouldn't even need a pool if we lived near the beach," she bargains. Her compromise when I told her Florida is going to be very expensive.

Can't argue with her reasoning. She hasn't really spoken about her mom, but I know she's hurting. Therapy is going to be another must whenever we get settled. I want her healthy, and that includes her mental health.

"Are we going to fly?" she asks as she zips the suitcase.

I remember then that the thing belongs to Dom and here I am being presumptuous that it's okay for me to take all of the things he's bought. I have a duffel bag of cash provided by my brother, but not one item of clothing except the boots on my feet are mine.

"I think we'll take a bus."

Her face falls. "I've never flown on a plane."

"Me either, but I think being able to say we've been to all of the states we'll ride to is pretty cool," I say hoping she buys it. There's no way I can get through security at the airport with all the cash I have. Plus, the TSA are assholes, and I hate cops. Avoiding them at all costs, even if it means spending days on a crowded bus, is my plan.

"Can we get a map? And I can color all the states as we go through them?" She claps her hands together, appeased by the prospect I've suggested.

"Perfect plan," I say. "Now jump in the shower. We may not get a really good bath until we get to where we're going."

"Florida?" she pleas.

"Sure, sweetheart. We can live in Florida."

She squeals like the eight-year-old she is and heads to the bathroom. I wait for her, sitting on the edge of the bed and running our plans through my mind. If we can make it to Tampa or Miami, I know I can get a pretty decent job waitressing or tending bar. I'd fit right in with the crowds there, my pink hair helping rather than hindering opportunities like they would've in Ohio. I pull the burner Dom gave me and call to order a cab, but leave it on the bedside table when I'm done. I may take the clothes because I need them, but bringing the phone will only make me want to contact him, and the only way I can walk away and stay gone is cutting him out completely.

Calmness settles over me after making plans. Something to work toward, plans for our future soothe the anxiety that has been creeping in since Jasmine showed up yesterday.

She's dressed, but still running a towel over her hair when she steps out of the bathroom.

"There's one other thing we need to talk about," I say as she sits on the floor to pull on her shoes. "When we leave here today we will no longer be Makayla and Jasmine."

Tears immediately pool in her blue eyes. "I like my name." The croak in her voice pains me. "You said we were safe. If we have to change our names, it means we're not safe."

"Changing our names is what will keep us safe." The new identities have more to do with the enemies the Renegades have all over the place than a need to make a fresh start. "Scorpion wants to make sure no one bothers us when we get to Florida."

She nods, understanding fully. She's seen too much of the stuff going on at the club to not comprehend the need for change. "What will my name be?"

"I'm Pamela Isley, and you're my daughter Lillian Isley." I do my best to keep the sneer off of my face. Not only did my brother name us both after DC Comic's Poison Ivy, playing on my club name, the asshole also made me four years older. I know he did it because of Jasmine's age, but it still bothers me.

"Can you call me Lilly?" I nod. Her eyes fill with love. "And I get to call you Mom?"

"I'd love that."

"Me too," she whispers as her eyes lower to finish tying her shoes.

"Ready?" I ask slapping my hands on my knees before standing from the end of the bed.

"Yep." She rises from the floor. I give her the handle of my suitcase to pull behind her and grab the two duffel bags.

I was hoping that Dom would be gone, or in his room when we left, but his boots on the coffee table as we round the end of the hall come into view.

He's on his feet the second we enter the living room. The sway in his gait from last night is gone. He looks exhausted, but he's no longer drunk. His sobriety and ability to think straight will hopefully make leaving a little easier.

I swallow roughly when my eyes meet his. Sadness not acceptance fills his eyes, and I know this is going to be harder than I ever could've imagined.

"Hey, Jasmine," he says offering his hand. "We didn't really get to meet yesterday. I'm Dominic."

She smiles at him but stays behind me, reaching her hand around my legs to shake his. She's tiny in comparison, her hand getting lost in his. "Call me Lilly."

His eyes meet mine in understanding. He's well aware of the shit storm that surrounds my brother.

He smiles back down, releasing her hand. "Nice to meet you, Lilly."

"And you are?" he asks reaching to shake my hand as well.

I shake my head, refusing his request. I can't tell him my new name, can't tell him where we're going. I can't take the chance that he'll try to track us down. When I leave his house, I don't plan to ever look back, and he needs to get in the same mindset.

"She's *Mom*," Jasmine offers.

He gives her a sad smile before looking back up to me.

"Mom," he says softly, letting it play over his tongue. "That sounds perfect."

Tension is building, and I haven't a clue what he's going to say next, so I bend at the knees and speak to my sister. "How about you keep an eye out front for the cab?"

She smiles and heads to the front door, pulling the suitcase behind her.

"I left money on the dresser for the clothes and suitcase," I tell him once I'm standing again.

"I don't want your money, Mak." His warm hand runs the length of my arm, and I allow it, drinking in his touch one final time. "I want you."

I shake my head. "Don't make this harder than it already is."

"Stay," he begs. "Let me love you, let me love *her*. I'll never stop loving you, baby. I heard every word you said last night. I'd never grow tired of you. I'd never want another woman if I know you're here. I wouldn't be at the clubhouse looking to climb in bed with anyone else because you'd be sitting on my lap while I'm there."

I shake my head again. I know he's saying all of the right things but words mean nothing.

"I'll be a good dad to her, Mak. Let me show you."

"Cab's here," Jasmine says.

Tears are streaming down my face when I turn from him.

"I love you," he calls after me when I shuffle my sister out the door and down to the cab.

"I'll always love you," he yells as my chest constricts.

"To the bus station," I tell the cab driver as he pulls away.

I cry all the way, Jasmine holds my hand, comforting me until the driver pulls up outside of the bus station. My first day as an adult responsible for a child and she's the one helping me hold it together.

Chapter 40

Dominic

My head hanging in my hand, I wait for the ringing in my ear to be answered.

"Hey, brother." Kincaid's voice through the phone isn't the one I want to hear, but calling Makayla's phone only led me to where she'd left it in the guest bedroom.

"Dom?" The concern in his voice is thick and laced with apprehension.

"She's gone," I mutter.

He's the silent one now.

"That was quick."

"She couldn't get out of here fast enough," I explain.

"I thought she'd give it a few days. Get a plan together. Do you know where she's heading?" he asks.

"Not a clue. Fucking Scorpion gave them new identities. She wouldn't even tell me who she's going to be now."

"That's easy enough to get from him," Kincaid offers.

"You giving me permission to beat the shit out him for the info? I already want to gut him for killing Grinder."

"He stole that from you," he says with understanding.

"You can easily solve this, brother."

"She rejected me." Damn, that's hard to say out loud. "I laid it out, asked her to stay, and she turned me down."

"And you're going to take no for an answer? Doesn't sound like the man I know."

"She's afraid I'll stop loving her, that she's a burden."

"She's got that kid now, Dom. She kind of is a burden." He's baiting me, and he knows it.

Fuck if it isn't working.

"They're not a Goddamned burden, Kincaid. I want what she has. I want her pain and her feistiness. I want to raise that little girl as my own." My voice is rising with every word, and if he were here right now, I'm not so sure I wouldn't punch him in his damn face for saying such shit about Makayla and Jasmine.

"Yet you're sitting alone in the house, talking on the phone with your asshole brother?"

I'm on my feet pocketing the keys to the SUV before I can even talk myself out of it. I know they went to the bus station. It's the only way she can travel. The weight of those duffel bags means there's a lot more than clothes in them. Scorpion may not openly love his sister, but handing over a wad of cash to help them get on their feet speaks volumes of his concern.

"And when she turns me down again?"

Kincaid laughs. "I'd say find a dark room and do what you do, but that little girl is with her. If she walks away again, wait a few weeks and go to where she is, try to convince her then."

"Let her walk away and travel to God knows where with a child?" The idea sinks like a brick in my stomach.

"I know it's not ideal, Dom, but she's a strong girl, has a good head on her shoulders. She'll be fine." I agree with him, but it doesn't mean I have to like knowing she doesn't need me.

"Talk later," I tell him.

"Good luck, brother."

I end the call as the garage door opens and I climb inside. The bus station is only ten miles from the house, but I know it can take up to half an hour to get there depending on traffic. I back out of the garage and don't even wait for the door to close before I'm peeling off. My bike would be faster, but it would be impossible to transport all three of us back to the house. My mind considers Jasmine. If I can convince them to come back, she would probably need a booster seat since she's so damn tiny, but I can't focus on that now.

The drive seems to take forever, as I try to think of a different way to tell her how I feel, a better way to explain how much I need her.

The sight of the bus already outside of the Navajo Trading Company makes my hands tremble, but it's the pink haired woman I know I'll love for the rest of my life, waiting in line to board that nearly makes my heart stop.

I pull directly in front of the bus, parking so close the passenger door won't even open.

"You can't park there," the driver yells as I exit the vehicle, his hand pulling from the suitcase he was about to lift and load onto the bus.

I ignore him, opting instead to keep my eyes locked on the woman that's watching with widened eyes as I step on the sidewalk. I pause, taking in her gorgeous eyes and tear stained cheeks. Leaving me hasn't been easy for her. I'm an asshole knowing this will work in my favor, but at this point, I'll take all the help I can get.

"Dom?" she whimpers. "What are you doing?"

I shake my head. "You didn't think I could just let my two girls walk away from me, did you?"

"Please don't," she says squeezing Jasmine's hand so much it causes her to wince.

"You said that last night," I remind her. "Told me to stop loving you. I'll tell you again, baby. I'll never stop loving you. Are you really going to do this, walk away from the man you love, the man who wants to give you the world?"

"And a pool," Jasmine says softly.

"And a pool," I repeat to her stubborn older sister.

Makayla looks down at Jasmine, and I know she can read the hopefulness in the kid's eyes.

"I saw ducks outside yesterday," Jasmine bargains as if those filthy fucking creatures sweeten the pot.

I know then that I'd spray shit off the docks for hours a day, every day for the rest of my life if it means they came home with me. If that isn't true love, I don't know what is.

"How do you know I love you?" Mak asks.

"If you didn't this wouldn't be hard for you. You don't cry for a guy you just sorta tolerate." She grins a little, a small smile twitching the right corner of her mouth. "If you didn't love me you'd be on that bus."

She looks over, realizing for the first time that the bus, unhindered by my parking job, just backed up a couple of car lengths and drove right around my SUV.

"There's another one coming in an hour," she counters.

"By that time we'll be at the hardware store, picking out paint for Jasmine's room."

"Turquoise," my new teammate insists as she releases Mak's hand and picks her side by stepping closer to me.

"Two against one," I tell her with a wink.

I hate the tear that forms and runs down her cheek because I don't know what it means. This can go either way. I take two steps closer to her. She leans in closer, rather than pulling away.

"I do," she whispers only loud enough for me to hear. "I love you."

My eyes soften, but I can't celebrate just yet. The look on her face is still one of indecision.

"Go with that," I urge.

She shakes her head. "I can't choose a man over my sister because it will make me happy. She's been second her whole life."

"She deserves to be number one," I agree. "She will be."

She glances from me to Jasmine who's watching on with eager eyes. "Don't break our hearts."

She's in my arms a second later, her tears wetting my shirt. Mine wetting hers.

"Fuck, baby," I mutter. "You had me worried."

"I'm glad you came for us," she sobs. "Saved me from having to pay a cab back to your house."

I pull her away from my chest, staring into her eyes, wondering if I'd heard her wrong.

"You were coming back?"

She nods, a wicked grin on her lips. "The driver was taking our bags off the bus, not putting them on."

I kiss her then, crush my mouth on hers until Jasmine clears her throat at our public display of affection.

"I'm going to spank your ass so fucking hard tonight," I warn before pulling away and reaching for their bags.

"I can't wait," she teases.

With the world back together and future looking bright, we make our way back to the SUV while Jasmine begins to bargain with what kind of dog she's going to get.

Epilogue

Dominic

1 Month Later

"You don't even want to tell Khloe?" I look at my wife warily. Kid's woman and she have become best friends. Toss Itchy's weird ass into the mix, and they are the strangest triple threat you can picture.

"No," she says again. "We still have some time. Besides, Misty and Shadow just announced her pregnancy. I don't want to steal their thunder. It's rude."

"I want everyone to know," I insist.

"You probably told them last night when you couldn't keep your hands off my damn stomach," she says with a grin.

"Swear jar," Jasmine says from the breakfast bar where she's been working on homework.

"Damn isn't a horrible word," Mak says.

Jasmine raises her eyebrow. "Can I say it?"

I laugh when Mak doesn't answer her but pulls a dollar from her purse and shoves it into the jar on the counter.

"Happy?" she snips playfully.

"I'll be happy if you cuss a lot more. Motorcycles are expensive. I'll never get my own if everyone keeps watching what they say."

"Jasmine," I warn as Mak hisses and turns glaring eyes back to me. "You can't keep a secret for shit."

Jasmine smiles and points "Swear jar."

"You are not getting her a fucking motorcycle," Mak yells.

"Swear jar," Jasmine sing-songs again.

I glare at my eight-year-old daughter before turning back to my wife. "Stress isn't good for the baby, baby." I pull her close and put my hands on her flat stomach. I lean in close to her ear. "She's purposely riling us up, so we fill the jar faster."

Mak chuckles, but doesn't see me glaring over her should at our little girl. I give her the *'you sure as shit ain't getting a damn motorcycle now'* look, but she just grins at me.

My life is perfect. A wife that married me the week after I picked her up from the bus station. That's how she tells the story since she was on her way back to me. I have a little girl we're in the process of making official through adoption, and the baby growing in her stomach. The baby we'd created at the clubhouse a week before the shit even went down with Grinder. My skin still crawls when I think about everything I could've lost that night.

Every vision I have of my future includes exactly what I have and more babies if Mak's willing to let me keep her pregnant for the next ten years or so.

"What are you thinking about?" my obsession whispers against my lips.

"What makes you think I got anything on my brain?" I ask against her neck.

"Your cock is pressing into my stomach, not fifteen feet from our daughter." *Our* daughter, man I love how that sounds.

"The things I'm thinking can't even be put into words. Last time I mentioned your tits and how much I couldn't wait for them to grow heavy from the pregnancy, I ended up tied to the bed."

She chuckles against my lips, the memory making my cock grow even more.

"You loved it," she argues.

"My dick was sore for days," I remind her.

"I kissed it and made it better." That memory makes me groan.

"Done," Jasmine says, oblivious to our embrace.

She'd mentioned before that she likes that we're so in love, and how much of a change it was from the things she's seen before. Some of the stories she's told the counselor she's seeing would make a grown man blush. We had to explain more than once that the home she came from is not the home she lives in now. It's a work in progress, but she's making great strides.

I smile against Makayla's mouth. "You know what that means?"

She nods, turning so her back is to me, giving me the time I need to settle things down low.

I clear my throat and step around her when I'm good to go. "Did you decide which one?"

Always a neat little girl, I watch as she puts her school books away.

"I'm thinking the girl. I think her and Ollie will make beautiful puppies."

"Oh lord," I mutter. "I sure hope Kincaid doesn't mind becoming a granddad so soon."

I laugh and follow my world out into the garage to pick up the puppy we promised Jasmine earlier in the week.

Another Epilogue

Makayla
7 Months Later

I can't stop the hot tears streaking down my face as I watch my amazing husband hold our little girl. Less than an hour ago, Sofia Gayle Anderson entered the world with lungs so strong I was sure the walls were going to collapse around us. She didn't stop crying until she was bundled and placed in her father's arms, and that's exactly where she's been the entire time.

My husband, the strongest man I've ever met, hasn't once wiped at the tears that began falling the second the doctor told me I was ready to push. He fought wars for twenty years, has been through hell and back, and yet a tiny, six and a half pound little girl brings him to his knees. It's the most amazing sight.

"She's perfect," he whispers, not looking up from her. His voice is filled with awe and vulnerability.

"I wouldn't know," I tease, trying to lighten the mood.

His lip twitches when he finally looks up at me. "You want to hold her?"

"Please," I say with my hands reaching out for her.

He sincerely looks torn between allowing her mother to hold her and his arms being empty. I couldn't ask for a more dedicated man than the one I have.

"Why don't you spend a little more time with her," I offer. Patting the bed beside me, I urge him closer. "Just sit here so I can watch her sleep."

He obliges, looking like a giant with such a tiny little bundle in his arms. I feel protected, safe, knowing Dominic will protect our family at any cost.

"Jasmine?" I whisper, sleep nearly taking over after such an exhausting day.

"Kincaid and Em took her back to the clubhouse. She was asleep in the waiting room," he explains. "They'll be back in the morning."

"What time is it?"

"Four in the morning," he's answers softly keeping his eyes on Sofia. "They thought labor would've gone quicker."

"Me too," I mumble as my eyes flutter closed.

"Get some sleep, beautiful."

I smile, letting the warmth of his body wash over me.

So many things have changed since I came back with him from the bus station. He took to parenting Jasmine like it was his destiny. She took to calling him dad like it was the most natural thing in the world. He got rid of the photo album he'd been holding onto for decades the same day he removed the guns Scorpion sent with Jasmine. The money went into a savings account for Jasmine, and we never looked back.

Dominic, once broody and mad at the world, seemed to come to life. He released his past as if it hadn't controlled all of his adult life. He loves me with a fierceness I never imagined was possible, and every day I'm thankful for the new lease on life he's provided for me.

We haven't heard a word from the Renegade MC, just as my brother promised. Precarious ties between the two clubs have been broken, severed eternally, which I know is a relief for Dom. With that gift, I'm able to raise my children in safety, happiness, a life filled with love and devotion rather than pain and tears.

I fall asleep to the sound of my husband softly singing to the little girl he's never allowed himself to dream of.

Snatch
Cerberus MC Book 5
Releases July 2017
TBR IT
UNEDITED SNEAK PEEK

Prologue
Snatch

Blackness surrounds me when the power to the building we're infiltrating is cut. Somehow tipped off, the insurgents knew we were coming and prepared in advance. Back to the nearest wall, I'm so pissed I want to kick my own ass. Both Itchy and Kincaid urged me to wear night vision, but I waved them off. The green tint, even with the infrared gives me a headache that lasts for days. Besides, we've been watching this place for almost a week and it has always been lit up like the fucking Christmas tree in Rockefeller Center.

"I'm blind," I whisper yell into my mic.

"Fucking told you," Itchy taunts. "Just stay against the wall, pretty boy. Let the men handle this sh—"

His word is cut off the exact moment gunfire echoes around us. I crouch low to the ground tucking my chin to my chest so my Kevlar helmet is facing the action, making myself as small as possible, and hold. I'm no use to them, having to wait until the dust settles before I can move without risking getting my head blown off.

The sound of bullets hitting the concrete walls as well as small explosions to my left reverberate off the walls. The guys communicate through their mics on where the threats are and systematically take each one out. I know I'm going to catch shit over this once they're done, and Kincaid will never let me opt out of the night vision headset again.

The same sense of calm I always feel in these situations is with me even without being able to see what's going on around me. The only difference is the guilt I feel because I know that they're taking care of the combatants as well as making sure I don't get a bullet in my melon since I'm practically a sitting duck. It leaves them distracted; Itchy especially.

I shake my head, refusing to run the last two years through my head, refusing to let my own stubbornness take hold while in the middle of a deadly combat.

I don't initially freak out when I hear Kincaid come over the mic. "Itchy's been hit."

We sometimes take a shot to the chest, that's why we wear the best Kevlar money can buy. It isn't until Shadow yells that makes my blood runs cold.

"Right leg!" Shadow screams. "He's down, Snatch. Eight meters up and six to your left. I'll cover you but you have to go now."

Without thought, without consideration of my own safety, I crawl toward him. I slip and nearly face plant when I get within a foot. I realize immediately when I pull my hand from the wetness, that it's covered in blood. My best friend is fucking bleeding out and I'm blind, wrapped in a darkness that grows more ominous with each passing second.

"Stay with me," I beg. "I got you."

I run my hand up his right leg, looking for the wound. Finding the tear in his cammies, I shove my finger into the bullet hole. God damn it, I think but barely keep the words inside. Inside of his right leg, he's been hit in the femoral artery. I hate the feel of his pulse as each burst pushes more blood past my finger, and I struggle to keep the injury plugged against the force I'm working with.

"Fuck," he hisses.

"Sorry, man," I mutter as I use my free hand to pull my belt off.

It isn't until it's wrapped high on his leg and pulled as tight as I can get that I pull my finger from the bullet hole and reach for his night vision.

"You're crying," he whispers, voice already growing weak and ragged from the blood loss.

My eyes flutter closed when his fingers reach up and caress my cheek.

"Don't get all soft on me know," I tease as I situate the headset.

I told myself not to react, no matter how bad he looked, but I can't help the cuss word that slips from my mouth when I look down at his leg. What I had assumed was a small puddle is actually a full on pool of his blood.

"I'm cold," he says and I can hear the shiver in voice.

"Don't," I hiss. "Save your energy."

"I love you," he whispers. "I'm so sorry I couldn't be what you needed."

In the green haze of the goggles, I see his eyes close. I did the same thing when my back was against to wall earlier because it's easier to zero in on your other senses that way. The pained look on Itchy's face, however tells me his eyes are closed due to loss of strength.

"Please," I beg him. "Stay with me. You're all I'll ever need. I love you, too. Please open your eyes."

They flutter but he no longer has the strength to obey my order. Before resting my head on his chest, I tug on the belt turned tourniquet around his leg and get it a quarter inch tighter. His breaths are shallow and intermittent and his pulse is thready.

"I love you. I love you." I chant over and over. I confess the words for the first time out loud with each compression of his chest.

I'm repeating it still when I feel someone's hand on my shoulders. I'm still saying it when the lights are turned on and I'm staring down at the ashen grey body of my best friend, lover, and the greatest man I'll ever know.

We Said Forever

Sneak Peek

Rock bottom.

They say the only way to go from there is up, but what is "up" when you're born into someone else's rock bottom?

At ten, football became my first love. It's what got me out of the house away from my self-destructive family. My love for football landed me at Las Vegas University with a full ride scholarship, and the orange on my jersey was my favorite color...until my eyes landed on the red dress Fallyn wore the night we met.

At twenty-one, I jumped off the cliff into the unknown the second Fallyn McIntyre danced in my arms at a party. I had the greatest girl in the world and the opportunity to play college ball every Saturday. My rock bottom was looking up, thanks to my two first loves.

Parties, sex, and football—life was perfect. But one drink too many, and my world came crashing down. When I chose pills over my second love, my head told me it was the best decision I ever made. The pills keep me warm and protect me from the distance Fallyn created. Percs don't judge me. They make me feel alive.

Threes.

They say the best things come in threes, but one leads to a stable future, one is my salvation, and the other drags me to hell—a hell I'd willingly burn in for eternity...if it weren't for my second love.

Prologue

The stagnant, filthy air of the one bedroom apartment stings my nose as I make my way down the short hall to the living room. The worn, tamped down carpet sticks to the soles of my shoes, the years of built up grime well past the point of being able to be cleaned.

My stomach roils in disgust, the shame of where I live and what I deal with daily sitting heavy in my empty gut. A familiar buzz surrounds me, and I swat at the fly permeating my space—one of God knows how many. My gaze darts to the couch, and true to form, my mother is passed out, a rubber band around her arm and needle sticking out of her vein. I drag my hands through my hair as a sigh bursts from my lips. Exasperation, desperation, disgust—it lands straight in my sour stomach. She couldn't even be bothered to pull the frequently used hypodermic needle out of her arm before passing out. Closing my eyes, I pinch the outer shell of the needle with sure fingers, tug it free of her arm, and place it next to the empty baggie and heroin residue on the weathered piece of wood that's served as the coffee table for as long as I can remember.

Muscle memory is all that's involved as I grab the tattered blanket from the end of the couch and pull it over her sleeping form, her chest rising and falling with each shallow breath. Gooseflesh is already visible on Mom's skin—a surefire sign she's coming down from her high. Helping her isn't out of love, but a sense of survival, self-preservation. Waking up warm decreases the chance of an altercation when I get home from school this afternoon.

I used to love my mother—years ago, when alcohol was the only thing she needed to get through the day, when she used words rather than her fists. Taking care of Mom always allows thoughts of my deadbeat father to trickle in—the man who ruined my once loving mother when I was eight. One tiny bag of chunky brown powder was all it took for my mother to turn from a semi-functioning alcoholic to a full-blown heroin addict. He got her high, beat her bloody, and left like he always does. I took care of her when he deserted us again. I held her to my chest and begged her never to do it again as her stomach emptied on my clothes. She promised me she'd stop it all. No more drinking, no more drugs, no more Dad.

Those promises lasted as long as the high did. Six hours later, she was gone, looking for her next fix. That was four years ago, and every day since has gotten progressively worse.

I shake my head, trying to rid my thoughts of the failure my parents saddled me with as I walk out of the apartment. Pulling the broken door closed is the best I can do. The lock and door jamb were busted long ago, but that's what happens when a drug dealer comes around looking for payment. Sometimes she's able to trade with stolen goods or cash, but most often, she settles her debts on her back—another thing a twelve-year-old boy should never have to see when coming home from school.

Tears sting the backs of my eyes. One minute—that's all I ever give myself for self-pity each day. For sixty seconds, I allow myself to wish things were different while cursing God for giving me this life.

I hitch my backpack farther up on my shoulder, the weight of my football uniform and second-hand cleats a welcome distraction. Football is my escape. The smell of the grass, the thud of shoulder pads as they collide, the sound of Coach's whistle when we can do better...all of it helps me clear my head—helps me keep hope alive that one day my life will be different.

"If you don't like it, change it." Coach's words, his mantra, echo in my head as I take the three flights of stairs to the ground level. I hold my head high as I walk out of the apartment building in ratty clothes. There's something to be said about living and surviving a childhood in East Las Vegas. Not many people know some of the worst neighborhoods in Sin City, even competing with the ganglands of Los Angeles, are a mere ten miles from where millions of people vacation each year. Unbelievable to many, but true nonetheless. Mention the area surrounding UMC Hospital to anyone from around here and wait for the crinkle of their noses—it's inevitable.

This may be my life now, but there is nothing about this situation that will be involved in my future. I look up at the sky—blue, cloudless, much like my destiny.

Chapter 1

Fallyn

"No freaking way." I cringe at myself, then look over my shoulder at Charity's reflection in my mirror. Familiar narcissistic emotions tingle at the edge of my subconscious. I despise the awareness after it's been dormant for years.

"You look hot," she cajoles as her hands swipe down the front of her equally ridiculous dress.

"Where in the world did you even find clothes like this?" I tug at the bottom hem of the micro-mini, only to have a nipple pop out from the top. If the length of the dress doesn't scream slutty, the red, shimmery fabric ensures everyone who sees it will think just that.

"From that novelty store near Excalibur."

I glare at her in the mirror. "That's not a novelty shop, Charity. It's a damn sex toy shop."

She shrugs, pushing me out of her way so she can apply the fourth layer of lipstick to her already bright red lips. "Semantics. This party is a big deal," she assures me.

"For you, maybe. You know parties don't interest me at all." I've managed to separate myself from the college party scene the last two and a half years, sans one other, which cemented the notion that I don't belong in that world. Why I relented tonight, I'll never know. I give up on stretching the dress and pull on my favorite denim jacket. At least I won't be flashing everyone my breasts the second we arrive. I can't say the same about my ass.

"The Tigers will be there—all of them," she explains, referring to the players for the Las Vegas University football team. "It's the weekend before the Championship game, so the house is going to be filled with them!"

Her excitement over possibly scoring with a college-level football player is almost admirable. Almost.

"I don't know a damn thing about sports. I won't fit in." *I don't want to fit in.*

She narrows her eyes at me, and she chuffs an indignant laugh. "I know for a fact you give zero fucks about fitting in. It'll be fun, I promise. You'll regret not going. Plus, football players just mean hot, sexy, incredibly fit guys, which honestly has nothing to do with sports."

"Tons of fun," I snipe, walking out of the cramped bathroom in our off-campus apartment. "Just what I need, egocentric, self-serving jocks who think they're God's gift to every woman."

I stop long enough to grab my purse from the table and walk out the door, Charity on my heels. The energy radiating from her is palpable. The girl acts as if this is the very first party she's gone to with football players in attendance. How easily she forgot the party after the first game of the season and the player who told her to "get fucked"—his words, not mine. At least she's resilient. My plans for tonight include drinking water and blending into the wall until she's so wasted and rejected, she begs me to get her home, just like the one and only other party she convinced me to attend last fall.

I glance down at the time on my cell phone as we huddle together in the brisk January air calculating how long it will be before I can crawl back into my warm bed.

"At least pretend to be excited," she chastises with a quick shake of my shoulders. "It's New Year's Eve, Fallyn, second semester of your junior year. Eventually, you're going to have to act like a damn college student."

I nod, my lips clamped in a thin line. "Right. College student. Getting messed up and sleeping with random guys—"

The smile on her face halts my words. "Exactly," she mouths.

I watch the puff of warm air mix with the cold around us until it dissipates completely. "Why don't I just skip the trip to the free clinic next week by going back inside and watching the damn ball drop on TV? It's nearly midnight on the east coast, so I could be in bed within the hour."

"Unbelievable," she mutters as the cab pulls up to the curb. She shoves me into the back and climbs in behind me, giving the driver the address to a house on the other side of campus.

I regret agreeing to do this as much as I'm going to regret the blisters I'll have on my feet from these ridiculous shoes and the frost bite that will cover more than half my body when I wake up tomorrow. What a way to start the New Year.

***

My head pounds in rhythm to the beat the DJ seems to have on repeat. I ignore the catcalls and wandering eyes of the beyond drunk people surrounding me. Safely tucked into the corner of the room with my back against the wall, I contemplate using drunken college parties and the failure rate of students who attend as my thesis next year, but then I remind myself my degree is in marketing and that makes no damn sense.

I look at my phone for the millionth time since arriving at this near orgy and realize it's only been six minutes since the last time I looked at it. With a soundless sigh, I push myself off the wall and weave through the group of half-naked, gyrating bodies. My water bottle has been empty for the last forty-five minutes, and if I have any hope of surviving the humid air in the small living room, a refill is mandatory.

"Orange," I mutter, squeezing past a girl with her legs wrapped around a tall guy in a jersey. Her dress is to the point of indecent hanging around her hips as they dance together—and by dance, I mean practically have sex in front of a group of easily a hundred people.

His jersey, her dress, and the tiny scrap of lace between the cheeks of her ass—all of it is orange. Welcome to an LVU party. Does anyone involved in picking colors for colleges even consider how hideous the color looks against tan skin and dark hair? Gag me. I'm drowning in it. Everywhere I turn, orange and white assaults my vision. School colors were the furthest thing from my mind when the college offered me a partial scholarship, and since I'm not one with very much school spirit, it wasn't really an issue.

Firm hands grab me as I attempt to squeeze through another clump of rotating hips and breathless, slutty moans.

"No thanks," I say without even looking over my shoulder, swatting at the unrelenting grip on my body.

Turning to face the guy who is either too stupid or too drunk to take a hint, my eyes land on the handsome face of a tall blond with the lightest blue eyes I've ever seen.

The smirk on his face clearly indicates he believes I should be impressed. And I am. There's no doubt about it. I'm completely fascinated by the ego this douchebag emits with one simple look. Without a word, I let my eyes trail from the top of his purposely mussed hair that probably took longer to fix than mine to the orange chucks adorning his big feet.

He allows the perusal, awaiting my approval. Cocking an eyebrow at his blatant, pompous attitude, I push his hands off my hips.

"Not a chance, buddy," I say before turning back toward the kitchen.

My legs tremble, wobbling on my already unsteady heels. I release a long, slow breath, hoping he disappeared into the crowd. The last thing I need is for him to notice the way my eyes lingered on his stubbled jaw and the muscles of his chest even his clothes can't hide. I'm almost certain he could sense my quick, unmasked arousal. One look was all it took for this man to creep his way under my skin and throb in my core. He's got self-entitled, bad boy, asshole written all over him—character traits I would have dropped anything for a few years ago. Not today, though. Those are flaws I left in Utah when I graduated high school.

The same firm grip reaches for me again, wrapping all the way around my body and pulling my back against an incredibly strong chest.

I close my eyes for a moment, allowing only a second of contact before turning around and readying my hand to slap him across the face for taking such liberties without my permission—just another alpha asshole attribute that used to make me swoon.

"You need to get your—"

His finger covers my lips, preventing me from getting my words out. My attempt at what I'm sure was going to be a very eloquent threat against his manhood falters as he pulls me closer to his body. His leg somehow finds its way between mine as he squats a couple inches to decrease the differences in our height.

The steady hand that has reached for me twice tonight is around my back, fingers splayed against the thin red fabric. The finger that halted my words trails down the column of my damp neck before gripping around at my nape. Gooseflesh follows the trail, racing over my fevered skin. He holds me against him, guiding me to the rhythm I hated until this very second. Like the traitorous slut she is, my body molds against him, every soft inch against his hardness.

"I don't," I begin again, only to have his hand leave my neck to push another finger against my parted lips.

I watch, enthralled and utterly stupid, as his bottom lip rolls between his teeth at the same time his thumb sweeps over mine.

I cave, wholeheartedly capitulating to the moment. Ignoring the warning bells going off in my head, screaming at me to bolt through the front door and not look back, I grip the silky athletic fabric of his jersey and pull him closer. A knowing grin lights his face and sparkles in the crystal blue of his eyes.

One song blends into another as our bodies close every millimeter of distance. No words are spoken as the countdown begins. No promises are made when the clock strikes midnight. No way I'll survive this man when his breath becomes mine. No chance I'll see him again when swaying all night turns into dancing tongues. No possibility of keeping my promise of no bad boys when one hand grips my nape and the other squeezes my ass.

Alcohol has never really been my thing. The memory of the first time I drank heavy liquor in high school is enough to make my stomach sour, but the bourbon on this guy's lips is the perfect mix of sweet and spicy. It's, hands down, the most satisfying thing I've tasted since the ice cream I had after getting my tonsils removed when I was seven. I savor every fraction of a second, every slow glide of his tongue against mine, each time his lips pull back a fraction and turn up to smile against mine.

Without so much as one spoken word, this man has managed to master my body, persuading it to beg for more, coaxing whimpers from my mouth when he pulls away, only to ensure it pants a seductive moan when those skilled lips find my neck.

Warm breath hits the opposite side of my neck a split second before the weight of another person presses against my back. My seducer pulls his lips from my skin and the cold air mixes with the wet warmth his mouth left on my neck. Icy blue eyes glare over my shoulder for a brief second before calming to a cooler, if annoyed, slightly darker cerulean.

Turning my head a few inches to the right, I notice the familiar shock of bright red hair hanging down my arm and roll my eyes as Charity clings to my shoulder. I do my best to resist the urge to shove her off me and pretend I don't know her. The compulsion to stay in this moment with Mr. Nameless in lieu of helping a friend, who, in her obvious state, has no chance of making it home safe, makes me realize just how fast I've transitioned into the same girl who disgraced her loved ones several years ago.

He sees the decision in my eyes before the words can make it past my lips, so I don't even bother to speak them aloud. Unwilling to accept what he knows is going to happen, he reaches for me, and I do the only thing I can fathom: I grasp my drunken friend, arm under hers to lend a steadying hand, and get both of us out of there as fast as her stumbling legs will allow.

More Than a Memory
Sneak Peek

Chapter 1
Olivia

"You look better." I smile at my computer screen.

What were once vibrant blue eyes peer back at me, red-rimmed and dull.

"I still feel like shit."

Prominent shadows under his eyes, lines of exhaustion across his forehead, and the downturn of his once always smiling lips are evidence of his tiredness, but it's to be expected.

"You're gorgeous. Even better looking than the day I fell in love with you."

"And what day was that, sweet cheeks?" His eyes brighten marginally. We've had this conversation more than once.

I love the nickname he gave me so long ago. He was trying to act mature and look important in front of his friends. In high school, many guys thought acting like a douche was the best way to get the girl. It was never "beautiful", "pretty girl", or hell, even my first name. Years later, the intentionally derogative name stuck. I used to hate it, but now I wouldn't want to be called anything else.

"First day of freshman year," I say with a knowing smirk. Even when he was propped up against the wall with a small group of buddies our first day of high school, spouting offensive comments my way, I knew he was mine.

"I was covered in acne and had braces."

"Like I said, even better looking than the day I fell in love with you." He chuckles at my wink. I love the sound of his laugh. I haven't heard it as much lately, and today, it's a balm to my saddened heart.

His face grows serious and his Adam's apple bobs with a rough swallow. "I miss you so much."

"Can't be more than I miss you." My face falls and my eyes tear up, unable to keep the pain contained at hearing the devotion in his voice.

"I'll be home soon. I promise."

I reach out and stroke his face on the computer screen. I miss him more with each passing day. "I love you."

"I love you, sweet cheeks. Chat with you later?"

I nod just before the screen goes dark. Chat with you later...never goodbye.

***

I'm knee deep in YouTube videos when my phone rings. I ignore it like I always do the first time, and continue to watch the panda bear as it swings upside down on a rope ladder. The phone rings again and I sigh, scooping it up off the table.

"Yes, Mother?" I don't even have to look at the screen. She's the only one who calls me anymore, and for that, I'm grateful. I lost my tolerance for fake, nosy people months ago.

"How are you?" The lighthearted tinkle of her voice drives me nuts. At least, it seems to these days.

"Fine." *Miserable.*

"You know why I'm calling, Olivia. Are you ready to discuss it?" She's been hounding me for weeks. It's either talk about it now, or wait and try to put her off again tomorrow. The longer I take to discuss the issue, the greater the chance of her showing up on my doorstep—and that's the last thing I need.

Closing my computer, I sit up straighter on the couch, strengthening my resolve for what's to come.

"Now is fine," I say, the words coming out in a huff. I pick at the stickers covering my laptop, my lips purse as I wait for my mother to preach the same sermon she's been shoving down my throat for months.

"Are you planning to go back to school this semester?"

"No," I say, blinking into the empty room, my voice portraying every bit of the shitty attitude I have toward the topic. She already knew the answer. It's the same every time she asks.

"You need to come home then." Her voice grows deeper, which means she's losing her patience—another thing that seems to be happening more readily these last few weeks.

"I'm not coming home."

Her sigh is so loud, I have to pull my phone away from my ear. "I knew you were going to say that."

Then why did you ask?

"I'm going to rent the other room," she says, a coolness in her voice, as if she didn't drop a damn bomb in the middle of my living room.

I chuckle with a flippant defiance. "Don't be ridiculous."

"I need help with the rent."

Annoyed, I almost hang up on her. She's clearly lost her mind. My mother hasn't worked a day in her adult life. My father has been beyond successful in numerous business endeavors. We're what people would consider upper-upper class. She spends half of my apartment's rent on her hair each month. She's far from desperate in needing assistance to pay for the empty room.

"Think of something else. The rent excuse isn't going to fly." Frustrated with the broken record, I grab my laptop and head to my bedroom. A long nap after this conversation is a must.

"I'm tired of you being alone." Her voice holds more emotion than I'm used to. It's genuine. She's dedicated her entire life to me, and I know it breaks her heart to see me making decisions she can't control. I feel like a failure, but it's what happens when life fails you.

"I'm fine. I promise," I say with growing frustration. Lying back on my bed, I focus on the rotation of the fan blades—constant, never-ending, reliable when so many things in life aren't.

"Are you taking your medicine?"

I clench my teeth until I swear they're about to crack. "I don't need the medicine."

"The doctor said—"

"I know my body. I don't care what the doctor said."

"Have you been eating?"

I sigh, not caring if the sound rings loud in her ear. "I eat."

"Have you left the apartment this week?"

I scrub my hand over my face. "What's with the twenty questions? I'm not coming home. I like it here. I'm not leaving."

"Well," she says with more indignation in her voice than before.

I sit up on the bed and listen with sharpened focus for the first time since she called. Not one good thing ever comes from my mother using *that* word.

Well, pads are better than tampons. Insert embarrassing middle school volleyball game here.

Well, trucks are better than cars. They don't have a back seat. Almost lost my virginity in the bed of a truck.

Well, I sold that desk because you don't use it anymore. All of my money from working the previous summer was stashed in a hidden compartment in one of the drawers.

"A young lady is coming in an hour to look at the apartment. I suggest you make it presentable."

I roll my eyes so far back, I can almost see my own ass. Like this damn place isn't spotless already...

"Damn it, Mom! I don't want a roommate."

"It's time. She'll be there shortly." With that, she hangs up the phone.

I fall back onto the bed with a huff and toss my phone to the side. My last roommate was my best friend from high school. We started college together, full of hopes and dreams last fall, then I dropped out shortly after spring semester began and she continued her journey. She's now in a sorority on campus, and I haven't seen her in months. I could say I miss her, but we've changed so much over the last year, I guess I miss who we used to be.

Refusing to sit idle any longer, I get up with a renewed determination and a devious plan. Fifteen minutes later, the apartment is a wreck. Dirty clothes everywhere, the mini-blind cords pulled so they hang askew, food wrappers from the trash on the floor and counter, and dishes piled up in and around the sink—clean dishes, but enough for a good visual alarm. I'm not crazy enough to dirty a bunch of dishes.

I sit on the couch and can't help the calculating smirk settling on my lips when the doorbell rings. My antisocial mask in place, I pull the door open.

"Olivia?" The pretty brunette standing in the doorway takes in my appearance and has the class not to wrinkle her nose. My hair is all over the place and my clothes are practically torn to shreds. "I'm Emerson Daniels. I spoke with your mother about the room available."

"Ollie," I offer, ignoring her outstretched hand.

I almost feel bad for what I've done to the apartment—almost. Looking at her bright smile brings more sadness. In a different lifetime, I could've been friends with this girl. She has an air about her, sophisticated yet down to earth.

Stepping away from the door, I sweep out my arm, indicating for her to come inside, and point down the hall. "Last door on the left."

I ignore her as she tours the apartment on her own. My fingers itch to open my laptop, but I space out, watching a penguin documentary on Netflix instead.

"Is there a laundry room?" she asks, walking back into the room. I pop up on the couch, startled by her reappearance, and search for the time. The apartment is only so big, how long had she been checking it out? *What* had she been checking out for so long?

She picks a towel up between her forefinger and thumb and places it on the end of the couch near my feet before settling in to the armchair.

I put that towel there to deter anyone from sitting and getting comfortable. I almost smirk at her—almost.

A soft smile tilts her lips up and I overanalyze the response, wondering just what in the hell my mother told this girl. "Laundry room?" she asks again.

"Stacked washer and dryer just off the kitchen."

She acknowledges me with a quick nod, but doesn't get up to verify. I turn my attention back to the television, praying she takes a hint.

"This is a great apartment," she says, talking more to herself than me as she gazes around the living room.

I know it is. I also know trying to trash it up was a futile attempt at giving it less appeal. There's only so much damage that can be done on short notice.

"Only two blocks from campus," she murmurs, and I wish she'd take her contemplation out to her car. "How far is it to the baseball complex?"

I cut my eyes to her, but refuse to give the appearance of her owning my undivided attention. The last thing I need is a cleat chasing roommate.

"All the way on the opposite side of campus," I say, even though it won't make a difference. She doesn't seem deterred.

"Okay then," she says with a quick slap to her knees before standing. "We'll make it work. Can't beat furnished with a laundry room."

"Great," I mutter without getting off the couch.

"I'll contact your mother and make sure the contract is signed and emailed back. Move in next week," she says, clapping her hands. "I'm so thankful we found this place. I think he'll be pleased."

The door closes behind her with a thud and my eyes narrow in annoyance. All the work I put into destroying my apartment was futile.

If she shows up with her boyfriend and the expectation he's either moving in or spending all his time here, she's got another thing coming. A roommate is bad enough. One who has a man glued to her isn't even an option, unless she stays mostly at his place. That would totally be acceptable.

I spend the next hour de-trashing the apartment. I wish I could leave it nasty as a way to try to deter her one last time when she arrives next week, but I couldn't live in the filth for a couple hours, much less several days. My mother calls it OCD, but it's just due diligence.

An email alert draws my attention as I settle on the couch with a dry box of cereal. Opening my laptop, I check for the unread mail. Just as I suspected, it's a copy of the signed contract from a Bryson Daniels. Well, at least rent will be on time if her father is taking care of the lease.

Chapter 2

Bryson

Just my damn luck. I lean forward and tilt my head, angling it closer to the windshield, trying to find a break in the pelting rain. The sky opened up five minutes ago and hasn't relented since. This is what I get for complaining about the heat when I had to pull over an hour ago to change my flat tire, which I'm sure was karma for driving past the crazy-eyed hitchhiker ten miles outside of my hometown. I was finally leaving La Grande and Eastern Oregon University behind me, the last thing I needed was to get shanked in my truck by a man with more desire to get away than I had.

Taking a fortifying breath, I push my way out of the truck and manage to grab my duffle bag, but everything else will have to wait. The apartment I'm moving into is furnished, so everything I brought with me is in the backseat, at my mother's insistence. Apparently, she actually bothered to look at the forecast before I left.

Making a mad dash to the covered awning over the apartment door, I manage to step in a puddle large enough to soak both of my damn shoes. I'm frustrated as hell by the time I knock on the door. As if traveling over five hours from home isn't stressful enough, let's add sopping shoes and planning to live with a dude before meeting them to the tension of the day.

I knock again when the first rap goes unanswered.

Finally, the door pulls open and the most adorable blonde looks up at me. Petite and almost fairy-like, she only comes up to my shoulder. My frustration washes away as my award-winning smile floats across my face. That's not false advertising either—I was named "best smile" in high school, and it's caught more women than I care to mention.

Her eyes narrow at the sight of me and my face falls. She must be Ollie's girlfriend. The last thing I need is to get kicked out of the only apartment we were able to find on such short notice. Plus, poaching really isn't my thing.

"Hey, I'm Bryson." I drop my duffle bag to the ground and stretch my arm out for a shake, but she ignores it. *Tough crowd.* "You Ollie's girlfriend?" Her eyes narrow further. "Sister?" I ask, hope filling my tone.

"*I'm* Ollie," she says, venom in her voice. "Who the hell are you?"

"Bryson," I answer. "Daniels? I guess we're roommates."

"Like hell," she says, crossing her arms over her chest and taking a step back. "I thought Bryson was that girl's dad."

"It is. He just happens to be my dad also. I'm a junior. Look," I say, trying not to let my renewed frustration rear its ugly head, "it's no big deal. You have a room. I need a room. Two plus two equals I'm your new roommate. I'm paid in full through the end of the school year."

I grab the strap of my duffle and walk farther into the apartment. Brushing past her, I ignore the look of confused disgust on her face and take in the small, yet very tidy apartment. The snap of the door closing either means she's accepted my arrival, or she's planning to kill me and doesn't want any witnesses. I can't discern the look in her eyes, but since I see no weapons, I'm hoping it's the former.

"My room?" I hold up my arm, indicating my heavy ass bag.

"Stay here," she demands as she swipes her phone off the living room table and stalks down the hallway.

I follow, unable to take my eyes off her. Even in sweats, this woman is deadly. She disappears behind a door, and I take it upon myself to wander down the hall, ducking my head inside rooms until I find mine—not a difficult task with only a couple options to choose from. The room is simple. Dresser, bed, night tables—more than I'll really need. A place to crash and not having to drag baskets full of dirty clothes across town were my only two requirements, and Emerson assured me there was a washing machine inside the apartment. Seems like the perfect setup.

"No," I hear Ollie hiss through the wall, "I'm not saying that, Mother."

Two things. One, what kind of name is Ollie? I need to find out, because I'll be damned if I call that woman Ollie. Two, why are the walls so damn thin? So much for getting any action. Here, at least.

"Well, he's not ugly, that's for sure." I can't help but smile. "No. I said no. He doesn't seem like a serial killer."

I find myself leaning closer to the wall to hear the rest of her conversation, ignoring the slim ounce of guilt trying to sneak its way up at invading her privacy.

"You're not one bit sneaky. I know exactly what you're doing—and it's not going to work."

Having heard enough, I drop my duffle bag on the bed and head out of the room in search of the washer and dryer. I have a meeting first thing tomorrow, and being the procrastinator I am, I didn't wash my clothes before packing everything up.

I find the small laundry room and look in awe at the pristine labels on the shelves beside the stacked washer and dryer. Turning around, I take in the rest of the kitchen. I only thought the apartment was tidy when I first walked in, but this place is beyond spotless. I was concerned before, but now I'm not sure this is even going to work.

I pull my phone from my pocket and call my sister.

"You told me I'd fit in here. You said my roommate is just as filthy as I am. You also failed to mention she's a fucking girl!" I say as soon as she picks up, before she can utter a "hello".

She's silent for a long moment, and I actually wonder if she's taking me seriously for the first time in our lives. A second later, raucous laughter comes through the line before a clatter echoes in my ear, bursting that dream. I can picture her dropping the phone on the floor and holding her hands to her chest in the same way she's done all her life

I wait, my eyes fixed on the ceiling as I tilt my head back. It's the only thing I can do. Emerson does what she wants, at her speed, and won't be rushed.

"First," she begins with a snort, "that apartment was disgusting. Well, not as bad as your old one, but it was up there."

"This place is surgical room clean. Everything is fucking labeled." I turn in circles, scanning every inch of the kitchen, and tug open the refrigerator door. "Even her damn food is all neat with the product labels facing the front." I cringe at the obsessive order of this place.

My sister giggles again. "I knew she made that apartment dirty on purpose. The towels in the bathroom were perfect and the tub was sparkling clean."

I look around the corner to make sure her bedroom door is closed before whispering, "You don't even know, Emerson. This place is so clean, I think she may murder me if I leave clothes on the floor."

"So quit being such a slob and don't leave clothes on the floor."

I huff. *Like that will ever happen.*

"She's pretty, right?" she asks with the same misplaced hopefulness she always gets when she's talking to me about women. I groan in frustration. My sister is always in my business.

"Don't start that shit. This girl is about to throw me out. I'll be homeless. Once she gets off the phone with her mom, I'm out of here."

And it's not like I can just go home, I mentally add, since saying it out loud is pointless. I fought to get out of La Grande for two years and finally put my foot down this summer. My mother insisted I stay close to home the first couple years to "acclimate" to college life, and I did, since she and dad were footing the bill my scholarship didn't cover, but not anymore. There's no way I can get anywhere in baseball stuck at Eastern—hell, they haven't had a first round draft pick since Ron Scott skated into the minors in 1970. This is my shot, and running back isn't an option.

"You're so damn dramatic. How I ended up with such a sissy for a brother, I'll never know. Sharing a womb with such an awesome girl must have increased your estrogen or something."

I scrub my free hand over my face at my twin's broken record on the subject.

This isn't the first time Emerson has mentioned being the power twin.

"Besides," she continues, "her mother knows exactly who's moving in to the room. I was very upfront with her. She knew you wouldn't be able to make it up there to check the place out. She told me that was fine as long as someone looked before signing the lease. Now, whether or not she relayed that information to Olivia is on her."

Olivia.

It's a perfect name for the tiny blonde hiding in her room— so much better than Ollie.

"She had no clue I was the one staying here. She didn't say as much, but I think she was under the impression you were going to be her roommate. You didn't mention it?" I leave the small kitchen and head into the living room, which is sparsely furnished and almost surgically sterile.

This situation doesn't surprise me. Emerson pulls wild shit like this all the time.

"I don't remember *not* mentioning you. I never said I was moving in, though. Nonetheless, you're there. Her mom knows who you are, and she's fine with you living there. Her mother made it very clear Olivia wasn't going to be happy about anyone moving in, but she did say she wouldn't be openly rude about it. So, don't worry. Get unpacked and make sure you make it to the field house for the meeting tomorrow." Always mothering me. Four minutes older and running my life.

"How do you know about my meeting tomorrow? You're worse than Mom."

"I linked up your email calendar with mine. I don't want you missing any important stuff while you're on your own for the first time." Meddling ass.

Before I can berate her for sticking her nose in my business once again, I hear the door down the hall open. "Hey, sis, gotta go. She's coming out of the room and I don't want to seem rude."

"Since when? You're always ru—"

I hang up before she finishes her sentence, prop myself against the counter, and wait for the gorgeous blonde to make her entrance.

Other Books by Marie James

<u>Cerberus MC</u>

<u>Kincaid Book 1</u>

I am Emmalyn Mikaelson.

My husband, in a rage, hit me in front of the wrong person. Diego, or Kincaid to most, beat the hell out of him for it. I left with Diego anyway. Even though he could turn on me just like my husband did, I knew I had a better chance of survival with Diego. That was until I realized Kincaid could hurt me so much worse than my husband ever could. Physical pain pales in comparison to troubles of the heart.

I am Diego "Kincaid" Anderson.

She was a waitress at a bar in a bad situation. I brought her to my clubhouse because I knew her husband would kill her if I didn't. Now she has my protection and that of the Cerberus MC. I never expected her to become something more to me. I was in more trouble than I've ever been in before, and that's saying a lot considering I served eight years in the Marine Corps with Special Forces.

<u>Kid: Cerberus MC Book 2</u>

Khloe When Khloe Devaro's best friend and fiancé is lost to the war in Iraq, she's beyond distraught. Her intentions of joining him in the afterlife are thwarted by a Cerberus Motorcycle club member. Too young to do anything on her own, the only alternative she has now is to take Kid up on his offer to stay at the MC Clubhouse. As if that's not a disaster waiting to happen, but anything is better than returning to the foster home she's been forced to live in the last three years.

"Kid" Dustin "Kid" Andrews spent four years as a Marine; training, fighting, and learning how to survive the most horrendous of conditions. He never imagined that holding a BBQ fundraiser for a local fallen soldier would end up as the catalyst that turns his world upside down. Resisting his attraction for a girl he's not even certain is of legal age was easy, until he's forced to intervene when her intentions become clear. All his training is wasted as far as he's concerned, since none of that will help him when it comes to Khloe.

Will the self-proclaimed man-whore sleep with a woman in every country he visits as planned, or will the beautiful, yet feisty girl living down the hall throw a wrench in his plan?

Shadow: Cerberus MC Book 3

Morrison "Shadow" Griggs, VP of the Cerberus MC, is a force to be reckoned with. Women fall at his feet, willing to do almost anything for a night with him.

Misty Bowen is the exception. She's young and impressionable, but with her religious upbringing, she's able to resist Shadow's advances... for a while at least.

Never one to look back on past conquests, Shadow is surprised that he's intrigued by Misty, which only grows more when she seems to be done with him without a word.

Being ghosted by a twenty-one-year-old is not the norm where he's concerned, and the rejection doesn't sit right with him.

Life goes on, however, until Misty shows up on the doorstep of the Cerberus MC clubhouse with a surprise that rocks his entire world off of its axis.

With only the clothes on her back and the consequences of her lies and deceit, Misty needs help now more than she ever has. Alone in the world and desperate for help, she turns to the one man she thought she'd never see again.

Shadow would never turn his back on a woman in need, but his inability to forgive has always been his main character flaw. Unintended circumstances have cast Misty into his life, but will he have the ability to keep his distance when her situation necessitates a closeness he's never dreamed of having with a woman?

Hale Series

Coming to Hale

The only time she trusted someone with her heart, she was just a girl; he betrayed her and left her humiliated. Since then, Lorali Bennett has let that moment in time dictate her life.

Ian Hale, sexy as sin business mogul, has never had more than a passing interest in any particular woman, until a chance encounter with Lorali, leaves a lasting mark on him.

Their fast-paced romance is one for the record books, but what will happen when Ian's secrets come to light? Especially when those secrets will cost her everything she spent years trying to rebuild.

Begging for Hale

Alexa Warner, an easy going, free spirit, has never had a problem with jumping from one man to the next. She likes to party and have a good time; if the night ends in steamy sex that's a bonus. She's always sought pleasure first and never found a man that turned her down; until Garrett Hale. Never in her life was she forced to pursue a man, but his rejection doesn't sit well with her. Alexa aches for Garrett, his rejection festering in her gut. The yearning for him escalating until she is able to seduce him, taste him.

Garrett Hale, a private man with muted emotions, has no interest in serious relationships. Having his heart ripped out by his first love, he now leaves a trail of one night stands in his wake. Mutually satisfying sex without commitment is his newly adopted lifestyle. Alexa's constant temptation has his restraint wavering. The aftermath of giving into her would be messy; she is after all the best friend of his cousin's girlfriend, which guarantees future run-ins, not something that's supposed to happen with a one night stand.

Yet, the allure of having his mouth on her is almost more than he can bear. With hearts on the line, and ever increasing desire burning through them both, will one night be enough for either of them?

Hot as Hale

Innocent Joselyne Bennett loves her quiet life. As an elementary teacher, her days include teaching kids then going home to research fun science projects to add to her lesson plan. Her only excitement is living vicariously through her sister Lorali and friend Alexa Warner.

Incredibly gorgeous police detective Kaleb Perez was going through the motions of life. His position on the force as a narcotics detective forced him to cross paths with Josie after a shooting involving her friend. On more than one occasion Kaleb discretely tried to catch Josie's eye. On every occasion, he was ignored but when her hand is forced after a break-in at her apartment Josie and Kaleb are on a collision course with each other.

Formerly timid Josie is coaxed out of her shell by the sexy-as-sin Kaleb, who nurtures her inner sex-kitten in the most seductive ways, and replaces her inexperience with passionate need. The small group has overcome so much in such a short period of time, and just when they think they can settle back into their lives, they are forced back into the unknown.

Can Kaleb protect Josie from further tragedy? Can she let him go once the threat of danger is gone?

To Hale and Back

Just when things seem like they're getting back to normal and everyone is safe, drugs, money, and vengeance lead a rogue group into action, culminating in a series of events that leave one man dead and another in jail for a wide range of crimes, none of which he is guilty of.

This incredibly strong and close-knit group of six will be pushed to their limits when they are thrown into adversity. But can they come out unscathed? The situation turns dire when friendships and bonds are tested past the breaking point. Allegiances are questioned, and relationships may crumble.

Hale Series Box Set

Love Me Like That

Two strangers trapped together in a blizzard. One running from the past; one with no future. Two destinies collide.

London Sykes is on her own for the first time in her life after a sequence of betrayal and abuse. One man rescues her only to destroy her himself. An unfortunate accident lands her in a ditch only to be rescued by the most closed-off man she's ever met, albeit undeniably handsome.

Kadin Cole is at the cabin in the woods for the very first and the very last time. Since his grief doesn't allow for him to return home to a life he's no longer able to live alone, he's finally made what has been the hardest decision of his life. His plans change drastically when a beautiful woman in a little red car crashes into his life.

How can she trust another man? How could he ever love again? Will happenstance and ensuing sexual attraction be enough to heal two hearts enough that they can see in themselves what the other sees?

Teach Me Like That

Thirty-three, single, and loving life.

Construction worker by day and playboy by night. Kegan Cole has what many men can only dream about. A great job, incredible family, and more women fawning over him than he can count. What more could he ask for?

Lexi Carter spends her days teaching at a private school. Struggling to rebuild her life after tragedy nearly destroyed her, she doesn't have the time or energy to invest in any arrangement that could lead to heartbreak. That includes the enigmatic Kegan Cole whose arrogance and sex appeal arrive long before he enters a room.

It doesn't matter how witty, charming, and incredibly sexy he is. She plays games all day with her students and has no room in her life for games when it comes to men, and Kegan Cole has 'love them and leave them' written all over his handsome bearded face.

When Lexi doesn't fall at his feet like every other woman before her, Kegan is forced off-script to pursue her because not convincing her to give in isn't an option.

How can a man who hates lies be compatible with a woman who has more secrets than she can count?

Can a man set in his playboy ways become the man Lexi needs? More importantly, does he even want to?

This is a full-length novel that has adult language and descriptive sex scenes. It is NOT a student/teacher book. Both main characters are consenting adults.

Made in United States
North Haven, CT
26 February 2023

33212622R10124